******

To God –
For the Gift

"Bring the best of the firstfruits of your soil to the
house of the Lord your God."
Exodus 23:19

Safe & Sound

Danielle Singleton

This book is a work of fiction and any resemblance to persons, living or dead, or places, events, or locales is purely coincidental. The characters are productions of the author's imagination and used fictitiously.

ISBN: 1481907786

ACKNOWLEDGMENTS

First and foremost, I am eternally grateful to my Lord and Savior Jesus Christ, for without Him I am nothing. I dedicate this book to Him.

Thank you to my family, who have loved and supported me all of my life, especially Mom, Dad, Amanda, and Joshie. Thank you also to my extended family and friends . . . y'all make my world a happier, better place and I'm blessed by the presence of each and every one of you.

I also owe a great debt of gratitude to the members of my "Reading Committee" – your first comments on the novel were both encouraging and constructive and I credit y'all for helping the book become what it is today. Especially Jamie McGinnis and Amanda Singleton – y'all have no idea how much your enduring support has meant to me. Thanks also to Lisa McElroy for your advice.

To my many teachers over the years, especially Coach Hunter, Mrs. Berman, Mrs. Rhodes, Dr. Sheehan, Mr. Reynolds, Father Schall, Professor Hull, Professor Carfagna, Professor Feldman, Professor Dershowitz, and Professor Glendon – y'all helped mold and shape my mind and pushed me to be more, be better, and "stand up and be counted." Thank you for giving so much of yourselves to the younger generations. Thank you also to General Martin Dempsey, whose parting words of advice to my class - to "live an uncommon life" – have remained at the forefront of my mind ever since.

And finally, last but not least, thank you to my wonderful dog, Gus, for not eating the pages of my novel as it was being written.

I hope y'all enjoy the story.

Safe & Sound

****

ONE

"Is today the day that Amy Millhouse is coming in?"

The curious question from her longtime receptionist was the first thing Dr. Susan Vilsek heard as she entered her townhouse-converted office on a sunny late-spring Thursday morning. Dr. Vilsek could hear the excitement in the other woman's voice. Even though Christine had been her receptionist ever since Susan started her own practice over ten years ago and had interacted with dozens of high-profile clients, the highly-regarded psychologist could tell that the other woman was particularly interested in this new patient. After all, who wasn't? Amy Millhouse had become a household name in the United States and many places around the world after her dramatic kidnapping by a violent drug gang in Mexico. And now the young woman had turned to Dr. Vilsek for therapy, after having reportedly tried several other therapists to no avail.

"Yes. She has an appointment for this afternoon. But you could have already known that if you looked at today's schedule." Susan couldn't help but include a good-natured jab in her response. She and Christine liked to keep a pretty happy office atmosphere at all times, but especially before patients started arriving in the mornings. Christine knew that Susan had to deal with some very serious topics every day, so she did what she could to keep things upbeat. And Dr. Vilsek appreciated the banter. "But, as with all of our high profile patients – "

"I know, I know," Christine cut off her boss before she could finish the sentence. "Don't say anything out of the ordinary. Treat her like any other patient."

"Right. Good. So, who do we have first today?"

****

Several hours later, in the middle of the afternoon, the patient Christine had been waiting for finally arrived. The middle-aged receptionist recognized the girl immediately from newspaper and magazine photos and some of the home video footage that the Millhouse family released to the public in the hope that someone in

Mexico would see it and recognize their daughter. Amy Millhouse was on the tall side but not awkwardly so, skinny but not too skinny, with blonde hair that glistened when the light hit it. Walking in with the young woman was very obviously her mother. Even if Christine hadn't also recognized her from television, she would have been able to tell based on the uncanny resemblance between Amy and Mrs. Millhouse. The older of the two looked exactly like her daughter, only a few inches shorter and a few pounds heavier.

"Good afternoon," said Christine with a smile, remembering to act like this new patient was no different than all the others. "Do you have an appointment?"

"Yes," answered Mrs. Millhouse. "She has an appointment for 3pm. Amy Millhouse."

"Wonderful. Well, if you'll just please fill out these forms here, and I'll need a copy of your driver's license and insurance card."

As Amy and her mother took a seat in the small reception area that once served as a dining room and began to fill out the standard new patient registration forms, Christine rose and walked from behind her desk, across the Oriental rug-covered room, through the townhouse's foyer and knocked three times on Dr. Vilsek's door – the signal that the next patient had arrived.

By the time that Amy finished checking in and filling out all of the new patient paperwork, Dr. Vilsek's two o'clock appointment was leaving. The therapist stood in the doorway to her office and motioned to Amy, inviting the young woman to come inside.

TWO

"Why don't we start with just some simple background information? We can get to the other stuff later," offered the middle-aged trauma therapist seated in front of Amy Millhouse. The therapist, Dr. Susan Vilsek, seemed nice enough so far. She had given only the slightest of smiles when Amy arrived at her office, which Amy had learned from experience was the closest thing to genuine that she could hope for. No smile meant the doctor was too process-driven, too scientific, too serious to really care about her. A big, welcoming smile was a dead giveaway for a person who was too self-absorbed, too excited at the prospect of being the one who 'cured' such a famous patient. The slight smile, though, might actually be worth talking to. The slight smile meant 'I know who you are and I want to help you, because I can see that you're in a lot of pain.'

Dr. Vilsek's office was a positive indication, too. No weird couch to lie on, nothing super frilly, but not austere either. Dark cherry wood, leather sofa chairs, one wall covered in shelves full of psychiatry books, one with print copies of corporate art. Bright colored flowers in lush green meadows had been chosen to fill the frames. The doctor's desk had a few family photos and scattered manila-envelope case files. And Amy already had a favorite part of the office: the giant bay window behind the chairs, complete with a window seat and pale yellow pillows that looked like the perfect size for hugging while crying. The townhouse where the office was located was set far enough back from the street and the window had just the right type of curtain so someone could sit there and still not really be seen from the sidewalk. Which was good. Amy didn't want to be seen.

Actually, that wasn't true. Amy wanted to be seen, really seen. She had spent far too much of her life, even before the kidnapping, being viewed but not really seen; examined but not understood. Tears once again began to well up in her pretty oval-shaped eyes that changed color from blue to gray to green depending partly on her mood and partly on which outfit she was wearing that day – her grandmother called them 'chameleon eyes.' Amy had preferred to play with the boys growing up and was the neighborhood's ultimate tomboy, to her father's delight and her very proper, Junior League President mother's horror. Playing cops and robbers instead of dress up with dolls had made Amy tough, resilient, and outgoing. There wasn't a person in the world she was afraid of talking to and felt inferior to no one. Previous therapists had concluded that was because she had to be doubly tough as the only girl playing with a group of boys who would look for any excuse to prove that boys rule and girls drool and send her home. The strength of personality of her tomboy years still remained, even though her ponytails and cut-off shorts had long ago been traded in for perfectly manicured nails and the latest in preppy fashion. That tough personality also likely contributed to Amy always being a leader among her peers, from fifth grade class president to varsity cheerleading captain to homecoming queen and sorority president.

More than one teacher had suggested to Amy that she should enter politics and maybe even run for Congress or President one day, to which the young woman would smile graciously, say "maybe," and then change the subject. For her secret, cleverly concealed from all those who only view and examine instead of seeing and understanding, was that the only organization that Amy ever wanted to be president of was the local Parent-Teacher Association. She knew a lot of her friends and college professors and certainly feminists on television would be disappointed and tell her that she would be wasting her talents and her time by being a stay-at-home mom, but Amy couldn't disagree more. Her mother had stayed at home to raise Amy and her younger brother, just as her grandmother and great-grandmother had done before them. Amy honestly couldn't think of a more important or noble endeavor – or a better use of her talents and her time – than to make sure that her contribution to the next generation was raised properly.

"Amy? Did you hear me?"

"Huh?" The psychiatrist's words snapped Amy back to reality. "Sorry, yes, I heard you. Background info. If you don't mind, I'd rather not. My entire life story has been displayed all over the country for the past year; I don't see a need to repeat it."

"Okay, that's reasonable," replied Dr. Vilsek in her indistinguishable, I-could-be-from-anywhere accent. "Where would you like to begin, then?"

Amy paused. The problem wasn't where to begin, but the fact that she didn't want to begin at all. And yet, in a way, she did. She wanted to begin all over again. Wanted to rewind her life by twelve months and not get on that plane to Mexico. Or, better yet, rewind a year and a half and have never even planned the trip at all. Who voluntarily travels to a country racked with brutal drug violence, anyway?

"Amy?" Again Dr. Vilsek invaded Amy's thoughts, reminding her that there were supposed to be two people in this conversation.

"Let's start at the very beginning. I hear it's a very good place to start," Amy finally responded, trying to crack the tension in her mind and in the room.

"'The Sound of Music,' very nice. Do you like that movie?" Dr. Vilsek was obviously trying to match Amy's lighter approach, even though her patient's mind was clearly someplace other than the office. Which wasn't really all that surprising for trauma victims like Amy.

"Everything I tell you stays private, right?" Amy suddenly blurted out, dramatically shifting her tone. "I mean, I tell you stuff and you can never ever tell anybody. Like, you take it to your grave or whatever the saying is?"

"Yes," replied Dr. Vilsek, confidently yet cautiously, curious to see what her young patient would say next.

"I had a baby," said Amy quietly, stopping and lifting her eyes to see if the woman sitting across from her was as shocked as she expected. No one knew that part of the story. Remarkably, Amy and her family had been able to keep that bombshell out of the tabloids. "I had a baby nine months after I got back to the United States. Nobody knows about that. And nobody ever will." Amy punctuated that last sentence, intent on reinforcing to this complete stranger that just because she had a bunch of fancy degrees from fancy schools didn't mean that Amy trusted her.

"Of course they won't," answered the doctor, fully understanding the message in Amy's words. "Not unless you want them to." Dr. Vilsek paused, trying to determine where to go from there. She had indeed been shocked by the revelation that Amy had a child, or had at least given birth, but she didn't feel like exploring that topic was the best way to start her therapy relationship with Amy. Easing into things from the beginning, like the patient proposed, would likely be a better opening. Putting her curiosity aside, Dr. Vilsek asked the safer question. "Why don't you tell me about the trip, before the kidnapping? You went with a group of girls in your sorority, right?"

"Yes," Amy replied, grateful to have someone ask about something other than 'it.' That was how Amy referred to the entire experience: it. She didn't want to give it some corny label like "the event," but she couldn't handle calling it what it actually was: a violent kidnapping and hostage situation that had captivated the entire world with its brazenness and brutality. So Amy just called it 'it.' That was more than enough. "We planned the trip to celebrate graduation. Some of our parents were worried about us going to Mexico because of the drug wars, but we were convinced – and managed to convince them – that the *narcos* (short for *narcotraficantes*, or 'drug traffickers' in Spanish) wouldn't bother such a big group of American tourists. Especially since the resort area where we went was supposedly safe."

"Supposedly," Dr. Vilsek repeated, trying to gently prod Amy into talking about what happened.

"Yeah. I even printed out a copy of an article where the President of Mexico said that the only 'shots' Americans get in Mexico are made of tequila." The 22-year-old blonde then shook her head and snorted in disgust before turning in her chair to stare out the big bay window, sitting cross-legged in her pink shorts that stopped mid-thigh and matched perfectly with the white halter top she was wearing.

"Why don't we call it a day," suggested Dr. Vilsek, who could sense that her patient had returned back to whatever parallel universe that her brain had been in when she arrived in the office forty-five minutes earlier. "We can pick things up again tomorrow when you come see me."

"Mmm hmm, okay," mumbled Amy, as she rose to walk across the room and pick up the sorority-labeled beige tote bag that she had lain beside the chair closest to the door. "Tomorrow."

THREE

Amy Millhouse arrived the next day at the modest townhome that housed Dr. Vilsek's office promptly at 3:00pm, but Susan Vilsek had been in the psychiatry industry far too long to believe that Amy got herself there on time. No, the promptness was due entirely to the efforts of Mrs. Millhouse, who not only drove her daughter to the therapist every day but also sat in the waiting room the entire time – partly in case she was needed for some reason, but mostly, Dr. Vilsek surmised, so she would know exactly where Amy was at all times. Mrs. Millhouse was determined to never be any significant distance away from her daughter ever again. Or at least not for the foreseeable future.

"Come on in, Amy, and we'll get started," said Dr. Vilsek, standing just inside the doorway and gesturing behind her to her right and Amy's left toward the chair where Amy sat the day before. The young woman, tall and slender, handed her mom the magazine she had been reading before crossing the townhome's foyer and entering the office. Once inside, Amy headed straight to the bay window and grabbed one of the big pillows that she had spotted the day before. "Those are my 'hugging pillows,'" offered the doctor. "Almost every patient I've ever had has held on to those pillows just like you are now."

Amy responded by pulling her knees to her chest and squeezing the object even tighter.

"I have a question for you, Amy. About something you told me yesterday."

"Okay," Amy mumbled, her mouth half-covered by the yellow pillow.

"Why did you tell me about the baby?" Dr. Vilsek asked, using one of her favorite techniques to get trauma patients to open up: blunt honesty. "You had just met me, and neither your file nor any news reports say anything about a baby."

"I don't know," answered Amy as she continued to stare out the window. "I guess I'm just tired of not being able to talk about it."

"Why can't you talk about your baby?" Dr. Vilsek pressed, wanting to get Amy to reveal the whole story, even though she could tell how painful the subject was for the young woman. She could sense that the baby held the key to helping this poor girl finally begin to heal.

"It's too painful for my parents. I saw the looks on their faces when my doctor told them I was pregnant; the way they acted around me for nine months; the pain in their eyes on the day she was born."

"So it was a girl," noted the therapist.

"Yeah, a little girl," continued Amy. "I didn't see her, though. I didn't want to. We had arranged for the delivery to be at home so we wouldn't risk having someone at the hospital recognize me. Then the doctor drove the baby to a fire station about an hour away and dropped her off, since at that time the state had a no-questions-asked policy about giving up babies. We knew there would be medics at the fire station and my doctor could get in and out of the area without being spotted." Amy stopped talking, having reached the end of the factual, non-emotional description of what happened. It was Dr. Vilsek's job, however, to uncover the emotional side.

"So you have no idea what happened to your child? She could be anywhere?"

"Yes and yes," answered Amy sharply, trying her very hardest to avoid reopening this wound.

"Why did you give the baby away?" continued the relentless therapist.

"Funny, I was expecting you to ask why I didn't have an abortion," Amy replied bitterly.

"Well, why didn't you? No one would have blamed you for aborting the pregnancy."

"It wasn't that baby's fault."

The sharpness of Amy's defensive retort was dulled by the fact that it was delivered in between sobs and sniffles, with the sound partially blocked by a hugging pillow. "She didn't do anything wrong. That's also why I gave her away. She deserves a chance to grow up in a family that loves her and can support her. No child deserves to live their entire life knowing that one parent is an emotional wreck because the other parent is evil. Talk about needing therapy." Amy paused to wipe tears from her cheeks before continuing: "I watched an interview one time with the daughter of a lady who had killed her other kids. At one point she said, 'I was born of a child killer. People judge me for that.' I didn't want my baby to be judged that way." Amy grabbed a tissue from the box on the window sill and blew her nose when she finished talking, then took another tissue to wipe away the tears that continued to cascade down her face.

"That was a very selfless thing you did, Amy."

"Don't make me out to be a saint," the girl quickly replied, her tears stopping as suddenly as they had started. "I also gave her away because I knew I couldn't stand to live every day of the rest of my life with that constant reminder of what they did to me. They already haunt my dreams at night; I couldn't handle them haunting my days as well."

Dr. Vilsek rose from her chair and walked over to sit next to Amy on the windowsill. She then gently rested her hand on the younger woman's shoulder, saying, "that's a perfectly natural feeling to have. But I still maintain that it was a selfless act. Carrying the product of a rape full-term and then giving her a chance at a better life was a major sacrifice on your part. So is not talking about it in order to spare your parents the pain. But in here," Dr. Vilsek gestured around her office, "you don't have to be selfless. In fact, I want you to be selfish. While you're here with me, you come first. Put yourself first, okay?"

Their conversation was interrupted by the soft three-knock rapping of the assistant Christine's hand – the signal that it was time for the next appointment.

"I'm afraid our time is up. Tomorrow is Saturday but I'll see you on Monday, right? And remember: in here, you are your top priority."

Amy nodded her head in acknowledgment as she walked past Dr. Vilsek to the door. As the girl turned the brass doorknob to leave, her therapist couldn't help but notice that Amy looked sadder than she had the day before. And all Susan Vilsek could do was hope that healing Amy would be like spring cleaning: everything has to get messier before it can truly get clean.

FOUR

"I want to try something different today, if that's okay with you," began Dr. Vilsek at her third session with the young Amy Millhouse.

"It's your office," replied Amy in resigned agreement to the proposal.

"I want you to tell me a story. A story about a young woman who went on vacation with her friends to Mexico but ended up staying longer than she anticipated – or wanted. Tell me what happened, Amy. From the beginning. I want to know everything." Dr. Vilsek knew this was a pivotal moment in Amy's therapy. The girl would either decide to open up and tell the doctor everything or she would continue to live and suffer silently in her pain.

"Do I have to?" asked Amy, sounding like a young child who was told that she would have to check for herself to see if there was a monster in her closet.

"Yes. I think it's time," came the parental reply.

Amy exhaled deeply and grabbed a stronger hold over the pillow in her lap. "Okay. But it's not pretty. You're going to be haunted just like I am. You'll close your eyes at night and instantly be in the holding room, surrounded by them. Every time you get into an elevator or a tight space you'll feel like you're in a cornmeal sack in the back of a car and start praying they don't discover you at a roadside checkpoint. Once you hear it, once I take you there, you can never leave."

"That's okay," said Dr. Vilsek softly. "The point is for you to not have to be there alone."

****

Amy didn't start talking right away. She couldn't. She opened her mouth several times to start telling Dr. Vilsek about what happened but the words simply wouldn't come. What came instead were tears. A seemingly endless flood of tears and sadness and exhaustion poured out of Amy until she could barely breathe. The pillow that she had a death grip on was soaking wet and Amy had a headache from crying and sniffling so much. But it felt good. Strangely enough, even without saying a word, this outburst of emotion was making everything feel better. Amy looked around the room and the blur that had existed since her return to the United States was gone. The pain and heavy pressure in her chest had lifted a little bit. Amy laughed.

"What is so funny?" asked Dr. Vilsek, confused by the sudden change in emotion.

The young woman turned from the window to face Dr. Vilsek. "It's nothing. It's just that every once in a while when I was growing up, my mom would go back into her bedroom and my dad would tell my brother and me not to bother her because it was a 'crying night.' Even if she wasn't upset about anything in particular, she'd force herself to think about something sad so she'd start crying. I always thought she was crazy when she talked about the healing powers of crying. Turns out she was right."

Dr. Vilsek waited. She could've responded; could've continued the dialogue now that Amy had obviously cried out some of the toxins in her mind. But instead she waited. She waited for Amy's story.

FIVE

"There were seventeen of us on the trip," Amy began slowly.
"All but one of us were in the same pledge class and had just
graduated a few weeks before. The other girl was the younger sister
of a member of my pledge class. The vacation website that we used
when researching our trip had the slogan "Come for the Weather,"
but aside from it being sunny enough to lay out at the beach, the
weather was probably the least of Acapulco's attractions for us. I'm
sure we were quite the sight at the airport: seventeen coeds in our
short skirts and sorority t-shirts, giggling and talking about drinking
margaritas and getting tan and if we thought there would be any cute
guys at our resort.

"Although I never really thought of myself as someone who
stood out in a crowd, I was told later by people who had been on the
flight with us that it was easy to tell that I was one of the leaders in
the group. They said it was something about the way I carried myself
and the way the other girls interacted with me . . . I dunno." Amy
shrugged her shoulders and then glanced over at Dr. Vilsek. "I was
my sorority's president, you see. So that's where the leadership part
comes in." Amy then turned back, fidgeting in her chair and
alternating between looking out the big bay window and staring at
the bookshelves in front of her, with the occasional quick glance
over her shoulder towards Dr. Vilsek.

"The biggest party girl in our group was Laura Ann. Well, party
girl is a nice way of putting it. Every sorority has their resident slut,
and ours was Laura Ann. I don't know a single guy in Delta Chi who
she didn't hook up with – including the two that were married. But
anyway, she was the one in our group who had to sit next to a
stranger on the plane. Seventeen people, odd number, so somebody
had to do it. In hindsight, knowing her, I should've made sure she
was sitting somewhere on the plane where she couldn't talk to
anybody we didn't know. Then again, in hindsight, there are a lot of
things about that trip that I'd do differently."

Amy paused, resting her chin on the pillow that was in the lap of
her criss-crossed legs. She exhaled deeply as she stared down at the
floor, regret washing over her face. *What a terrible burden for her,*

thought Dr. Vilsek, *to have to go through life replaying every part of that trip and wondering if she had only done this one thing differently would it have changed what happened. Would it have prevented tragedy?*

****

"What happened with Laura Ann?" Dr. Vilsek prodded after a few minutes of silence. Hesitantly, Amy continued her story:

"Laura Ann is one of those people who could make a doorknob talk, you know? So I didn't really think anything of it when I heard her talking. Plus the guy sitting next to her, the one she was talking to, was really cute and I heard him say that he was flying down to meet some of his friends from college. Kinda like our trip except they didn't all travel together. I turned on my iPOD as soon as they let us use our 'approved electronic devices,' so I didn't hear any more of their conversation. But I know what they talked about because Laura Ann wouldn't shut up about him during the whole drive from the airport to the resort. Apparently she told him where we were staying and he said he and his friends were just down the road at a different hotel. Laura Ann was super excited, and we had all seen him on the plane so we knew how hot he was. When she told us that Ricky – that's what he said his name was – wanted all of us to meet up at a bar in between the two hotels, it wasn't hard to convince us all that it was a great idea. I mean, after all, the area where we were staying was advertised as being totally safe for tourists. It was even one of the spots where the State Department said if you insist on vacationing in Mexico, go here." Amy rolled her eyes and laughed in disgust. "Little good that travel warning did for us. Thanks for nothing, State Department."

Dr. Vilsek was about to cut in and comment about the federal government's active role in searching for the missing girls and then, later, tracking down those responsible for what happened to Amy and her friends, but the young woman continued talking:

"The thing about Ricky, or whatever his name was, the thing that really bugs me about him is that he sounded completely American. He didn't even look Mexican. He was like one of those spies in World War II that my history professor told us about. The

Nazi ones that Hitler sent to grow up in the U.S. so they wouldn't have funny accents when they infiltrated the American troops during the war. Ricky was that guy. He was their plant. The cartel recruited him to be their bait. He was on the flight for the sole purpose of trying to pick out rich tourists that they could kidnap and hold for ransom. It's actually pretty common among kidnapping gangs to have a spotter like Ricky. There was even a famous Mexican soccer player who was arrested for being part of a kidnapping ring . . . the police said his job was to pick out wealthy targets since he ran in the same circles as them.

"You know Ricky told me one time, after the other girls had been released, that he 'hit the jackpot' with us. That he got a $1,000 bonus for every tourist he trapped, so we earned him $17,000. Seventeen grand. Our lives were ruined for a measly 17 grand."

Amy's words trailed off as she rose from the chair and walked to stand facing the bay window. Dr. Vilsek couldn't help but marvel at how 'normal' Amy seemed on the outside as she stood at the window, her tight-fit jeans and white oxford shirt betraying no signs of a body that had given birth just three months earlier. Mrs. Millhouse had informed Dr. Vilsek that running every morning was how Amy kept her demons under control, and it showed.

"Let's call it a day, Amy. Tomorrow you can tell me about what happened when y'all went to the bar."

SIX

The shopaholic in Dr. Vilsek had grown to enjoy the steady parade of early summer fashions that Amy wore to the office for her daily therapy sessions. Always bright and cheerful and the latest in preppy style, from simply looking at the young woman one could never tell that she had gone through so much. Dr. Vilsek's intuition was that Amy always dressed so perfectly for precisely its illusionary quality: passersby on the street wouldn't stare (at least not any more than they would normally stare at a pretty girl) and, maybe more importantly for Amy, it wasn't painful for her parents to look at her. Because just looking at her, you couldn't see the scars.

Today's outfit was no different: a bright yellow sundress and matching flip flops, with a navy blue ribbon in her hair that went perfectly with her ever-present sorority tote. She looked like something straight out of a Vineyard Vines catalog.

"Do you remember where we left off?" asked Dr. Vilsek, eager for Amy to resume her story.

"The bar," replied Amy as she sat down in what was quickly becoming her favorite chair. "You want to know what happened when we went to meet Ricky at the bar."

Dr. Vilsek nodded her head yes, and Amy started back into her story:

"Like I said yesterday, Ricky had told Laura Ann about a bar that was in between our hotel and the one where he and his friends were supposedly staying. It was our first night in Mexico and we wanted to have fun, so we agreed – well, Laura Ann agreed for us – to meet up with the guys that night. He said he and his buddies would show up around 11pm, so about 10.45 we went downstairs to the concierge and said we'd need enough taxis to take us all to the bar. I remember the guy at the concierge desk looked surprised when we said we were going there, and he even asked us if we were sure we wanted to go. I should've known; should've listened to that little voice in my head that said the concierge dude knew what he was talking about. But Laura Ann had talked to Ricky nonstop during the long flight, so she felt like she really knew him. Enough to tell the concierge that we were going to meet up with friends. – Friends.

Ha," Amy harrumphed, shaking her head and rolling her eyes at the concept of this Ricky character ever being referred to as a friend.

"So they got the taxis for you?" asked Dr. Vilsek, trying to keep Amy on track.

"Yeah. It took four taxis to get us all in, but we headed to the bar right before 11pm that night." Amy paused, because this was where the story turned painful.

"We never made it to the bar. I know some news reports said we were taken from inside the bar or the parking lot, but we never even made it that far. You see, they were having us watched. Thanks to Laura Ann and Ricky the scout, they knew exactly where we were staying and the exact route we'd have to take to get from our hotel to the bar. They – they being the kidnapping gang – even had somebody stake out our hotel and call when we left with a description of our cars."

"A professional job," commented Dr. Vilsek. "How do you know all of those planning details?"

"Some from the police reports when they arrested the kidnapping group, but mostly because they told me. They all thought they were the shit and could get away with anything. That's why they didn't wear masks and let us see what they looked like. Why they called each other by their actual names around us, and why they weren't worried about telling me how it all went down."

****

"And how did it all go down?" Dr. Vilsek asked, repeating Amy's phrasing.

"There was a roadblock," Amy began, keeping her words slow and deliberate in an attempt to tell the story without crying – something she hadn't yet been able to do. "I guess that's a common tactic for the cartels, because the taxi drivers told us to sit quiet and we'd be fine. 'They leave the American tourists alone' was what my driver said. Only when we got up to the row of black SUVs blocking the road, they didn't leave us alone. A lot of them – I don't know how many, just a lot – swarmed our taxis and started yelling at us. They were all wearing black ski masks and carrying big army guns, and they pointed the guns at us and told us all to get out of the cars."

"What were you feeling while all of that was happening?" inquired Dr. Vilsek.

"What do you think?" replied Amy caustically, having now assumed an upright fetal position on the window seat. "I'm sorry. I just don't like telling this story." As she gripped a big pillow even tighter, Amy continued, "I was terrified. We all started screaming and nobody knew what to do so we all kind of froze. That's when the gunmen started pulling us out of the taxis and dragging us over into the SUVs. Some of us bigger girls were able to put up more of a fight, but the tiny ones didn't stand a chance. I remember one girl, Caitlin, who is like 5'0" tall and 90 pounds soaking wet, was just picked up and carried under a guy's arm like a football. In the end, I guess none of us ever stood a chance. Those of us who had more strength to fight just ended up getting hit more. They knocked me out cold. I don't remember anything from when the guy dragged me from the car until I was in the basement of the house where we were held captive."

"You were unconscious that whole time?"

Amy nodded her head in the affirmative. "Completely out. That's actually why the police think I was able to stay calmer and more defiant later on. Because even though the other girls told me what happened, I didn't actually see it so it didn't affect me as much."

"I don't understand. You've lost me," said Dr. Vilsek.

"Oh, sorry. I keeping forgetting what was in the news and what stayed classified." Amy took a deep breath, the lines of pain and stress clearly visible across her face. "There were two things, actually. While I was knocked out, after they put all of us in the SUVs, the gunmen made the taxi drivers stand up in a line about ten yards away from where we were. The last thing the rest of the girls saw before they were blindfolded was the taxi drivers being shot. Execution style." Amy bowed and shook her head. "Everybody was so traumatized by that that they were willing to do whatever the kidnappers told them to."

"And the second thing?" Dr. Vilsek asked.

"The kidnappers were smart, right?" Amy began, speaking rapidly and with more hand gestures than she normally did. "Some people said they were stupid but really they weren't. It was a sophisticated operation and they knew what they were doing."

"Okay . . ." replied Dr. Vilsek, wondering where Amy was going with this story.

"The obvious thing to do would be rape all of us as soon as we were kidnapped. I mean, there we were, seventeen pretty girls literally sitting at their feet. It wouldn't even be shooting fish in a barrel – we were for all practical purposes already dead fish in that regard. But if they sexually assaulted us right away, we might have adopted the attitude of 'what else do we have to lose' and not done what they told us to." Amy took a deep breath, then continued: "so they didn't go after everybody at first. They picked out one girl and raped her, making the rest of the group watch. That way they scared everyone into submission."

"But not you," countered the therapist.

"No, not me. Because I didn't see that," replied Amy, with the look on her face betraying her doubt over how things might have been different if she had.

SEVEN

Dr. Vilsek didn't see Amy again until the following Monday. Mrs. Millhouse had called the morning after Amy's revelation of the taxi driver executions and said that her daughter wasn't feeling well. Such breaks in therapy, while not encouraged, were hardly unexpected with trauma patients like Amy. Dr. Vilsek knew that Amy wasn't just telling the story; she was reliving it. Every detail, every sight, every sound, every horrifying memory was running through her young patient's mind yet again. That intense healing process was both emotionally and physically exhausting.

"Good afternoon, Amy," welcomed Dr. Vilsek with a smile as the young woman entered her office Monday afternoon. "How was your weekend?"

"Not that great," replied Amy, and Dr. Vilsek could immediately tell from her tone that today would be a tough session.

"Why? Because you were sick?"

"No. I wasn't really all that sick," Amy admitted. "My baby turned three months old on Saturday."

The therapist wasn't expecting that response. Of all of the things that she had gone through and discussed so far, Amy seemed the most stable and most resolved about her decision to give her daughter up for adoption. Dr. Vilsek paused, treading carefully with her next question. "Do you regret your decision to give up the baby?"

Amy's head snapped up from its bowed position. "No. Absolutely not. She has a chance at a better life. A normal life." With tears beginning to fall down her cheeks, Amy added, "but that doesn't mean I don't miss her."

Dr. Vilsek handed Amy a handkerchief and sat back, waiting while the girl cried. It seemed as if the Hoover Dam had burst with the amount of tears that Amy shed, but her therapist was beginning to agree with the girl's mother: crying has healing powers of its own.

When the tears and the sobbing and the sniffling finally stopped, an entirely different Amy emerged. Composed and serious, this was the Amy Millhouse that Dr. Vilsek did not like to see. The Amy from a catalog. The Stepford Amy. The Amy who neatly packaged up her emotions in a box and shoved them in the attic where no one could see them. Yet the good doctor also recognized that if she ever wanted to hear the whole story of what happened in Mexico, this version of Amy would be the one to tell it. The other Amy wasn't strong enough – yet.

****

"Where was I in the story?" Amy coolly asked, as if she was recounting her latest trip to the mall rather than her experience as a hostage.

"You had all been put into the vans and blindfolded," replied Dr. Vilsek, careful not to mention the taxi drivers' murders.

"Right. Well, like I said, I don't remember being taken to the compound. The last thing I saw was the butt end of an AK-47 swinging towards my head."

"And when you woke up, when you came to, where were you? Tell me what it was like where they kept you all," prompted Dr. Vilsek.

Amy closed her eyes, doing her best to travel back to the large dungeon-like room where she had been held in Mexico. She remembered that it was hot, and humid, and smelled like a rotten combination of the barn where she went horseback riding and the weight room in her old high school . . .

EIGHT

Amy's head was pounding. She hadn't had a hangover this bad since sorority rush her freshman year. It was strange, though, Amy thought as she lie on an unfamiliar dirty concrete floor, because she didn't remember drinking a lot at the bar the night before. In fact, she didn't remember anything about the place where she and her sorority sisters had gone to meet up with Ricky the Hottie and his friends.

"¿¡Por qué ella todavia está durmiendo?!" The harsh male voice startled Amy. *Who is that? Why is he in my hotel room? And why is the bathroom floor so dirty?*

"Ella es inconsciente," responded a second man. *Unconscious?!* Amy thought. *I can't be unconscious! I've never even blacked out from drinking, let alone passed out!*

And then things started to slowly piece themselves together in her brain. She couldn't remember drinking the night before because they never made it to the bar. The group of girls had been on their way, happily harassing the taxi drivers to play music that didn't involve a mariachi band, when they saw a line of cars blocking the road ahead. Amy's cab driver had told them not to worry; this was like a toll road in the United States, except you paid the toll to the drug cartels instead of the government. "They never bother American tourists," he had reassured them. Then the supposed toll booth operators started dragging her friends out of the other cabs. Amy had tried to resist when they got to her car, but there were simply too many men who were all stronger than her. Amy suddenly had a flash vision of a gun being swung at her head. *That must be what knocked me out,* she thought.

Amy had never been more grateful to have chosen to major in Spanish in college. Her parents told her it was a waste of time, but she liked the language and she wanted to be a stay-at-home mom anyway so, the way she saw it, her college major didn't really matter. Amy had enough sense and had seen enough kidnapping movies to have kept her eyes closed and her body still this whole time. She was about to open her eyes when she heard the first man speak, but she could tell by his tone and that of the other man that the longer she could stay 'unconscious' the safer she would be.

"¡Despiertala!" commanded the first man, who was clearly in charge. *Uh oh*, thought Amy. *There goes my 'stay unconscious' plan. The other guy was just told to wake me up.* Deciding it was better to avoid whatever method the man might use to wake her up, Amy began to stir and did her best to appear groggy and confused as she opened her eyes.

What she saw, though, shocked her. There weren't just two men in the room. There were five. The ski masks from the abduction were gone; she could see what her enemy looked like now. *Is that bad? Good?* Amy felt like it was supposed to mean something, but her head was still too foggy to figure it out. All but one of the men – the boss, 'el jefe', Amy presumed – were heavily armed with the same type of weapons that had been used to kidnap her and her friends. *My friends!* Amy was overcome with panic when she remembered the sixteen other girls she was travelling with and realized that she couldn't see or hear any of them.

"Good. You're awake. I was beginning to think Emiliano had killed you."

Amy gasped. She knew that voice. And then there he was. Standing in front of her, staring down at her dirty, bruised body: Ricky. The guy from their flight. The one they were supposed to meet at the bar. Despite the oppressive heat in the room, a shiver ran up Amy's spine as she realized that this was going to get a lot worse before it got any better. *If* it got any better.

NINE

Ricky continued to stand over Amy, a smug look of satisfaction on his face and evil gleaming in his eyes.

"Where are my friends?" Amy croaked, her voice stiff from her involuntary sleep.

"Oh, they're here too, don't you worry about that," replied Ricky with a smile. "Emiliano wanted you kept away from the group until you woke up."

Amy got halfway through her next question of 'where am I' when the unarmed man in the room strode over to the spot where Amy had now pushed herself up to sit on the floor.

"No questions!" the man barked in heavily-accented English. He then motioned from Amy to the door and told Ricky "al otro cuarto," which Amy assumed meant that she was being taken into another room to rejoin her friends. At the jefe's command the other men in the room sprang into action, lifting Amy off the floor and practically carrying her out the door and across a short hall into a much larger room. On the other side, away from the door, were her friends.

Amy burst into tears at the sight of them, and many of the other girls did the same. A man who looked like the enforcer of the group put a quick end to the hostages' joy when he took a large baton of sorts and whipped the women who had been crying.

"¡Siéntate! ¡Y no hables!" were Amy's instructions as she was unceremoniously dumped on the ground next to her sorority sisters. Amy began to ask her 'where am I' question once again, even though she knew she had just been told to sit down and be quiet.

"He said don't talk!" came Ricky's translation, and Amy knew her mission had been accomplished. If she was going to make it out of wherever she was alive – and she fully intended to – then she needed to use every advantage she could. And keeping the kidnappers unaware of her Spanish skills was definitely a huge advantage.

****

For what seemed like an eternity, the enforcer guy stood close to the group of girls, watching them with a glare that was almost daring them to talk. Like he was thinking 'go ahead, try to say something, because then I get to hit you.' As Amy looked around at her friends joining her on the hard, dirty concrete floor, she could see her own fears reflected in their eyes. Ashley was immediately to her left, a brunette with shoulder length hair that was now falling over her face as she bent her head in prayer. Ashley wasn't what Amy would call a devout Catholic, but she always attended mass on the important holidays, and there are no atheists in foxholes, right? Okay, so maybe they weren't soldiers, but Amy definitely felt like a prisoner in a war that she hadn't known she was fighting.

Amy's eyes continued to scan the rows of semi-circles comprised of frightened sorority girls. She wasn't surprised to see Lindsey, Allison, Amanda, and Emily all sitting together, since they had kind of been the four musketeers ever since freshman year. They were all dressed alike too, wearing cute sundresses that were at least one season out of style but could certainly pass for current fashions in Acapulco. Next to the four musketeers sat girls named Tanner and Kristen, both tall, pretty blondes who had made the unfortunate decision to wear jeans last night. *Was it last night? What day is it?* Amy's survey of the other girls was sidelined by her realization that she had absolutely no idea how long she had been there. In reality, it was the middle of the night, only a few hours after the girls were abducted on the side of the road, but she had no way of knowing that in this windowless room. Amy shook her head to clear those thoughts from her mind, instead focusing back on the other girls. Tanner and Kristen had both already rolled up the legs of their jeans as far as they could, and were looking with jealous eyes towards Elizabeth and Sarah, both of whom had chosen to wear shorts and tank tops to the bar and were therefore undeniably the most comfortable in the group.

Amy saw Kennedy next, a redhead with freckles that somehow worked for her and politics that were the exact opposite of what her name would suggest. The red rims of her eyes matched her hair, and the only reason she had stopped crying was because she had run out of tears. The two young women next to her hadn't reached that point yet, as the tears continued to fall while they held tight to each other. Brittany and Heather were sisters, Irish twins, and, although Heather was a year younger than the rest of the group, she had quickly become a member of their social circle.

The mental accounting of the rest of the girls was interrupted as, finally, the enforcer dude walked to the other side of the room to join Ricky and the other men. When he was out of ear shot, a girl named Sophie whispered to Amy: "Are you okay?" Amy could hear the concern in the other girl's voice. She could only imagine what they thought had happened to her while she had been kept in the other room.

Amy, fearful of the ever-present watch of the men on the other side of the room, simply nodded her head yes. She then began to try to get a better feel for her surroundings. Amy's younger brother, Josh, had been a Boy Scout when he was a kid and had always annoyed her by constantly talking about being prepared and knowing your environment. Amy told herself she'd have to thank Josh for that when she got home. When, not if.

The room she was in now was significantly larger than the one she had just been in. Probably somewhere in between a squash court and a basketball court, Amy guessed. The walls and floor were concrete, as if they were in a basement of some sort. It was old concrete, though, evidenced by the brown stains on the walls from water damage and years without cleaning. The basement theory would also explain why it was so damp and humid, although it was still oppressively hot and basements, in Amy's experience, were usually somewhat cooler. *Maybe not in Mexico*, Amy thought. Even the parts of the concrete that weren't stained were turning to a tan color – it could definitely use a good power-washing – and the ceiling was solid wood, not the kind of drop ceiling that Amy was used to from school buildings. *What is this place?* Amy wondered. *A storage spot for drugs? A holding cell for prisoners? Have they brought other kidnapped people here before?*

Kidnapped. That word sent shivers up her spine. In the next instant, though, it gave her hope. *Kidnapped. We've been kidnapped. Bad guys kidnap people to get ransom money, right? They'll contact our families, demand money, our families will pay, and then they'll let us go. Kidnapped. Secuestrada. Okay. I can handle kidnapped.*

Amy had never liked uncertainty; she hated surprises and always wanted to have a plan for everything. One year when she was a teenager her parents had planned a surprise birthday party, but after listening to their daughter explain in detail one day how much she didn't like being surprised, they told her about the party four days before it was scheduled to happen. Consequently, once Amy remembered that kidnappings were followed by ransom demands, payment, and release, her nerves calmed down a considerable amount. She knew what was supposed to happen now.

TEN

Amy had been super excited about the trip to Mexico. But not only for the reasons that people thought. When asked, she said that she was very excited and it would be so much fun to go on the trip with so many of her college friends. And to work on her tan, of course . . . with the last line being delivered with her trademark wink and smile. Her combination of pretty blue eyes and sparkling white teeth had become a powerful tool over the years, as Amy cultivated and tweaked it for use with her parents, teachers, and the few boyfriends she had. In reality, though, the trip had symbolized something more for Amy. A capstone to her graduation. A jumpstart to her freedom and independence. She knew it didn't make much sense to attach notions of adulthood to a trip that had all the hallmarks of a typical college spring break, but Amy didn't mind that inconsistency. The good girl, type-A go-getter had begun her plan of defiance by even going on the trip at all, since her parents had been among the loudest objectors to the girls' desire to vacation in Mexico. Amy could still hear her mother's impassioned declarations of how dangerous it would be, especially without any men in their travel party. Amy, while mindful of the travel advisories and news stories about drug violence in Mexico, had dismissed her mother's concerns as being 'paranoid' and driven by her overexposure to television shows like *CSI* and *Law & Order*.

Jack and Linda Millhouse's arguments against the vacation had been considerably weakened by the other parents' agreement to the trip and the fact that, at twenty-two or twenty-three years old, none of the sorority sisters actually needed their parents' permission to go to Mexico. They had also been taken somewhat by surprise by the new, defiant, 'I'll do what I want' Amy that had appeared in her final year of college. And the new, defiant, 'I'll do what I want' Amy had gotten her way regarding the trip to Acapulco.

The 'new Amy' had no plans of going away any time soon, either. Instead, she would continue with her teaching job starting that fall. Amy had told her father that Teach for America was a great service opportunity and she would use it to increase her chances of getting accepted to law school. However, the new Amy (or the old, real one who had just been hiding until now) fully intended to 'fall in love with teaching,' never even take the Law School Admission Test, and keep that job until she got married and could become a stay-at-home mom.

It was a bit backwards, Amy knew. A lot of the time women told stories of being stay-at-home moms but longing to go out and join the workforce. Amy's college career counselor had laughed and called Amy a 'feminist boomerang,' but Amy was completely serious. All that this high school valedictorian, cheerleading captain, and sorority president wanted to 'do with her life' was be a wife and a mother.

By all accounts, until the kidnapping, Amy had lived a charmed life. Her parents were both still alive and married to each other. Although one of her grandfathers had died several years earlier, she was fortunate enough to have gotten to know him and her other still-living grandparents, as well as several of her great-grandparents. While her younger brother could be supremely annoying at times, he was a good kid (well, young man now) and Amy knew she could always count on him. The biggest stressors in Amy's life had always been the high expectations of those around her. 'To whom much is given, much is expected, darlin''' was what her father loved to tell her. His father, the one who passed away, had told her the exact same thing several times; except he said "sugah" instead of "darlin'."

The truth was that Amy shouldered a large amount of guilt over the fact that what she was expected to do and what her talents allowed her to do were far different from what she wanted to do. But now all of that was far less important. In the face of possible death, of maybe never making it home, the charades that Amy had been playing with her family and friends for years seemed petty and childish. The only thing that mattered now was surviving. Taking whatever tortuous treatment the kidnappers might throw at her until the ransom was paid and she got to go home.

ELEVEN

In the wee hours of the morning, after the girls had been reunited in the big holding room and their belongings carefully searched for any valuables or identification, after the sorority sisters had collapsed in exhaustion on the concrete floor and fallen into a deep, terror-induced sleep, a young man stood nearby, watching them, crowing with pride at his accomplishment. In Ricky's world of spotting potential kidnapping victims, he had established certain guidelines to go by. Richer was always better, of course. Children of the rich were to be avoided if possible, because although the chance of ransom payment was greater, so were the odds of private security teams and retaliation. If a Mexican national, pick a man. If a foreigner, pick a woman. The lighter skinned the better. And boy had he followed the guidelines with this group. Seventeen Americans, all female, all white, all pretty, and – if their clothes, jewelry, and hotel were any indication – all from relatively wealthy families. Ricky, standing proud over his catch like a fisherman in the Pacific Northwest or a hunter on safari in Africa, would receive 1,000 U.S. dollars for each of these girls. Not to mention his cut of any ransom money from their families. This was his best operation by far.

The young man brushed his brown hair back away from his eyes as he reflected on his career to this point. Ricky's mom was from Cuba and her parents were from Europe, and with such light skin he could easily pass for a tourist when he wanted to. Some of his aunts and uncles had escaped Cuba to the United States as refugees, and the long stretches of time he spent visiting them in America as a kid meant his English was nearly perfect. No Spanglish like some of the other men; he barely had any accent at all. Those traits had quickly vaulted young Ricardo from cartel foot soldier to a highly-valuable niche position in the organization: victim scouting. Ricky's job – he had quickly dropped Ricardo for the more ethnically ambiguous Ricky several years ago – was simply to blend in with the moneyed crowd at the resorts, find out details about where they were from, what room they were staying in, and any plans to leave the secure resort area to sample the 'local scene.' He then passed that information along to whichever group of *narcos* had hired him, collected his finder's fee, and went on to the next job.

His first had been a low-level mark, a local merchant, chosen more to hone his skills at picking targets than out of any desire to make the man pay any money. This selection, though, these girls, were different. This was his fifteenth scouting, as he called it, but the first one where he would stay with the operation through the end. Although being a spotter gave him more job flexibility, this was where the real money was. And Ricky knew he had hit the jackpot this time.

One of the girls stirred in her sleep and it reminded him that he was tired too. It had been a long last couple of days. With one final, gleeful glance over the group of Americans lying at his feet, Ricky turned, walked back across the room, and headed up the stairs to go to bed.

TWELVE

Was it just a dream? Maybe? Please?

The sound of chairs scraping against the concrete floor and men talking rapidly in Spanish gave Amy her answer. It wasn't a dream. This was real.

The guards were obviously changing shifts, and the three men who stood watch during the night were being replaced by the daytime guards. *Five of them. Seems a bit much*, Amy thought. *They must really be worried about us trying to escape. Like we'd ever be able to overpower grown men with machine guns.*

The other girls had also woken up by now, since the men on the other side of the room refused to be quiet and the smoke from their cigarettes spread through the air. Amy coughed as the smoke filled her lungs – she had always been particularly sensitive to cigarette smoke – but she knew that the irritation she was feeling in her chest was nothing compared to what one of the other girls, Katie, must be going through. Katie had a pretty bad case of asthma and always carried an inhaler with her. She didn't have the inhaler with her now, though, since the kidnappers had taken all of their purses and jewelry and other personal belongings. *I hope she doesn't have an asthma attack while we're here*, Amy thought, crossing her fingers.

"Pssst, Amy." Amy slowly turned her head around to see who was whispering to her. It was Emily, a member of the four musketeers with mousy brown hair and a squeaky voice to match. She had never been close friends with the girl, and in fact Emily was probably her least favorite member of her sorority pledge class. There was just something about the girl that rubbed her the wrong way. "Amy," Emily repeated in the same low whisper.

Rather than answer the girl, since they weren't supposed to talk, Amy simply nodded her head and raised her eyebrows a little bit to signal that she had heard her.

"Do you think they're going to feed us?"

"How should I know?" Amy whispered back. "They don't talk things through with me."

"I don't know," Emily responded. "I just thought they might have told you while you were in the other room."

"Well, they didn't," Amy sharply replied and then turned her head back around. She knew Emily was just curious – and hungry – but they didn't need to push their luck with the guards by whispering all the time. Especially for questions that didn't need to be asked.

Seemingly on cue, though, the girls heard what sounded like footsteps on stairs and then a man walked into the room carrying a big steel cooking pot. Another man followed him with two plastic shopping bags in one hand and a large pitcher of what looked like water in the other. One of the guards at the table stood up and walked alongside the newcomers, bringing his big, black pistol with him.

The man with the pot set it down on the floor in front of the girls, and then took one of the shopping bags and began pulling out small plastic bowls.

"You eat," he barked at the sorority sisters in a gruff, accented voice.

Eat what? Amy thought, before her question was answered by the nasty-looking gunk that the man began ladling out of the pot and plopping into the bowls. The man who carried the bags then started handing the bowls to the girls.

When Amy received her bowl she just stared down at its contents, amazed that anyone would think that this was food suitable for human consumption.

"What is this?" Amy asked boldly, knowing the risk she took by speaking.

"No talk! You eat!" the pot man growled back at her in response.

Amy opened her mouth to protest, but it was quickly shut for her by the cold, hard blast of a 9mm pistol slamming against the side of her face.

"He said don't talk!" the guard declared angrily.

So that's what it feels like to be pistol-whipped, Amy thought as she instinctively covered the right side of her face with her hand. Big alligator tears and a few lines of blood streamed down her face and Amy could feel her cheek and eye begin to swell. A large number of the tears dripped from Amy's chin into the bowl in her hands, mixing with whatever congealed, gray mush the girls had been served. *Maybe the salt from my tears will add some flavor*, Amy couldn't help but think as she set the bowl down on the ground and gratefully accepted the small glass of water that the bag-carrying man was handing her. *A bowl of concrete mix and a glass of water. These guys should audition for Top Chef,* Amy mused, her head pounding from the impact of the gun ramming into her cheek.

Once the 'breakfast' had been served, the three men walked back across the room and away from the girls. The guard who had hit Amy rejoined a card game, and the other two kidnappers left the room entirely. Amy and the other girls could once again hear footsteps on stairs as the men returned to wherever they had come from. *So we are in some sort of basement,* Amy thought. *Or at least a lower level of something.*

"Are you okay?" her good friend Caitlin asked in a worried whisper. "He hit you really hard."

"I'll be fine," Amy whispered back. The right side of her face was still on fire and was probably at least double its normal size, but there wasn't anything that Amy could do about that now. She instead returned her focus to the bowl sitting in front of her, and realized for the first time that they had not been given spoons or any other kind of utensil with which they could eat. *Oh well,* Amy thought as she raised the bowl to her mouth. *If we're going to be having dog food we might as well eat it like dogs.*

This wasn't how this trip was supposed to go. It was supposed to be fun. But this, this room, this 'food,' this pain, was definitely not fun. It would be so easy to just give up, Amy thought. Suddenly, Amy could hear the words of her old gym coach ringing in her ears as she sat slumped on the hard concrete, stars and tweety birds still dancing in front of her eyes. "Don't quit on yourself!"

Don't quit on yourself, Amy repeated. *Don't quit on yourself.*

THIRTEEN

A few hours after their first "food" was served, Amy noticed that, in addition to the lingering pain from the pistol whip, her face began to itch. She usually washed her face twice a day, morning and night, and now it had been almost twenty-four hours since she'd last had access to soap and water. Her makeup from the night they headed to the bar was now a mixture of smudged off and caked-on, leading to what she knew must be a lovely, splotchy look. She knew she also probably looked a bit like a raccoon from her smeared eye shadow and mascara, even though Amy had tried her best to wipe away the smudges from under her eyes – a task made more difficult by the fact that she really didn't want to lick her finger with her tongue to get it wet, given that it had also been a long time since she'd washed her hands. Her teeth had long-since acquired a nasty, filmy feel to them from a lack of brushing, and she grinned a little at the thought that her best attempt at escape right now would probably be breathing on the kidnappers, since her breath undoubtedly reeked.

Amy knew it didn't matter what she looked like or how bad her breath smelled – the other girls were in just as bad of shape in that regard and it wasn't like they were trying to impress the kidnappers. No, Amy just wanted to look good because doing so made her feel good. Like the rest of her sorority sisters in the room, like her mom, heck, like every proper Southern woman Amy had ever known, she took pride in her appearance. But that appearance right now was, well, less than spectacular.

Amy could only imagine what the pictures would look like if they were suddenly rescued now. *Eww, gosh that'd be terrible*, Amy thought. *My face, immortalized for all of the world to see me, looking like a cross between the work of a three-year-old makeup artist and a Picasso painting.*

Will we be rescued soon? Amy couldn't help but wonder. She also couldn't help the next thought that came creeping into her mind: *will we be rescued at all?* Amy shuddered. *Surely, somebody will find us. They have to know we're missing by now, right? We never came back from the bar that first night – we never even made it to the bar that night – surely someone noticed?* Maybe that concierge dude, the one who Amy should've listened to when he asked, voice full of paternal concern, if they really wanted to go to that bar. *Or what about the taxi drivers? Wouldn't they have told the police about their passengers being kidnapped?* Not that the local Mexican police forces were known as being bastions of justice.

A wave of bad feelings suddenly rushed over Amy. *What happened to the taxi drivers?*

"Psst. Caitlin," Amy whispered to her friend and former roommate, seated beside her on the dusty floor. She had two questions for her friend – the only two she couldn't seem to figure out on her own.

"What?" Caitlin whispered back. Amy didn't usually initiate conversations when kidnappers were in the room, so the other girl knew something must be going on.

"What's up with Laura Ann?" Amy nodded her head in the direction of the third girl, who Amy had noticed was curled up in a ball, her skimpy, all-white outfit ruined by dirt and grime and blood. Laura Ann hadn't yet made eye contact with her . . . come to think of it, she wasn't really making eye contact with anyone.

"They made an example of her," Caitlin slowly answered, her eyes glued to the ground as she picked at the concrete beneath her. She didn't elaborate, but she didn't need to. Laura Ann had been raped.

"Just her?" Amy whispered back.

Caitlin simply nodded her head. For the first time in her life, the naturally curious Amy didn't want to know any more. She didn't need to. Instead, she continued on to her next question.

"What happened to the taxi drivers?" Amy asked, giving voice to the question that had run through her mind just moments ago. Amy knew the answer wasn't a good one by the look on her friend's face.

"You don't remember?" Caitlin asked, her eyes glancing across the room to check and make sure the guards hadn't noticed them talking.

Amy shook her head no in response. "I got knocked out. I don't know what happened."

"They're dead," Caitlin whispered, her voice shaking as tears welled up in her eyes. "They . . . they shot them," she continued.

"They grabbed us all and put us in the vans and SUVs, then they lined up the drivers and – "

Caitlin's sentence was interrupted by the hard glare of one of the men from across the room. Amy followed her friend's gaze and realized that she wouldn't be hearing any more of the story anytime soon. Also not going away anytime soon was the terrible feeling in the pit of her stomach. *Laura Ann was raped. To send a message to the rest of us. And the taxi drivers are dead. Killed. Because they happened to be the ones to answer the hotel's request for cabs to drive a group of girls a couple of miles. Because of me. They're dead because of me.*

FOURTEEN

Laura Ann could tell that Amy and Caitlin were talking about her. She saw the eyes dart over toward her, the grimaces and looks of pity on the two girls' faces. Laura Ann wouldn't lie, she had been enormously relieved when Amy was brought into the room to rejoin the rest of the group. Their fearless sorority president had been missing ever since they arrived in the big room, and no one would tell them where she was. But Laura Ann also couldn't help but notice that Amy didn't look much worse for the wear. Sure, she had a massive bruise on her forehead, which made sense after Caitlin said she remembered Amy getting hit in the head and knocked out by a gun. But aside from that, and the place where she got hit for talking, she looked fine. Laura Ann was anything but fine.

Truth be told, Laura Ann had never liked Amy Millhouse. Little Miss Perfect was what she and some other sorority sisters called their vener-hated president. Nobody was that good. That perfect. Everybody has secrets; flaws. They just couldn't seem to find Amy's. She was pretty, smart, nice, very organized, and even Laura Ann had to admit she made a great sorority president. If honest with herself, Laura Ann was jealous. Amy had everything she didn't – money, good grades, and a sterling reputation. Laura Ann had never cared much about that last one, though. She was pretty and she knew it, and her mother had taught her from a very young age how to use her feminine wiles to her advantage. Men were easy to manipulate and control, if you knew what buttons to push. Besides, Laura Ann liked men, and they liked her. And unlike pure-as-the-driven-snow Amy Millhouse, Laura Ann liked sex. In her opinion, previous generations of women hadn't fought long and hard for equal rights and women's liberation for her to throw it away by being a save-it-all-for-marriage Stepford Wife.

Laura Ann had seen the looks that Amy and her sidekick Caitlin had given her when she was talking about going out and meeting up with strange guys at the bar on their first night in Mexico. Not quite "you're a whore" – level judgment, but close. And yes, Ricky had turned out to be evil and their bar plans a trap. But it's not like she had known that would happen. Laura Ann couldn't help but wonder if the other girls thought she had it coming . . . thought she somehow deserved to be singled out by the kidnappers to be raped.

Laura Ann knew why the men had targeted her. Why they made an example of her. She knew exactly why. On the plane, talking to Ricky, she had been only too happy to put on her best sexy, flirting routine. Batting her eyelashes. Twirling a strand of hair around her finger. Leaning forward, across the arm bar separating the two seats, to whisper parts of stories to Ricky and then finish them with a coy smile. Laura Ann knew the tricks of the seduction trade well, and she had put them on full display for the handsome stranger. So, naturally, when the kidnappers declared that they were going to make an example out of a girl to show the rest what would happen if they didn't behave and do as they were told, Laura Ann had immediately known that she would be the one who was raped.

Part of her wished they had killed her instead. Every terrible thing she had ever heard or read about what it's like to be a rape victim – the fear, the violation, the pain, the shame – it was all true. After it was over, she had huddled by herself in the corner, as far away from everyone as she could get, her knees pulled up to her chest as she rocked back and forth to the sound of her own tears.

****

Ricky had watched Laura Ann from across the room after one of the other men had raped her, only several hours removed from the actual abduction itself. He started to feel a little better about selecting her as the example. Ricky had told Emiliano that they should pick someone else, pick a different girl. After the way she had come onto him on the plane ride from the U.S. to Mexico, Ricky had no doubt that Laura Ann was a little slut – a *jinetera*, as his Cuban mother would call her – and he felt like the girls wouldn't be as affected by Laura Ann's rape as they would be by making an example of one of the other ones . . . like the little brunette with the feisty eyes that he heard some of them call Caitlin.

But now, looking across to the corner at the shell of a woman who remained, nearly twelve hours after the rape, still hugging her knees and slowing rocking herself back and forth, Ricky knew they had picked the right girl. Emiliano had been right. Picking the slut as the victim had actually doubled the impact of the rape. Now the other girls were sitting across the room, alternating between trying not to stare at Laura Ann and glaring in his direction, and undoubtedly thinking that if being sexually assaulted impacted Laura Ann that much – Laura Ann with all of her experience with men – then what an impact it would have on them too. Ricky slowly unveiled his trademarked evil grin. Everything was going according to plan.

FIFTEEN

It's funny the things you think about when the only thing you have to do is sit and think. The things that catch your attention. Emily, the girl with all the questions, couldn't stop watching one of the other girls, Tanner, as she absentmindedly rubbed her left thumb back and forth over the spot where her engagement ring had once been. There was no denying that it was a gorgeous ring. Just over one-carat, in a beautiful white gold setting. Tanner's fiancé, Matt, clearly had help from his parents in buying it, but who cares when you end up with a ring like that.

The kidnappers had taken Tanner's ring and the rest of the jewelry that the girls were wearing, along with their purses and anything they had in their pockets. The jewelry that Emily brought on the trip was all from Target so she wasn't really all that upset, but a couple of girls had been wearing nice pearl necklaces that their families had given them. *Gone now*, Emily thought. Also gone were the paper copies of their passports that the girls had all been carrying, although she knew that the passports wouldn't really give the men all that much to go on – unless they planned to call the U.S. Embassy and read off a list of names of who they had kidnapped. Emily didn't think that would be the smartest move on their part, and these guys seemed smart. Practiced. Professional.

Emily was upset, though, about losing the purse she had been carrying. It was a designer handbag from Kate Spade, a gift from an ex-boyfriend. Maybe the bad guys hadn't taken it. *Maybe it got left behind at the spot where they took us.* If that was the case, then the police might have found it and she could get it back whenever they got out of this hell hole. It was a really nice purse – went with almost everything. Classy enough for dinners out but could also be an everyday bag. *I really hope I get it back.*

It's funny the things you think about.

****

Caitlin was also watching as Tanner continued to rub her thumb around her ring finger. Caitlin hadn't lost anything of great value, since her mother taught her at a young age to never bring any nice jewelry on a trip unless absolutely necessary. Even though Caitlin's earrings and necklaces were all insured, with the kind of jewels that women in her family accumulated, any benefit of travelling with them really wasn't worth the risk of losing them.

Caitlin wished this room had windows. She wanted so desperately to be able to see outside. She was a business management major, an economics minor, but Caitlin had always been fascinated by the weather. The other girls in the sorority teased her – good naturedly, of course – about the fact that her television was always tuned to The Weather Channel. There wasn't anything she would be able to do with the information if she could see outside, no one to tell, no advantage to gain against the men holding her hostage. That was demonstrated by the fact that one of the men, the one with the kind eyes and soft voice, would occasionally say things like "hot outside today" or "happy rain come tomorrow."

But oh, what she wouldn't give just to see the sun right now. Or maybe she would see rain or clouds . . . it didn't really matter. Any kind of reminder that there was a world outside of this God-forsaken room was all she was asking for. Instead, she got to look at concrete. Concrete beside her, concrete below her. *And for those desiring a change in scenery, there's a lovely solid wood display above you*, Caitlin mused, the voice in her head adopting its best impersonation of a Manhattan real estate agent. Her grandfather's Fifth Avenue apartment had solid wood floors. And an awesome view of Central Park. *I wonder if there are any parks nearby this place?*

It's funny the things you think about.

SIXTEEN

And there was evening and there was morning – the second day.
Amy couldn't help but wonder, as she sat on the cool, humidity-dampened concrete floor early in the morning of the second day, how many other girls had sat there before her. Something made her always picture the other kidnapping victims being like her – young, white, female – but she knew that logically it could've been anyone. Young, old, male, female, white, black, brown, or yellow. She also knew that the odds were that most victims were middle to upper-middle class Mexican nationals. She knew that, yet when she closed her eyes and imagined it, all of the victims looked like her. Amy figured there was probably some fancy psychology word to explain that, but she didn't know what it was and frankly didn't care.

Had there been other victims, though? The men holding them hostage certainly acted like they knew what they were doing. Had they demanded ransom for the other people? Had they raped some of the other women, too? Amy knew the answer to both of those questions was probably yes.

What about the big question, though – had they let those people go? Were they back home with their families now, maybe not sound but at least safe? Or were they dead, buried in a cemetery somewhere? Or, Amy shuddered, were they buried here?

****

Directly above Amy, on a wooden chair next to a round kitchen table, sat the man the girls all knew as Scarface. A jagged scar ran down the side of his face, from the outer edge of his right eye down over his prominent cheekbone and curling slightly inward to a stop just above where he shaved daily to keep his face clear of any beard or mustache. He had gotten the mark by which he would be defined for the rest of his life when he was in a street fight at age fourteen – a dispute over a girl that he thought would be settled with fists but was instead determined by the quick and unexpected slice of jagged metal across his face.

His real name was José María, but the girls didn't know that. To them, he was Scarface. He reminded Heather, who had played soccer in high school, of the French soccer star Franck Ribéry because of a similar scar that he had. Scarface reminded Amy of her dad, because Al Pacino's *Scarface* was one of Mr. Millhouse's favorite movies. That was where the girls got their nickname for him. And he reminded Laura Ann of her favorite childhood movie, *The Lion King*. But she didn't dare reveal that to any of the other girls. That would be way too childish for the girl who was always rushing to look and act older.

Right now, though, as he ate a quick breakfast after finishing night watch duty before heading down the hall to a bedroom for a nap, Scarface was having thoughts not completely unlike his blonde captive downstairs. This was José María's sixth kidnapping as part of Emiliano's gang. Several of the men, himself included, had once been low-level members of one of the bigger cartels, but they had gotten frustrated by the bureaucracy and lack of opportunity for advancement beyond foot soldier status. So Emiliano had formed his own group, claiming some territory in the Guerrero countryside and making most of their money through carjackings, roadside robberies, and occasional kidnappings. José María had been with Emiliano from the beginning. At age thirty-three, he was a seasoned veteran, having been doing work of some sort in the drug-trafficking/extortion/kidnapping realm for more than half his life. He often wondered when the government and the press would drop all of the various terms that they had for men like him and groups like his and simply refer to them as the Mexican mafia. Organized crime is what they did, after all. And José María knew the organization of every crime they had committed.

These new kids, though, didn't know the group's past. Didn't know their struggles, or what it took to start from scratch. Scarface knew they needed the manpower – even while heavily armed it takes a lot of people to pull off a kidnapping this big. Men to physically kidnap the girls. Men to drive the vans and SUVs. Men to guard the basement. Men to guard the outside of the house. Extra men to rotate in so no one got fatigued and made a stupid mistake. José María understood all of that; he had spent countless nights planning the operation with Emiliano and Paquito. Nevertheless, he sometimes felt like a babysitter in addition to a kidnapper. Davíd had been with their crew for a long time but was still too damn nice. The new driver, Ángel, looked more scared than some of the girls did. Marcelo, the big guy, definitely did his job well but also gave Scarface the creeps. There was a screw loose somewhere with him. And Alejandro, Emiliano's brother? The boy was practically still in diapers. All of these rookies made José María nervous. One of them would cause problems. He knew it.

Looking out a kitchen window into the back yard, Scarface reflected that finding this house had been a stroke of luck for him. He and Emiliano knew they needed somewhere relatively remote to serve as an operating base and a spot to bury the bodies they couldn't dump on the streets, but the location couldn't be so remote that it made operations difficult. And it wasn't like they had a ton of bodies to bury – their group much preferred the quick, clean operation of highway robbery or the use of extortion (keeping victims alive meant they could keep paying). Also, Emiliano generally believed in holding up his end of the bargain regarding ransom payments. Most of the people that they killed were from rival gangs or were locals who were either too curious for their own good or wanna-be saints trying to "clean up" the area. Clean it up . . . Ha. José María recognized, though, that they needed a good bit of land to bury the bodies, because the men all knew that nothing is worse than walking over a spot and knowing that there is a slowly-rotting corpse beneath your feet.

This spot, a former ranch house of some businessman from the city, was perfect. Centrally located between Acapulco and the state's capital city of Chilpancingo, with enough rooms for the men, enough land for the bodies, and a perfect basement for stashing drugs or hiding people. He had heard of some other *narco* groups having trouble with former land owners; other people who had abandoned their homes when the violence kept escalating and then changed their minds, only to show up and realize that drug traffickers had taken over the land. But Emiliano and José María had been using this spot regularly for the past five months or so without any trouble from its real owner. The perfect spot.

The sound of gunshots snapped José María back to the present. *What the hell?* he thought as he quickly grabbed the pistol lying on the table in front of him and headed for the door that led out of the kitchen into the carport. *No one should be shooting. No one should be shooting!*

Meanwhile, downstairs, Caitlin wondered if she had just heard thunder.

SEVENTEEN

Jesús Rodríguez never wanted to abandon his ranch in the Guerrero countryside. The Chilpancingo banker was really a cowboy at heart, and he had been prepared to fight fire with fire if any *narcos* tried to come take his land away from him. Fortunately or unfortunately, depending on who one asked, Jesús' wife had convinced him that it simply wasn't safe for them to spend any more time on the ranch. For the sake of his wife and children, almost two years ago he agreed to move to the city full-time. That didn't mean he had completely abandoned his property, though. Unbeknownst to his wife, every few months Jesús would drive out to the house to make sure no one else had taken up residence and no acts of vandalism had been done. He even cut the grass while he was there to make it look like someone still lived on the land. On his last visit out, about three months ago, Jesús noticed some tire tracks in the driveway and other signs that people had been there, but he didn't see anyone and consequently wasn't all that worried about it.

As his truck rattled and rambled down the long, curvy driveway and his house came into view, Jesús immediately knew that this trip wouldn't be like the rest. For starters, there were two big, black SUVs parked in the carport and what looked like the back end of another one sticking out from behind the house. *I've gotta get out of here*, he thought. Jesús stopped and shifted the truck into reverse, but as he turned his head around to look behind him, he quickly realized that going out backwards wasn't going to work. The driveway was too long, too curvy, and too bumpy for that. He would just end up crashing his truck, stranding him here in the middle of nowhere with yet-to-be-identified people who were undoubtedly up to no good.

Three point turn. It's my only option. Upon making his decision, Jesús quickly put his truck back into drive and went toward the house. As the stucco building drew closer and closer, Jesús glanced at the loaded shotgun lying in the passenger seat beside him. At that point, he actually wished he didn't have the gun. Feigning innocence would have been far easier if he wasn't armed. When it came down to it, Jesús realized, he wasn't a cowboy after all. He just wanted to get out of there. Back home to his wife and kids, where he would be safe.

The heart that had been beating at a frantic pace in Jesús Rodríguez's chest nearly stopped when he saw two men exit the house and walk toward the spot in the driveway where he had been planning on turning around, each carrying a machine gun in their hands. *Fuck. Shit fuck fuck.* The curse words tumbled through Jesús' mind as he recognized that he was trapped. And, based on the looks on the men's faces, probably going to die.

Jesús pulled his truck to a stop and rolled down the window, trying his best to appear innocent, nice, and not completely terrified. Before the scowling men opened their mouths, Jesús launched into his explanation. He used to live here a long, long time ago. He was driving through the area and thought, for old time's sake, that he'd stop by and see the place. He really didn't mean to disturb anyone and as soon as he got his truck turned around he would leave. *Please believe me*, he prayed. *Pleeeease let me go.*

Jesús could tell that one of the men was inclined to believe him. He was the one who spoke first. "Bueno, vete." *Leave.* Breathing a sigh of relief, Jesús began to execute his three-point turn in the driveway, careful to avoid going anywhere near the two men who had now moved off to the side. He never saw it coming.

****

"¿¡Qué hiciste?!" José María yelled as he got to the driveway. He wanted to know what they had done – wanted to understand why in the world two of his men had opened fire in broad daylight. It wasn't necessary, unless . . . *is that a truck?* Scarface's eyes focused down the driveway about ten yards to a silver crew cab truck. One of his men had jumped halfway inside to stop the vehicle from continuing to roll away. The other member of the duo who had been assigned outside watch duty that morning was standing a few feet away from José María, the look in his eyes a mix of pride in his shot and a quickly-developing fear that he would get in trouble for it.

José María listened as the shooter, Hector, scrambled to defend his actions. *He might have seen something*, came the first explanation. *He might have called the Federales and told them to*

come out here. Something had to be done. He had to be stopped.
José María simply pursed his lips and glared in disbelief at the young man's story. Turning around, he walked back to the house to let Emiliano know what all the commotion was about.

****

It certainly wasn't Hector's finest hour. The tongue lashing his bosses were giving him was worse than anything he had ever received from his father as a boy. So he shot the guy . . . big deal. Except it was turning out to be a very big deal in Emiliano's eyes. Someone could have heard the gunshots. The dead guy's family would probably come looking for him, and the last thing they needed during the middle of this kidnapping was more search parties snooping around.

Since Hector had been the one to shoot the guy, he was ordered to also clean up the mess. Along with Ángel, who Emiliano said needed some toughening up, Hector pulled the body out of the front and dumped it around back in the bed of the truck. He then had to get in the driver's seat, blood and brain splattered everywhere, and drive the vehicle around back of the house so it couldn't be seen. That night, he, Ángel, and José María would drive the truck and the body into the city and dump them – setting up the scene to look like a robbery. Hector knew that they usually sent the big, mean guy, Marcelo, to handle stuff like this, but he also knew that Marcelo had a tendency to get carried away with his victims and probably couldn't just settle for a robbery scene. Which meant Hector had to dump the body, with Ángel for help and José María for supervision. *Fan-freaking-tastic*, he thought as he walked back inside the house to take a shower and wash off the dead guy's blood.

EIGHTEEN

"Is this really the only food they're ever going to serve us?" Caitlin whispered to Amy as the girls stared at their second consecutive day of gray mush pudding. Breakfast had been delayed that morning, with some sort of commotion going on upstairs. For a split second the girls thought it might be someone coming to rescue them, but that hope quickly faded. "I know how to cook," Caitlin continued. "Not much, but better than this."

A small smile creased Amy's face at her friend's declaration of her limited cooking skills. Caitlin had a live-in housekeeper/cook throughout her childhood, an unlimited meal plan her freshman year of college, and had lived in the sorority house the past three years where the housemother doubled as a cook. Caitlin could find her way around a microwave, but that was about it. Nonetheless, Amy knew her friend was right – her cooking would be better than this.

A high-pitched scream jolted Amy out of her thoughts. It was Amanda, and she shrieked again before Amy could figure out what was going on. Everyone in the room had been caught off-guard, including the kidnappers, and one of the men on watch duty ran over, gun in hand, demanding to know why Amanda kept making that god-awful noise.

****

By the time Amanda realized her mistake, it was too late. Her response to the bug in her food had been automatic – she always screamed like that when she came in close contact with an insect. Amanda Hillis didn't like bugs. No, it wasn't just that she didn't like them. She hated them. She had never been a tomboy growing up, had never made forts in the woods or lived in a cabin at summer camp. She had had very little exposure to creepy-crawlers of any kind in her life, and she preferred to keep it that way.
And so she had screamed, loudly, when she looked down into her bowl of mush and saw a bug moving around, its nasty arms and legs and tentacles contaminating her one daily meal. Amanda didn't know if she was more afraid of the bug or the armed man glaring

down at her as she simply raised the bowl towards the kidnapper and pointed to the bug inside of it. The man, clearly confused, looked at the bowl, then down to Amanda, then back at the bowl before taking the mush from her shaking hands. For a split second, the thought crossed Amanda's mind that this kidnapper might actually show a glimpse of humanity and help her. Either pick the bug out of the food or, if she was really lucky, bring her a fresh bowl. That moment of hope left the girl's mind as quickly as it had entered it when the man turned the bowl in his hand and hurled it across the room into the bathroom corner. The hard plastic of the bowl bounced off the wall as gray mush splattered against the yellowing concrete and then began its slow descent to the floor.

The kidnapper then grabbed Amanda by the shirt, his strong hands lifting her partly off the ground as she was brought within inches of his sweaty, pockmarked face. The smell of his breath nearly made Amanda vomit as he growled at her: "no screams." He then dumped Amanda back on the ground and stomped across the room to the card table, clearly frustrated by the interruption of his game.

Amanda knew she wouldn't be getting any more food, but at that point she was so happy that the man hadn't hit her that she was more than willing to not eat that day. A small scraping noise caught her attention and she looked down to see Amy placing a half-empty bowl in front of her. Amanda couldn't stop the tears that began streaming down her cheeks as she realized that her friend was sharing her food with her. No, more than a friend, Amy was a sister. All of these girls were. However long Amanda had left in her life, be it several hours, several days, or several decades, she knew she would love these sorority sisters of hers forever.

NINETEEN

The girl's screams had scared Davíd. He was already on edge after Hector shot that guy earlier in the morning, and now this girl's hair-raising shrieks coming out of nowhere almost gave him a heart attack. As if he hadn't already known it, the past several hours simply confirmed that Davíd was not cut out to be a kidnapper. He wasn't that kind of person. He never wanted to threaten or steal or murder, although – thank God – he hadn't been made to kill anyone yet. Davíd knew that some groups said you couldn't be a full member until you got your first kill, but Emiliano and José María didn't have a rule like that. *Gracias a Dios.*

As his breathing finally slowed and his heart rate returned to normal, Davíd's thoughts roamed toward his father, sent to prison for drug running and murder. Davíd was twelve when his father went away – his mother was long-gone. The scared little boy with the beady eyes and mop-top hair had been left in the care of his uncle, who promptly sold Davíd to a cartel to settle debts and gain future protection . . . a sort of advance on extortion payments.

That was seven years ago. Davíd shook his head as he realized how long he had been living on the wrong side of the law. First the big cartel and then the members of Emiliano's gang had done more to raise him than his own family ever had. He'd become a man, but not the kind of man he was proud to be. Davíd, in his heart, in his soul, knew he was destined for greater things. He was born to do more than kidnap, rape, threaten, injure, or kill. He was born to be a football player. Not football like these girls would think of football, but the international football. Futból. On Saturday nights when he was a kid, before his father went away, Davíd would walk several miles across the city to see grown men get paid to play the game he loved.

He'd had a chance to be a great one; Davíd knew that. He was always the first one chosen for pick-up games, always the player that scouts for academy teams would rave about. But his father had outright refused to allow Davíd to play for any of the programs that would have led to a chance at a professional career. It would have made him forget where he came from. He would've gotten above himself. Or so he was repeatedly told. But now, at night, after his duties for the day were done, Davíd would lie in bed and close his eyes and dream of one day suiting up for Manchester United or Real Madrid, winning the Champions League and then leading *El Tri*, the Mexican National Team, to a World Cup title. Even kidnappers have dreams.

"Oye, Davíd, cambio." One of the older men, Paquito, alerted Davíd that it was time to change guards. Davíd nodded his head in acknowledgment and stood up from the card table where he always sat while on duty in the basement. Grabbing his pistol, the teenager then slowly made his way upstairs to begin his usual midday assignment of cooking lunch for the other men.

TWENTY

Caitlin liked to watch the changing of the guards in the basement – every five or six hours when some of the men got up to leave and others replaced them. Although not nearly as formal, as intricate, or as legitimate, this changing of the guard reminded her of the one in London at Buckingham Palace. She was a little girl the first time she saw the elaborate ceremony, with soldiers in what looked to her like costumes, funny hats, and the most beautiful horses she had ever seen. There were no horses here though. No funny hats. And certainly no costumes. But Caitlin had gotten a little better at telling the men apart, and she definitely had her most and least favorite guards.

Her least favorite, hands down, was the one the girls had nicknamed The Enforcer. Because that's what he was. Nobody dared step out of line or talk or even make eye contact with any of the guards while The Enforcer was in the room. Caitlin guessed that the man was a little bit older than her, a few years maybe, but looked like he was double her size. Caitlin was 5'0" tall, and The Enforcer looked like he was probably 6'3". She weighed right around 100 pounds, and he was probably 250. *He could bench-press me*, Caitlin thought. She shivered, a chill running down her spine as she realized that the big man was watching her. He seemed to do that a lot, but she couldn't figure out why.

Something else that the young heiress hadn't figured out was that the man's real name was Marcelo, the only child of a single mother who had been at her wit's end trying to keep him out of trouble. He was smart but oftentimes seemed to be controlled by his emotions, by rage, and one of his favorite childhood hobbies was to capture stray cats and dogs and invent new and increasingly gruesome ways to kill them. In the United States, Marcelo would have been in therapy from a very early age, since he exhibited all of the early warning signs of a future serial killer. But his mother had been too busy working and he skipped too much school for the teachers to notice his penchant for violence. Emiliano, though, noticed. He saw how the young man liked the sight of blood oozing out of a body, and didn't tell him that it was disgusting or weird. His boss recognized that Marcelo liked to feel and hear the snap of bones as they break, and that was okay too. He liked to dismember his victims, cutting them apart one limb at a time, and Emiliano didn't mind that either. In fact, he often encouraged it since it made it more difficult for the police to identify the person.

The rise of the drug trade and the escalation of the war between the cartels and the Mexican government had been the best thing that could ever happen to The Enforcer. It gave him a sense of purpose, steady employment, and protection from the police for his crimes. It also gave the twenty-four-year-old something else he had never had before going to work in this business: respect. Whether it was actual admiration or simply fear, he didn't ask. But nobody messed with Marcelo, and by his standards that was respect worth having.

****

The kidnappers weren't all like the Enforcer. In fact, one of them was actually kind of nice. Caitlin didn't know what to think about that, though. She didn't want them all to be like The Enforcer, obviously, because he was big and mean and very violent and the way his smoky brown eyes always lingered on her gave her the creeps. The men could've all been like the boss dude – that would've been fine. He was mean, sure. He had clearly defined rules and if you broke them you would get hit, but as long as you obeyed the rules you were safe. Or as safe as you could get while being held hostage at gunpoint.

The nice guy, though, messed with Caitlin's emotions. She had started to like him. Not like like him, as a guy – just as a person. In fact, that was the difference. His niceness enabled her to see him as a person, whereas the rest of the kidnappers fell into some "evil creature" category. Caitlin liked it better that way. "Dehumanize the enemy" was a phrase her grandfather used a lot when talking about work. "It makes it easier when you slit their throats." Caitlin had cringed the first time she heard her beloved grandfather talk like that, but as she grew older she learned that it was simply the language of the business. A business she couldn't wait to get into herself. She had her grandfather's killer instinct and eye for a good deal, and she always beamed with pride when he would turn to his aides and say "watch out for that one. She's gonna take over the whole damn industry one day."

Caitlin couldn't seem to apply that killer instinct to the nice kidnapper, though. 'Nice kidnapper' – an oxymoron if there ever was one. But it was true. His name was Ángel; she had gleaned that much from listening to the men speaking to each other. Caitlin, unfortunately, didn't speak Spanish. She spoke French and a little bit of German, the latter at the urging of her grandfather. "Learn German," he had told her. "It's a fucking ugly language, but they run the whole goddamn European economy so you gotta know how to deal with them." The only person who had ever been able to make Lawrence Van Oren censor his language was his wife, Caitlin's grandmother, but she died from breast cancer before Caitlin was born – "a fucking vicious disease," Grandfather always said. So French: yes. German: more or less. Spanish, however, was not a language she knew. But it was easy enough to pick out names.

Ángel. Angel. Amidst all of the angry, violent men, an angel. Caitlin and the other girls couldn't help but notice the little things Ángel did to try to make life a little bit easier on them. They had to be little things, of course, or else the other men would notice. But the girls appreciated his actions just the same.

Like how he hit them far less often than the others did. Or how, when he was ordered to hit one of them, he would pull his punch a little bit at the last second to take away some of the impact. At first they thought he just wasn't all that strong. He was on the small side to begin with, his floppy hair hanging down across his face and making him look even younger than he already did. But the weaker hits combined with the niceness in his eyes combined with the bathroom pot made them realize what he was up to. And of all of his angelic actions, the bathroom pot was the one for which the girls were far and away the most grateful. Seventeen young women had to use one five-gallon pot as their toilet. Seventeen girls. One pot. The kidnappers, by some magic olfactory mutation, didn't seem to notice the stench. But when the men didn't empty the pot for hours on end, it would overflow and the girls simply had to go on the floor. For Caitlin, it was the single-most humiliating aspect of this entire experience.

But Ángel, bless his heart, would empty the pot. Sometimes he would be assigned elsewhere and not be in the room for a while, but every time he came downstairs to what the girls had all concluded was a basement, the first thing he would do was walk across the room, pick up the nasty pot, and take it away, bringing it back empty. One time he also brought down some water and a broom and cleaned up where some of the girls had been forced to use the floor. Amy, who Caitlin knew spoke Spanish, told her that the other men yelled at Ángel when he did that and asked why he was cleaning up after the "putas," or whores. Ángel very wisely said he wasn't doing it for the girls . . . he just couldn't stand the smell any longer.

Ángel. He was an angel. Caitlin couldn't dehumanize this particular enemy. And she didn't want to.

TWENTY-ONE

"What are you doing?" Emily whispered to Amy, an interaction that had quickly become ritual each morning. Five days had now passed since the first time the girls were fed their daily 'meal,' and each morning, before the pot man and his assistant arrived, Emily would inevitably ask Amy a question about something. At first it was annoying (and dangerous), but by now Amy had realized that the other girl was just seeking some sort of reassurance and comfort. Even though the group of girls was on the far end of the large room where they were being held, the guards seemed to have eyes and ears like owls and had already caught several attempts at whispered conversations. Every observed communication had resulted in a pistol to the face for each of the girls involved. So Emily was doing what she and the rest of the group had done for the past four years: turning to their pledge class representative and then sorority president for guidance and support, trusting that she would know what to do even when they didn't.

This morning's question from Emily was actually somewhat valid, since the other girl did not have a way of figuring out the answer on her own.

"I'm marking our days here. Just to keep track," Amy whispered back. A piece of the concrete floor had come loose, and Amy had picked it up and was now using it to scratch tally marks in the floor in front of her – one for each day they had been in this hellish place. There were no windows in the room – no natural light of any kind – but Amy had figured out how to keep track of the passage of time based on their meal schedule. Morning brought with it their bowls of mush, and midday and evening were met with a glass of water for each girl.

The first mark that Amy scratched in the floor was for the time she had spent in the other room, unconscious from the events surrounding their abduction. That mark also encompassed her transfer into this room and reunion with her sorority sisters. Day Two, the first full day, was her introduction to pistol whipping and the unfortunate mush that they continued to be fed each morning. Day Three was when Ashley had asked the kidnappers for some rosary beads and, by some miracle, had actually received them. Amy still couldn't believe it.

It was rare, but not unheard of, for there to be a Catholic girl in Amy's pledge class. The vast majority of them were Protestant, and the Jewish girls all had their own sororities. Ashley had continued to pray a lot every day they had been in the basement. Amy prayed a good deal as well, but Ashley often whispered her prayers aloud so the other girls heard it. And then, on the second full day, the third tally mark, Ashley asked Amy how to say "rosary" in Spanish. Amy had told her to just ask the men in English – if she asked in Spanish then they would wonder how she knew what to say. So very politely, in her best innocent schoolgirl voice, Ashley had called out across the room and asked the men on guard duty if it would be possible for her to have some rosary beads. The men didn't understand her question, but after a few confused stares and murmurs among themselves, one of the kidnappers had gone upstairs and returned a few minutes later with Ricky.

"What do you want?" he had growled, causing Ashley's hands to shake and voice to quiver as she repeated her request for the rosary beads. Amy remembered the look of surprise on Ricky's face, as if he couldn't believe that any of these girls might be Catholic like him. He hadn't said anything in response, he just turned and walked away, but when the men came that night to deliver the evening water glass, all of the girls were shocked when Ashley received not only the water but also the beads.

****

The next three days had passed without much event, as the men guarding them played a seemingly endless number of card games and the girls attempted to talk to each other every chance they got without raising the ire of their captors. At this point, however, there were only a few girls left who hadn't felt the cold, hard rush of metal colliding with the side of their face, be it a pistol or the large, black baton favored by the man they all called The Enforcer.

Amy scratched her seventh tally into the floor and then blew on the ground to clear the spot of dirt and dust. *Seven days*, she thought. *A full week here.* The realization that so much time had passed since the girls had first arrived in this holding room made Amy suddenly get antsy.

What are they waiting for? The girls had not left the far end of the room where they were being held. They were still being fed as if they were animals: bowls of nasty, presumably corn mush thrown down on the floor in the morning, and a single glass of water to each girl three times a day. The restroom facilities were comprised of a pot in the adjacent corner. When one of the girls, Sophie, tried to tell their captors that she had started her period and needed a tampon or something of the sort, The Enforcer slapped her so hard with his nightstick that her eye was still swollen shut. Amy's face was also still considerably bruised from being hit several days ago, although the swelling had gone down enough that she could now see out of her right eye again.

It was that realization of just how much time had passed that led Amy, despite the obvious risk of more physical violence, to decide that she needed to speak up. Something should have happened by now. Maybe there hadn't been a ransom exchange because the kidnappers didn't know who they were and couldn't contact their parents. Or maybe they didn't know that several of the girls came from very wealthy families. Surely the prospect of a big ransom payment would help speed things up. Amy had read about these kinds of kidnapping gangs in her favorite Spanish-language newspaper. As the Mexican government started to make headway in shutting down the drug trade, the *narcos* began to turn to extortion and kidnappings in order to earn money. *Surely*, she thought, *that's what these people are after.*

Amy knew she would have to pick her moment carefully, and it arrived that afternoon. Looking across the room at the men guarding the door, she saw that The Enforcer wasn't there, which was good because he was the most violent. His Jim Crow-era billy club did much more damage than the pistols, and his eagerness to use it had managed to strike even more fear in the hearts and minds of the already terrified group of girls. While the other men clearly had no objections to hitting their hostages, The Enforcer actually seemed to enjoy it. In addition to The Enforcer's absence, the boss also wasn't there, which was a good thing because the other men always tried to impress him by being tougher. Amy took a deep breath, closed her eyes, and prayed for success. Then she called out:

"Excuse me? Can I talk to you?"

****

"No talking!" one of the men barked back at Amy. "No talking!"

"Can I talk to your boss, please? Jefe?" Amy purposely paused before saying the Spanish word, trying to make it seem like she was struggling to remember what it was.

"No talking!" the man yelled again, picking up a pistol from the table where he was sitting and starting to walk toward the girls.

"What are you doing?!" Elizabeth, her suitemate, whispered urgently. "You're going to get us all killed!" But Amy was determined. If their captors were going to kill them, they would've done so a long time ago. Besides, it was time for the girls to take back some control of the situation. Amy refused to continue living like a caged animal with no prospect of release any time soon.

"We can pay you," Amy continued. "Pesos? Dinero? If you let us go we will pay you."

Upon hearing the word for money, the guard stopped. He turned part of the way around and yelled something over his left shoulder, but he spoke too quickly for Amy to understand him. Things looked promising, though, because one of the other guards hurried out of the room. A few minutes later, the man returned. He had brought the boss, Ricky, and The Enforcer with him. The boss spoke harshly to Ricky, who then turned to translate to the group of young women.

"Do you think you can bribe the guards? Get them to let you go when we're not here? Do you?!" Ricky punctuated his last question by slapping Amy across the face with the back of his hand. *At least it was with his hand and not a gun*, Amy immediately thought.

"No!" Amy quickly replied to Ricky's allegation, her face burning like fire and tears welling up in her eyes. "Not a bribe. A ransom. To your group. All of you. Or your boss. Whoever. Ransom."

The boss' eyebrows raised and his brown eyes began to glitter when he heard the word 'ransom.' It was obviously a word he knew well. Amy seized on the opportunity.

"Our families can pay you. Our parents have money. They'll pay you."

Ricky translated Amy's latest words, and the gleam in the boss' eyes got brighter. The other men in the room inched closer, trying to hear the conversation.

"¿Cuánto?" Emiliano asked. He wanted to know how much money the girls' families would pay.

Amy reminded herself to pause and wait for Ricky's translation, even though it wasn't necessary. They still didn't know she spoke Spanish, and she didn't want them to get suspicious. After the young man spoke, Amy looked directly at the boss, challenging him by not breaking eye contact. "Name your price."

TWENTY-TWO

Amy didn't want to remember much of anything that had happened to her in Mexico, but in that moment, immediately after she told Emiliano that he could name his price for their ransom, she really wished she had a camera to document the look on his face. It was the kind of look one might see in a picture in a dictionary under the word 'evil'. The kind of look Amy had thought was only possible in a cartoon, like Ursula in "The Little Mermaid" or Jafar in "Aladdin."

The evil creature turned and murmured something to The Enforcer, who left the room and then quickly returned with a notepad and a pen. He gave the materials to Ricky, who in turn held them out toward Amy. "Write down your parents' contact information."

Amy reached out to take the pen and paper, but before she could begin writing she heard one of the other girls speak. It was Caitlin, the smallest girl in the group but also the richest in her sorority and probably the richest at her whole university. "Here, let me do it," Caitlin said, her voice trembling and hands shaking as she reached over to take the materials from Amy. "You'll want to talk to my grandfather. He has a fund set aside for this sort of thing."

As Amy handed her the paper, she remembered a conversation the two girls had their freshman year. Caitlin had to miss a couple days of class in the fall semester and asked to borrow Amy's notes. When Amy asked if everything was alright, Caitlin had cheerfully replied yes. She then explained that she was young for their grade and was just turning eighteen. Amy already knew that since a bunch of the girls had gone out to a celebratory dinner the week before, but she hadn't known that for most of Caitlin's life she had a GPS tracking device implanted in her hip. Her grandfather, a billionaire, insisted on it for all of his grandchildren in case someone tried to kidnap one of them. When she turned eighteen she had the option to get the device removed. Now, thinking back, Amy really, *really* wished Caitlin still had that chip in her. Then all the police would have had to do was plug in Caitlin's tracking number, almost like a package that had been shipped, find out where she was, and send in the Mexican equivalent of a SWAT team to rescue them. This whole ordeal could've been over almost as soon as it began. But Caitlin didn't have the device anymore and they didn't have a rescue team on the way, Amy reminded herself. *And I can't blame Caitlin for wanting to cut the cord, so to speak. This isn't her fault. It's the bad guys' fault. They did this.*

When the pint-sized brunette heiress finished writing down her grandfather's contact information, Ricky and the group's leader left. Sixteen pairs of American eyes watched as the handsome but evil young man and his boss made their way back across the room and turned the corner out of sight, and then sixteen matching sets of ears listened as the two men climbed the stairs on the other side of the wall, carrying with them the contact information for a rich man who they hoped would save them. But Amy's eyes weren't on the kidnappers, and her ears tuned out the sound of the footsteps on the creaky wooden stairs. Instead, Amy's focus was on the young woman sitting beside her. The young woman who had been Amy's friend for four years and roommate for three. All of the other girls knew that Caitlin came from money – her wardrobe alone was enough to tell them that. But only Amy knew how much money. And all of the other girls knew that Caitlin didn't like to talk about her rich grandfather, didn't want to be known only as Lawrence Van Oren's granddaughter. But only Amy knew how badly. Only Amy knew about the GPS chip that Caitlin had gotten removed nearly four years ago, and only Amy knew just how much strength it had taken for her best friend to drop her anonymity and direct the kidnappers to her grandfather and his money.

That was why Amy's eyes were still trained on her friend when the petite brunette turned her head to the side and made eye contact, and why Amy smiled, took the other girl's hand in her own, and whispered "thank you." Caitlin gave a half-smile in response, squeezed her friend's hand once then released it. The girls both knew that all they could do now was wait.

TWENTY-THREE

Lawrence Van Oren was the seventh richest man in America. He made half of his money the old fashioned way – he inherited it – and the other half through the shrewd business deals for which he was now legendary. It was the perfect combination, really. He had enough old money to have him be accepted at the right clubs and in the right groups, and enough new money to be able to do just about whatever the hell he wanted to. Except one thing, it seemed. Because the only thing he wanted right now was to find his granddaughter, Caitlin. And all the money in the world – or at least a pretty good chunk of it – wasn't helping him any in that regard.

Caitlin Mitchell was his oldest grandchild, the only daughter of his only daughter, and by far his favorite. He knew he wasn't supposed to have a favorite grandchild, but he did. It wasn't that he loved any of the others any less – he truly did love all six of his grandchildren equally. He just liked Caitlin more. Probably because they had so much in common. And where she wasn't like him – she was tiny and petite, he was a 6'4" giant of a man; she had moments of pure sweetness and compassion toward strangers, he wasn't exactly kindest person in the world – she was exactly like her grandmother, his late wife Louise. When it came down to it, that was probably why Caitlin was his favorite grandchild. Not because she was so much like him. Not because she wanted to go to business school and take over the reins of his company one day. But rather, it was because she was like a little Louise, a wonderful continuation of all of the best qualities of the lady who was once profiled in a magazine as "the woman who tamed a Wall Street bull."

Lawrence had been putty in Louise's hands, and the same was true with Caitlin. Both women reminded him of dainty little china dolls, and he always felt an overwhelming need to protect them. The brutal irony of the situation ripped through Van Oren as he realized that, once again, he was failing to protect the one living person who he needed to keep safe more than anything else in the world. He didn't protect Louise from the cancer that ravaged her beautiful body, and now he hadn't protected Caitlin from what police were telling him was a kidnapping in Mexico.

Goddammit, why hadn't that girl just kept in the tracking device like I told her to? Lawrence Van Oren was a billionaire, and a billionaire known to have a serious soft spot for his family. Consequently, his security team had convinced him to have GPS tracking chips implanted in all of his grandchildren so that they could be found if kidnapped. The problem was, once the grandkids turned eighteen, they couldn't be forced to have the chip anymore. And Caitlin, damn girl, had hers removed as soon as she possibly could. If she hadn't done that, if she hadn't insisted on being so goddam independent, she would be back in New York, safe and sound, and he would be having kidnapper heads served to him on silver platters.

But no, little miss Mitchell had declared that she wanted to be her own woman – whatever the hell that meant. She wasn't "her own woman" when it came time to pay her tuition bill or living expenses. Looking back, Lawrence knew he should've made paying for her school conditioned on her keeping the tracking device in her. Too late for that now (for Caitlin, anyway, but certainly not for the younger grandkids). He had even thought about telling the doctor to just not remove the chip and tell Caitlin he did, but his best friend and General Counsel, Philip Baker, told him he couldn't do that.

The only saving grace so far in this six-day nightmare, six days since the police first called his daughter with the news, was that the press had been somewhat decent human beings so far. Even with the different last names, it hadn't taken the reporters long to make the connection between the missing Caitlin Mitchell and the founder of Van Oren Investments. VOI had issued a press release asking for privacy and prayers, and Lawrence didn't know if it was actually a show of compassion by the press or just the results of his highly protective security team and staff, but he had – for the most part – been left alone. Left to wonder where his sweet little girl was. Left to torture himself over the "what ifs" that could've changed fate and kept her safe.

The sound of Bill Withers' "Lean on Me" blaring through his cell phone woke Van Oren out of his reverie and brought him back to the present. One of his other grandchildren had selected the ringtone for him for his family-only cell phone, and everyone else had thought it was so perfect that he hadn't had the heart to change it. He usually left that private phone at home – life was far easier when he could compartmentalize everything. Besides, Lawrence had long ago discovered that work and family had an oil and water quality to them, and work was the oil . . . always rising to the top of family. So he tried his best to keep them completely separate, to the point of having a separate cell phone that only his kids and grandkids knew the number to. But ever since Caitlin had been reported missing six days ago, he had kept that phone on and with him at all times. It was on his nightstand while he slept. On the bathroom counter within arm's reach while he showered. And on his desk right now while he worked.

Lawrence answered the phone just as the words "I'll help you carrrrrry onnnnnn" rang through the air.

"Hello?"

"Is this Lawrence Van Oren?" Caitlin's grandfather immediately stilled at the sound of an unfamiliar voice on the other end of the line. Without even asking, he knew he was speaking with one of the kidnappers.

"Where is she?" he demanded. "I swear to God if you touch a single hair on her head – "

"Mr. Van Oren, we don't have much time. I suggest you stop with the tough guy routine and just listen." Lawrence hated the way the other man sounded so calm, hated the way he was talking like this was some sort of business negotiation. And then it hit him. That's exactly what this was to the kidnappers. A business negotiation. Nothing more, nothing less. They had something that they knew Lawrence wanted, and they wanted him to pay to get it. Well, fuck them. And fuck any thoughts this prick had of winning this negotiation. Lawrence Van Oren was the best goddam negotiator that Wall Street had ever seen. This little shit was messing with the wrong guy.

"Go ahead," he finally replied, taking a deep breath. *Follow your business tactics. Listen more than you talk. Get him to show his hand.*

"Ten million dollars. U.S. currency. Cash."

It wasn't the amount of money that caused a chill to run through Van Oren's veins. Rather, it was the man's accent. He sounded . . . well, he sounded young. And *American*. Lawrence made a quick mental note to pass that information along to the police after this phone call ended.

"Did you hear me? Ten million," the man stated, clearly irritated by Lawrence's lack of response.

"Yes, I heard you," Caitlin's grandfather calmly responded. He was in full business negotiation mode now. As cool as a cucumber. Even though he was fully prepared to pay at least double that amount – hell, who was he kidding, he'd pay whatever they asked if it meant he got Caitlin back home – Lawrence continued with the business-like approach. "That's quite a large sum of money, young man."

"Are you saying you won't pay?" the kidnapper quickly sneered.

"No, no, I'll pay. It will just take a few days to put it together. I don't have that much cash just lying around." Before the other man could interrupt, Van Oren continued, "but I'll need a few things from you in return." *Keep the ball in your court. Make them show good faith.* The business tactics kept rolling through his mind as he talked.

"Such as?"

"For starters, proof that the girls are alive. All of them."

****

Ricky wasn't expecting that request from the rich American grandfather, although he guessed he should have been. He'd never done this part of the kidnapping before. He had always just handed off the victims' information and left. But it made sense that the guy would want to know his granddaughter was still alive before he paid out so much money.

"Hold on," he said gruffly into the telephone before putting his hand over the receiver and walking into the small room that Emiliano used as an office. Whispering to make sure the man on the phone couldn't hear him, he got his boss' attention and repeated Van Oren's request to know that the girls were still alive.

Emiliano nodded his head, as if he had been expecting that. "Él puede hablar con su nieta. Dos minutos."

Ricky turned and left the office, walking through the short hall and down the wooden stairs to the basement. He put a finger over his lips to silence the other men as he passed their card table and headed straight for the group of girls. Holding the phone out to Caitlin, he said "it's your grandfather. You've got two minutes. No specifics. Just tell him you're alive."

The tiny young woman's hands were visibly shaking and she started crying before she even took the phone from Ricky. *Stop it*, he told himself. *Stop caring*. He didn't know what it was about this little one, but she got to him.

****

"H-hello?" Caitlin said, her voice weak and full of fear.

"Ohmygod, it's you. Ohmygod."

At the sound of her grandfather's voice, Caitlin burst into a flood of tears. "Yes, it's me. It's me," she cried. "He said we don't have long. He said I'm supposed to tell you I'm alive."

"Oh thank God. Are you okay? Are you hurt?" the words tumbled out of her grandfather's mouth before he could stop them.

"I'm fine," she replied. It was a lie, they both knew it, but in the grand scheme of things she supposed it wasn't. She was alive. That was fine enough for now.

"And the other girls?" her grandfather forced himself to ask, even though at this point all he really wanted to talk about was Caitlin.

"We're all alive," Caitlin answered, knowing exactly what he was asking. She paused, then added, "I love you."

Her grandfather's voice, full of emotion, cracked as he responded, "I love you too, sweetheart."

****

Ricky knew it was time to cut this sob-fest short. Who cares if it hadn't been a full two minutes.

"That's enough," he barked as he reached down and ripped the phone out of the young woman's hand. Turning his back to the girls and his attention to the man on the other end of the line, he paused long enough to clear away the emotion that had built up in his voice after listening to the display of familial love in front of him. "There's your proof," he finally brought himself to say. "They're alive."

Ricky continued to walk back across the large, windowless basement room and slowly made his way up the stairs. He was surprised, though, when the rich man he was talking to wasn't finished with his demands.

"I also want you to give me your word that they will all be released. That nothing will happen to them." The businessman's demeanor slipped for a minute as anger rose in his voice. "Because I swear to God, if you touch a single hair on her head – "

Ricky interrupted his lecture. "You mean a promise that nothing else will happen to them?" he said gleefully, the sneer in his voice matching the gleam in his eyes as he knew that the grandfather knew exactly what they were talking about.

"You son of a bitch!" the old man yelled, and Ricky knew he had him right where he wanted him. Before, the man had been so calm, so collected, as if he didn't really care whether the girls would be released or not. As if it was some sort of business deal that he might walk away from. But now, he was angry. Emotional. Easily manipulated.

"Ten million dollars," came Ricky's reply. "Unmarked bills. No police. You have forty-eight hours."

The dial tone in his ear was Van Oren's first and only indication that the phone call had ended. And now he had forty-eight hours to pull together what would electronically be easily obtainable but was, in cash, an obscene amount. He couldn't begin to imagine how many banks it might take in order to pull this off, let alone the logistics behind the actual money drop itself.

Lawrence quickly picked up the office phone on his desk and pressed five, waiting as it speed-dialed his trusted General Counsel, Philip. If anyone could pull this together in that short amount of time, it was him.

TWENTY-FOUR

The Millhouse family home was exactly what one might expect from a Southern preppy family. It was large but not ostentatious, with only one extra bedroom for guests and every other part of the house actively used. It was brick on all four sides, two stories tall, and set back on a large lot surrounded by lush green grass in the front, woods in the back, and similarly sized and styled homes on either side. Linda Millhouse firmly believed it was the perfect place for an upper-middle class couple to raise a family, and her husband, Jack, agreed. They had both grown up in neighborhoods very similar to the one they now called home, with the only exception being that everything was now a bit bigger than in days past – the rise of consumerism making its mark.

But the happy, bubble-like environment of Maple Lane in the Pinewoods Estates neighborhood had been shattered when word spread that one of its most beloved residents, the young Amy Millhouse, had been kidnapped in Mexico. The Millhouse family was held in high esteem by everyone in the neighborhood and the surrounding affluent suburban community, and the flood of emotions and media attention had nearly overwhelmed everyone with any connection to the grieved family.

****

At first glance, the woman in the kitchen of the Millhouse home looked the picture of perfection. Linda Millhouse was a shorter, slightly heavier version of her daughter, with the same fashion sense and pretty blonde hair, even though her hair now had to be colored to keep the grays away. Linda still insisted on calling herself a natural blonde, though, because that's the color hair she had when she was born. She had met her husband of nearly thirty years at the same college that her daughter just graduated from, at a mixer thrown by the same sorority of which Amy had been president. She attended college back when it was still okay to admit that you were looking for your "Mrs." degree. A stay-at-home mom, or "homemaker" as she preferred to be called, Linda never regretted her decision to devote herself full-time to her husband and children. That said, she could see the potential in her oldest child and only daughter and knew the young woman would make an excellent professional one day – likely in Jack's law firm.

Just as she had taught her daughter, Linda began every day by putting on a full face of makeup and styling her hair to perfection, and today was no different – even though the middle-aged woman had absolutely no intention of leaving the house. Refined and polished over the years like a stone by water, Mrs. Millhouse was as smooth as she could be on the outside and solid on the inside. Her favorite movie was "Steel Magnolias," and the metaphor was accurate. Whenever the neighborhood association needed something done, they knew they could rely on Linda. The same was true for the local Junior League as well as First Methodist Church, where the Millhouses had been members for decades. Her friends jokingly said she was the Bree Van de Kamp of the neighborhood, only without the drama.

Linda's one and only weakness was her children. She loved and protected her two babies with a fierceness only a mother could understand, and the kidnapping was tearing her up inside. Every night, when the neighbors and family members and news crews finally left, Linda went into Amy's room, still decorated the same way it was before she left for college, and curled up on her daughter's bed, clinging to Amy's favorite stuffed teddy bear. Amy had loved that bear, nicknamed Max, ever since she was a little child and still slept with it, but she had left it behind this time because she hadn't wanted anything to happen to it on the trip to Mexico. Every time she saw the bear Linda began to cry, triggered by the guilt that Amy wouldn't let her bear go to Mexico to protect it but Mrs. Millhouse had let her daughter go.

TWENTY-FIVE

Linda Millhouse's husband hated the nighttime, precisely because he knew his wife would spend it crying and on any given night there was a 50/50 chance that he would cry too. There were simply fewer things to occupy the mind at night, and Jack Millhouse didn't like that. A lawyer by trade, ever since Amy had been reported missing Jack had spent his days comforting inquiring relatives and calling every former college and law school classmate of his with any connections in Washington, DC or Mexico, desperately trying to find someone with the power and authority to find his daughter and bring her home. The government had actually been a big help, with an FBI agent and a State Department official on call at all times and the U.S. Embassy in Mexico City and Consulate in Acapulco working around the clock.

The intense media coverage that always seemed to accompany the disappearance of a pretty white girl was multiplied by seventeen, because now there were seventeen pretty white girls who had gone missing. Jack had received multiple reassurances that the Mexican authorities were also working furiously to find the missing tourists, and, for the most part, he believed them. One particularly honest official explained to Jack one day that the Mexican authorities knew they had to solve this one. Even the corrupt officials were furious at the splinter group that was assumed to have done this, because it burst the bubble that they worked so hard to maintain. According to this officer, many Mexican states depended heavily on tourism, and everyone knew that that cash flow would dry up if people thought it was too dangerous to visit – that was why the police continually insisted that cartels weren't targeting innocent people. He told Jack that was a lie that the Mexicans didn't believe for one second but the naïve Americans were happy to gobble up. That was also why those same police regularly rounded up cartel members and then paraded them in front of the media, even though they all-too-often turned around and released them a few hours later. This, though, this brazen kidnapping of seventeen lily white rich college girls, complete with the mass execution of their taxi drivers, was too much. It broke the unspoken code that the *narcos* and their corrupt police, military, and government allies operated under. So the honest and clean officials, along with the corrupt ones, knew they couldn't screw this up. They had to find the girls. Alive.

Regardless of the justifications for their actions, Jack was glad to actually have the full force of the American and Mexican governments working to find his baby girl.

Still fit and trim at age fifty-two, Jack Millhouse was a pillar of the local community and the kind of man every mother hoped her son would turn out to be. There were also more than a few women in the area who had crushes on him, with his tall, muscular frame and full head of light brown hair that had only recently begun to go gray at the temples. Jack wasn't particularly fond of the gray, but his wife assured him that it made him look even more handsome and gave him a distinguished air. He had the same 'chameleon' eyes as Amy, but his changed color based solely on his mood whereas his daughter's mostly changed based on her outfit. His kids had figured out early in life to read his eyes before talking to him – blue meant you were good to go, gray was a sign to tread carefully because he was tired or annoyed, and green might as well have been red because it meant stay away.

In addition to working the phones and talking with relatives, the duty also fell to Jack Millhouse to console his wife. Even though he had lived in the South his entire life, it still amazed him the way Linda and other Southern women he knew held themselves together. Steel magnolia was the truth – his wife's hair, makeup, and clothes, always done perfectly, were simply the outer expression of an inner strength that he wished to God he had. He'd already cried once on camera when a two-bit reporter asked him to describe what he missed most about his daughter. But if there was one thing that his daddy had ingrained in him since the day he was born, it was that it was his job, as a man, to provide for and protect the women in his family. It was killing him that he had failed to protect Amy, and he for damn sure wasn't going to fail to provide his wife the comfort she needed. He knew, after twenty-eight years of marriage, that Linda – despite her still waters running deep – needed to have him be the one person who she could break down in front of. She needed him to sit beside her on Amy's bed, wrap his strong arms around her and stroke her hair while she cried, all the while saying "it will be okay, darlin.' I'm here. I'm here, baby. It'll be okay."

TWENTY-SIX

What Jack and Linda didn't know was that, on most nights, their son Josh was standing just outside of the door to his sister's room. A younger, taller, leaner version of his daddy, Josh Millhouse was otherwise nearly a carbon copy of his father. Indeed, the only thing distinguishing college pictures of Jack and Josh was their clothing style. And even that was still very similar, since khaki pants, button down shirts, and brown loafers or boat shoes weren't likely to go out of Southern preppy style any time soon. Josh had none of the gray that had crept its way into his father's hair, but he did have the same light brown color and hairstyle, just worn a little longer. Josh's grandmother lovingly called him her "little sheepdog" because of his shaggy hair. His eye color nearly matched his hair, since the Millhouse son had received his mother's honey brown eyes instead of the chameleons of his father and sister. A rising junior at the college that his sister had just graduated from, Joshie, as the family still called him, was also a member of the same fraternity that every male in his family had been a member of for as long as anyone could remember.

With a solid "B" average and sterling resumé of community volunteer efforts, the young Mr. Millhouse was supposed to have gone to New York City this summer for a prestigious internship at an investment bank. His sister was reported missing three days before Josh was scheduled to fly north, and he immediately called his summer employers to cancel. If there was anything his father had taught him over the years, it was that a man's obligation to provide for his family extended beyond just finances. His parents needed him right now . . . there would be other jobs. Besides, Josh knew he wouldn't want to work for a company that would force him to abandon his family at a time like this.

Even though Josh looked exactly like his father and up to this point was following the same path his dad had, Josh was different. He didn't want to go to law school and then work at his daddy's firm like most everyone expected. Instead, he wanted to work in finance in either New York or Boston. And while he loved home and the culture in which he was raised, Josh knew that he needed to explore the outside world. The way he figured, he would probably return home for the holidays one day, ten or fifteen years from now, with a Yankee wife and kids in tow. Thrilled to death to spend time with her 'grandbabies,' their appearance would also always make his mother a little bit sad, because those who aren't raised in the South can never truly understand it. But for right now, Josh's future career and explorations had to wait. His job this summer was to help his parents with anything they might need, playing second chair host to all of the people coming by to offer their sympathies and prayers and food.

Oh dear Lord, the food. He didn't think his mother would have to cook again for a year, what with all of the casseroles and baked goods that people kept bringing by. It seemed like every woman in the entire 200 home neighborhood had baked something, but the people from the church knew how to do it right. After generations of prayer chains and emergency cooking, the ladies at First Methodist knew that if everybody cooked all at once, most of the food would go bad before it could be eaten. So they made things on a rotating schedule, and the Millhouses had enjoyed a freshly baked meal every night for the past week and a half, ever since word got out that Amy was missing.

****

Josh's thoughts easily returned to the day when the police had given him the worst news of his life. He had woken up around 9am that morning, knowing he needed to get up and start packing for New York. His mom was already awake and ready for the day, coffee brewed and his father long-since gone to the office. Josh knew that his mom had talked to Amy the day before, after all of the girls arrived at their hotel in Mexico. He figured, given the time difference and the fact that his sister was travelling with such a big group, that they wouldn't hear from her again until at least that night.

Josh was upstairs in his room pulling clothes out of his closet and his mom was down in the basement grabbing another suitcase when the doorbell rang. It was a little too early for any deliveries and neighbors usually called before coming over, but Pinewoods Estates was the kind of place where someone from their street might literally be standing on the doorstep asking to borrow a cup of sugar. He looked out of his bedroom window and was surprised to see a police car parked in the street in front of the house. There was also an unmarked black car in the driveway. *What in the world?* Josh thought as he quickly left his room and headed down the front stairs just as his mom was reaching the top of the basement steps. "I'll get it," he said.

He opened the door to find two men, one black and one white, standing in front of him. They were both wearing cheap, off-the-rack black suits and grim expressions on their faces. Glancing past the men, Josh saw two uniformed police officers still sitting in their squad car.

"Can I help you?"

Josh's mom had joined him at the door now, as confused as he was by the situation. There was something else, though, Josh noticed. It was in her eyes. His mom wasn't just confused. She was scared.

"Are you Mrs. Linda Millhouse?" one of the men asked, looking past Josh and talking directly to his mother.

"Yes, that's me. Is something wrong?"

The man who already spoke pulled a black badge from his inside jacket pocket and flashed it towards the Millhouses. "I'm Agent Canady of the FBI. This is Mr. Gillam with the State Department. May we come inside?"

Josh could hear the concern in the agent's voice, could see the seriousness in his eyes as they all followed Mrs. Millhouse into the living room just off the foyer and sat down on opposite couches, the Millhouses facing the government officials. Normally, Josh knew his mother would send him to the kitchen for drinks for the two men. But she was too distracted, and he wasn't going anywhere until he found out what was going on.

"Tell us. Whatever it is, just tell us," Josh spat out. He could tell that the men in the cheap suits were surprised to get such a command from the kid in the baggy gym shorts and "AMERICA" t-shirt.

"It's about your daughter, ma'am. Amy," Agent Canady said, still training his focus on Linda.

"Tell us," she replied, her spine stiffening as she repeated her son's words.

Taking a deep breath, the FBI agent answered: "we have reason to believe that she has been kidnapped."

Josh immediately grabbed his mom and hugged her to keep her from collapsing off the couch and onto the floor. Gathering her composure, Linda Millhouse told her son to go call his dad and tell him to come home. While he was standing in the hallway on the phone, Josh overheard the agents filling in his mom on the details of the situation. The hotel concierge had kept an eye out for the group of girls, and when they didn't return after the time when the bar would have closed, he called the head of hotel security and sent him out to look for the guests. The concierge also called the cell phone of one of the taxi drivers who had picked up the Americans, but no one answered. Hotel security had found the four taxi cabs abandoned in a lot on the side of the road, the drivers dead and the girls missing. From there the federal police had been called, the U.S. Consulate in Acapulco notified, and now here these agents were, tasked with delivering the terrible news.

Josh's dad arrived home twenty-five minutes later and was told the heartbreaking story that his wife and son already heard.

That was eight days ago.

****

Josh admired his mother for continuing to put on such a good show of strength. For getting up every morning and getting ready with her hair and makeup and clothes on like they always were. She could have just as easily sent out word that she didn't feel like having visitors and then stayed curled up in bed or on the couch all day. People would've understood. The food still would've come. But Josh knew what his mother also knew: people were coming by with the pretense to check on the Millhouses, but really it was they themselves who needed comfort and reassurance that sweet Amy, who had worked every summer of high school and college as the neighborhood babysitter, would be alright. Josh believed that his mother appreciated having something to do to keep her mind occupied. It was at night, after the hostess duties stopped for the day, when he would stand in the hallway and listen to the muffled sounds of his mother crying in Amy's room and his dad trying to comfort her.

But right now it wasn't nighttime. There was no crying at the moment. Just Mrs. Millhouse in the kitchen cleaning up the plates from lunch, Mr. Millhouse on his cellphone with his cousin, and Josh attempting to watch "SportsCenter" but always finding himself switching back to the cable news channels just in case there was an update about his sister.

TWENTY-SEVEN

Linda Millhouse shook her head as she stared out the kitchen window at the crowd gathered in the street in front of her house. She knew that the other families were dealing with it too, but she just couldn't believe the amount of media coverage about her daughter's disappearance. Local police had to be dispatched to manage the traffic and keep the overzealous reporters and paparazzi off the Millhouse property. The crowds thinned out at night as the news crews headed back to their local hotels, but they were never all totally gone, and the hordes returned again every morning. There hadn't been any word from the girls in over a week, but the constant stream of press statements by government officials meant that the reporters always had a fresh sound bite to play and questions to ask if the Millhouses happened to leave their home. But they hadn't left, except to attend church on Sunday. At least there, in the confines of First Methodist, people had enough common sense and good manners to just leave the family alone.

In contrast, Linda felt like a prisoner in her own home, even though she was grateful for the steady stream of neighbors and friends who came by every day. The police had set up a background check of sorts, and people claiming that they knew the Millhouses or had something to deliver had to show identification and then be approved by Jack, Linda, or Josh before they could head up the driveway. Police from other towns had called with that advice . . . apparently reporters had been known to dress up like delivery people or pretend they were neighbors in order to get close to the house. Mrs. Millhouse was relieved and thankful that the police were being so helpful, and she'd already decided to give a significant portion of her charity donation money that year to the police department.

****

When the phone rang in the middle of the afternoon on Day Eight of Amy's disappearance, Linda didn't think anything of it. Probably just today's police officer, Joe Calamatti, calling to say that a neighbor was there with dinner for that evening. Based on the schedule, it should be Cindy Davis, a retired schoolteacher and wife of a local accountant. The first couple of days after Amy was reported missing, Linda and the rest of the family had always answered the phone on the first ring, hoping it would be Amy calling to say she was okay. By now, though, they had settled into a more realistic acceptance of things, hoping and praying just as earnestly for Amy to be found but steeling themselves that they could be in it for the long haul. Linda took her time getting over to the phone, picking it up on the third ring.

"Hey Joe, who's here?"

There was a pause at the other end of the line, and then an unfamiliar voice spoke. "May I please speak with Mrs. Linda Millhouse?"

Unsure if it was a reporter calling, the usually forthcoming woman replied curtly, "who is asking?"

"Lawrence Van Oren, ma'am. My granddaughter, Caitlin, was on the trip to Mexico with your daughter."

"Oh my goodness. Hello. I'm so sorry; I just never know who will be calling, and those reporters are relentless," Mrs. Millhouse replied, embarrassed by her opening exchange with the man on the other end of the line. She recognized the name, having heard it on the news. Lawrence Van Oren was a hedge fund investment guru – famous within certain Wall Street circles but noted for his extreme efforts to maintain a private life and protect his family from the glare of the media limelight. From what Linda had heard on television, the kidnapping had completely shattered the Van Orens' privacy bubble and turned the incident into a pop culture phenomenon: 'billionaire heiress goes missing.'

"No, no, no need to apologize," the man replied. "I completely understand. I probably shouldn't have contacted you directly at home. I suppose I'm just not quite thinking clearly right now." His New York-accented voice sounded strained and sleep-deprived, Linda thought, much like hers at the moment. "I'm calling you and the rest of the families personally in an attempt to keep the information out of the hands of the press," Van Oren began. "But I have been contacted by a man claiming to belong to a group that kidnapped the girls."

"Oh my gosh!" Mrs. Millhouse exclaimed, bursting into tears in an overwhelming rush of relief that the girls were alive mixed with fear about what would happen next.

Josh and Jack immediately dropped what they were doing and ran into the kitchen to find out what had caused Linda's emotional outburst. "What's going on? Who's on the phone?" they asked, peppering her with questions. Linda shook her head at them and waved them off as she tried to concentrate on her phone conversation.

"What did he say? Are they okay? What does he want?" Linda could hardly contain herself as she spit out the questions in rapid-fire succession.

Calmly, slowly, as if to not misspeak, the distinguished businessman replied, "The girls are all alive. And the men want money. All told they're asking for $10 million, in U.S. currency of course." Linda was surprised at the matter-of-fact tone in the voice on the other end of the line, but she supposed that when one is a billionaire one has to think about these sorts of things. "I've already begun making arrangements for the money transfer," Lawrence continued. "And I won't accept any contributions from the other families. After I made my first billion, my attorneys advised me that ransom demands of up to $20 million for one of my children or grandchildren would not be out of the question. I have a fund set up to cover it, so don't worry about it."

"Oh no, we couldn't possibly accept," Linda immediately replied, shocked that this man would offer to pay the entire ransom demand for a group of girls he had never met. As soon as she said that, though, reality set in as Linda realized that she didn't know where in the world she and her husband would come up with the $500,000 or so that would represent Amy's share of the total.

"Mrs. Millhouse, please. Caitlin is an only child and loves of all of her fellow sorority members as if they were her true sisters. If she loves them, I love them by extension. I just want to see all of the girls back home, safe and sound. The money is an afterthought."

"Why did they wait so long to call you? When will you give them the money?" Amy's mom asked, her questions endless.

"We're lucky we heard from them so soon. Apparently these kidnappings in Mexico can drag on for months or years before there is any word. And I don't know when I'll give them the money. They gave me forty-eight hours to put it together, so I'm guessing they'll call again when that time is up. I don't know if I will have all of the money by then . . . it's not exactly easy to get ten million dollars in cash. So I might have to ask for a little more time, and then the police are telling me to ask for more time so they can try to find the girls."

"They've had eight days to find them!" Linda couldn't contain her outburst of frustration.

"I know, my thoughts exactly. But you have to believe me, ma'am, I will pay the money and I will pay as soon as I can."

TWENTY-EIGHT

Caitlin's grandfather was livid. It should not be this complicated. He had money, people had his granddaughter, let's just make the switch and be done with it.

He understood that pulling together that much money in cash would be somewhat difficult. Having the government's help definitely sped things along, but it had taken the better part of a day and a half to get the money that was now in front of him in briefcases in the middle of a heavily guarded conference room. Ten million dollars in unmarked, non-sequential $100 bills. One million per briefcase. A little bit of a smile crossed Van Oren's lips as he thought about how easy it would be to catch the kidnappers when they went to retrieve the money. If they were smart, they would have set up an anonymous account and had the money wire transferred. That would be faster and less easy to trace. This way, though, this big of a money drop? All the police had to do was position someone to watch the spot and then follow the cash after it was picked up. The smile grew a little broader as Lawrence again envisioned kidnapper heads on silver platters.

When the phone rang, though, the billionaire stopped smiling. He waited, looking at the agents in the room as they scrambled to put on headphones to listen and record the conversation. The phone that the kidnapper used to call Van Oren the first time was a burner cell, untraceable. But the FBI wanted to listen in nonetheless. Getting a nod and a thumbs up from the agent in charge, Lawrence answered after the third ring.

"Hello?"

Not wasting any time, the man on the other end of the line declared: "it's been forty-eight hours. Do you have the money?"

Van Oren paused. He knew what he was supposed to say. How he was supposed to tell the kidnapper that he needed a little more time, that $10 million was a lot of money to get in cash but he was working on it. The FBI told him to ask for another two days. *Do I follow the instructions? Or make my own decision?* Using the gut instinct that had served him so well in business over the years, Lawrence chose the latter.

"I have the money," he began, and could hear the groans from the FBI agents, "but I recommend that you give me a little more time." Not waiting for the other man to ask why, he continued, "the police up here – "

"I said no police!" the kidnapper angrily interrupted.

"Come on now, son. We both knew that wasn't going to happen." The paternal tone in Lawrence's voice clearly took the young man by surprise, and so the grandfather continued:

"The police think they're smarter than the rest of us and gave me sequential bills. The money might as well have 'ransom payment' stamped on it." He paused to let that fact sink in. "Give me another twenty-four hours, and I'll put together the cash how you want it. Unmarked, nonsequential." Van Oren could tell by the tone in the kidnapper's voice that his ploy had worked. He had established a relationship with this son of a bitch. The bastard trusted him now. That was good.

"Okay," came the reply. "I'll call back in twenty-four hours."

Before Ricky had a chance to hang up, Caitlin's grandfather interjected. "One more thing, son," he said, adopting the same tone he had used countless times with business subordinates. "I just did you a huge favor. I could have left the cash as it was, easily traceable. But I didn't. I'm showing good faith here, holding up my end of the bargain. So I expect you do to the same."

There was a pause, with the kidnapper obviously trying to figure out the correct response. "If you pay, you will get your granddaughter."

Satisfied, Van Oren replied, "good. I'll talk to you in twenty-four hours."

****

Ricky didn't know what to make of this rich grandpa character. Was he telling the truth? Had the FBI really given him sequential bills and he needed more time to fix that? Or was it just a stalling tactic . . . lying to him to buy more time for the police to keep looking for the girls? This might have been Ricky's first time staying through the whole kidnapping, but he wasn't stupid. He knew this whole area was crawling with Federales and probably American FBI agents too, hunting for the missing girls. The more time it took to complete the money drop, the more time the police had to find them. But the old man seemed sincere on the phone, and Ricky liked how the billionaire was treating him like a business associate. Straightforward. Except for a few outbursts, free of the kind of crazy emotional stuff that Emiliano had warned him about.

Regardless, it would be another twenty-four hours before he called Mr. Lawrence Van Oren again with instructions for how to drop the money. Emiliano had it set up perfectly. The directions would be to put the money into duffel bags, $1 million per bag, and then put them in specifically designated lockers at the Acapulco bus terminal. Two bags per locker. Ricky knew that the police would be watching those lockers, waiting on someone to come retrieve the money. But Emiliano had that covered, too. Because one of the men, Hector, had a brother named Raúl who worked at the bus depot. The two men looked almost exactly alike, and Hector already stole one of Raúl's work uniforms. So the night after the money was dropped, Hector would go into the back, employees-only area. The lockers at the train station were cheap, flimsy, and Hector would be able to slide off the back and retrieve the duffel bags, without anyone on the outside knowing what was happening. It was brilliant. *We're gonna be rich. Filthy, stinking RICH.*

TWENTY-NINE

It was four days between the time when Caitlin talked to her grandfather and when Ricky and the jefe finally returned. Not that any of the girls had been allowed to keep their watches. Instead, Amy had continued to tell time based on their feeding schedule. Well, their watering schedule to be exact. Ricky had brought the phone down in between the midday water glass and the evening water glass, and it was after another four 'lunches' that the men finally came back into the room. The all-too-brief conversation between Caitlin and her grandfather had given all of the girls hope, and for the first time in a week and half they really thought they would be going home soon.

Ricky, the boss, and several other men first huddled with the guards, informing them of the situation, before the entire group turned toward the girls.

Amy shuddered deep inside when she saw the looks on all of their faces. She had seen something close to that look before on the drunken faces of men at bars and frat boys at big parties. A predatory, primal look. Except this version of it was much worse: more raw, more violent – like a hungry lion that had just come across a zebra with a broken leg . . . easy prey.

The group of men in the room now was much larger than those who were normally guarding the girls. *This must be all of them, or at least close to it*, Amy thought. From a quick count in her head, it looked like there was one male kidnapper for every female kidnappee. No one had said anything yet, but the equal numbers made Amy nervous. *What are they up to?* she wondered.

Finally, after what seemed like an eternity, Ricky stepped forward. *By the pricking of my thumbs, something wicked this way comes.* However, in addition to the predatory look in his eyes and the cocky grin on his face, Amy saw something else. Greed. She could almost make out the green dollar signs in his eyes where his pupils should have been. *Our families are going to pay the money*, Amy thought as a wave of relief rushed over her. *They're going to pay and we're going to go home!*

"You know," Ricky began, directing his speech toward Caitlin. "You shouldn't have told us about how rich your grandfather is. We usually only ask for $40,000 or $50,000 per person, but with you . . ." Ricky paused as his evil grin morphed into a full-blown smile . . . "We knew we could start the bidding much, much higher."

Caitlin's lower lip began to quiver at the mention of her grandfather, who despite his busy work schedule and immense wealth had always been a very loving, very involved person in her life. "Y-you m-mean, he, he's going to p-pay you?" Caitlin asked, stuttering and struggling to get through the sentence.

"Oh yeah, he'll pay," Ricky answered. "All of you lot," he continued, making a sweeping gesture with his arm to encompass the entire group of girls, "are worth quite a bit of money. Your families must really love you," Ricky commented, laughing as he said it. The few other men in the room who understood English also laughed, and once again Amy didn't like the looks on their faces. They were too happy. Sure, they were about to be paid an apparently large sum of money, much larger than they usually received. But the men weren't just happy about the ransom money. No, something else was going on here. Amy just couldn't figure it out.

"When will we be let go?" she asked boldly, demanding an answer to the question at the forefront of all of the girls' minds.

"Oh, soon enough," came Ricky's nonchalant response. "We're arranging for the ransom payment. Well, your families' part of the payment is being arranged."

"Our families' part?" asked Laura Ann, emboldened by the prospect of being granted her freedom and, like Amy, not liking the looks on the men's faces.

"We've been talking," Ricky began, looking around at the other men in the room, "and we decided that the money isn't enough. Ten million dollars is what we're getting from little Granddaddy Warbucks, but we want something from you girls, too."

Amy was taken aback by the amount of money their families would be paying for their release. *Ten million dollars?! There's no way my parents have enough money to cover my portion of that.* Her family was comfortable financially, but they didn't have that kind of money. Amy knew that Caitlin's grandfather, Mr. Van Oren, must be covering a significant part of the ransom payment. *But what do they want from us?*

The other men in the room began to chuckle and exchange looks amongst themselves when Ricky mentioned wanting something from the girls. "Granddaddy Warbucks will give us the money. Whether or not you all survive the trip to where we'll drop you off is up to you."

"What does that mean?" Amy asked, frightened by Ricky's suggestion that the girls might die en route from this holding place to wherever their families or, more likely, the police, would pick them up.

"It means," Ricky said slowly, as the chuckling and the predatory looks resumed, "that we will require an extra fee from each of you. A freedom fee, if you will. As you might have noticed, there are now seventeen men in the room. One for each of you. We're going to leave soon to finalize plans for the ransom drop. But when we get back, you girls will line up, side by side, in the middle of the room. Each man will then get a girl, and whatever he wants from you, you give. If you refuse, your family will get a corpse instead of a daughter."

"What do you mean, 'whatever he wants?'" asked Ashley.

"You're women. We're men. Use your imagination," Ricky replied. He then turned to walk away from the group of girls and out of the room, pausing to wink and smile at Amy as he left. She nearly vomited in response.

THIRTY

Once the majority of the men had left the basement and the ones remaining returned to the other side of the room, the girls huddled together in a small circle to talk about what had just happened. The men guarding them didn't seem to care if the girls talked now.

"This is outrageous," declared Amanda, the first one to speak. Her voice was still in a whisper, though, since they didn't want any of the guards to eavesdrop – even though they were pretty sure that none of the kidnappers in the room at that moment understood English. "They can't do this," Amanda continued. "They're getting the money; they can't make us do this too."

"Of course they can," chimed in Allison, one of the more serious, practical girls in the group. "They have guns. And absolute control over our freedom. We all saw the looks on their faces when Amy said 'name your price.' This is their price."

"Don't blame this on Amy," Laura Ann said defensively. "If she hadn't spoken up then who knows how long it would've taken them to contact our families." Laura Ann knew she had the attention of the group, even if it was attention gained through pity. Ricky and the other kidnappers were now asking the girls to give to them what they had already taken from Laura Ann. For one of the first times in her life, she realized that her friends were looking to her for guidance. Taking a deep breath, Laura Ann continued, "you all know how lucky you are that they haven't been demanding something like this from all of you from Day One. What's done to me" – Laura Ann paused as she choked up on the words – "is done. There's nothing that can change that. But y'all have to be realistic. We're all pretty girls. They're disgusting pigs masquerading as men. We never stood a chance of making it out of here without something sexual happening."

"You don't know that for sure," Amanda replied. She came from a very Puritan, almost-repressed upbringing and even the mention of the word 'sex' made her uncomfortable.

"Yeah, I do," Laura Ann shot back angrily. "They raped me. Do you not understand that? Have you already forgotten it? They raped me and they made you watch to scare you into submission. Do you want to go home, Amanda? Do you want to see your family again? Then do what they say."

"I just," Amanda haltingly replied, "I just thought my first time would be – "

"Oh, for crying out loud Amanda. Grow the fuck up," Allison snapped.

"Hey, y'all, calm down," interjected Amy, trying to put an end to the argument brewing between several of the girls. "Fighting with each other won't solve anything. This is obviously just a decision that each of us has to make for ourselves."

"There's no decision to be made," stated Allison. "You heard Ricky. Do what they want or die."

"But what if they have diseases?" Heather chimed in squeamishly. "Y'all know they've slept with prostitutes before. What if I get herpes? Or AIDS?"

Their end of the room fell silent at the mention of AIDS. None of the girls had thought about that before. Sure, there had been lots of advances in medical technology and treatments in the last several decades. But even amongst a group of young women who had faced death so many times in the past week and a half, that combination of four letters – A-I-D-S – still managed to strike fear into the hearts of all of them.

Kennedy spoke up for the first time. "Why don't we all say no? Surely if we all stick together and nobody agrees to it then they'll have to back down."

"Oh get real, Ken," Allison replied. "These are not the type of guys who will just back down. It's not like they were taught 'no means no' in their kidnapper training course. Look what happened to Laura Ann. If we don't give it, they'll take it. Or they'll kill us. Or both."

Laura Ann nodded her head in agreement. "Look, Allison is right. It's either do this and be released or stay here for God knows how long and maybe be killed. Y'all heard what Ricky said. Our families get a corpse or a daughter. End of discussion."

Amy had been silent for most of the conversation. She wanted to hear everyone's opinions, and she also knew how important it was to allow people to express their thoughts about this, especially since this was the first time they had been allowed to really talk since the kidnapping eleven days ago. But Amy had also already made up her mind. While she wanted to go home more badly than anything she'd ever wanted before in her life, and she had no doubt that her kidnappers were evil, soulless merchants of the Devil, she wasn't going to give in to their demands. She couldn't. She had known from the very beginning of this whole ordeal that the chances were pretty high that she would be sexually assaulted. But having it forced upon her was different than consenting to it. She couldn't sell her body like that, even if her captors were willing to pay her with freedom.

****

After what seemed like an eternity, but was in actuality probably only about thirty minutes, the men began returning to the room. First came Ricky, still sporting his now-signature arrogant smile. The boss man followed soon thereafter, along with The Enforcer. A steady stream of others then filled the room; men that Amy and the other girls had only seen for the first time half an hour earlier. Just like before, there was one guy for every kidnapped girl. All of the men looked like they hadn't showered in weeks, and the concept of clean clothes or a shaved face seemed entirely foreign to them. Amy certainly appreciated the scruffy, three-day-beard look on some men, but what this group had went far beyond that. This was closer to a mountain man, Eric-Rudolf-hiding-in-the-woods style. Not to mention the fact that the level of body odor in the room had now quadrupled. *I can't believe the other girls are going to do* that *with* them, Amy thought, shaking her head in disgust.

Ricky stepped forward, displaying his evil grin. "Ok, who wants to go first?" he more declared rather than asked, clearly not expecting that any of the girls would say no.

Two of the men, one of them The Enforcer, walked over to the corner that had been the girls' living space during their time in the basement. Armed with the same AK-47s that were originally used to kidnap the group, the same ones that had knocked Amy unconscious, the two men motioned for the girls to stand up. They were then herded into the center of the room, just like Ricky said would happen.

"You heard me. Who's up first?" Ricky asked again. Amy and her sorority sisters nervously looked back and forth between each other and the men, with no one wanting to be the first to step forward. Irritated, Ricky began to wonder if the girls were going to refuse. By this point in a kidnapping, their victims should have been little puppets. But amazingly, even after the kidnapping, witnessing the taxi driver executions, the rape of Laura Ann, and being held here for eleven torturous days, these precocious Americans still had some fight left. *Time to put an end to that*, Ricky thought.

"Don't think you'll just be able to keep standing there and eventually the terms of our agreement will change," Ricky warned the girls. "If you don't do what we want, you don't make it back to your families alive. It really is that simple. And it won't be a pretty end to your lives either. We have a tendency to, oh, how do you say, 'get creative' with the bodies." Ricky laughed as he said that, then continued: "You see Ramón over there? He scalped a guy once, just like your Indians used to. Paquito likes to tear out people's toenails before chopping off their heads." Ricky laughed more, imagining the first time he saw the man do that. "Hector used to run with a crowd that had a lion pit. Put the homies in a ring and then let lions loose on them. It was beautiful, or so he says.

"And don't think that just because I sound American that I don't know how to handle things. I got my first kill when I was fourteen. He was fifteen. We were just two local street kids who were picked up by a cartel one afternoon. Took us out to an abandoned fútbol field and made us stand toe-to-toe, facing each other. Then the guy in charge told me to pick a side, heads or tails. The loser of the coin toss would die. What he didn't say until after I won the toss – tails never fails – was that I was the one who had to kill the other kid. I shot him cold in the back of the head. Guillermo I think his name was. Anyway, don't fuck with us. We've been nice so far. Just be good little girls, give the boys what they want, and everybody is happy."

THIRTY-ONE

The young women were all shocked by Ricky's speech. *A lion pit? Scalping people?* Amy couldn't believe what she had just heard. Then again, she could. The people involved in the Mexican drug wars were notoriously brutal and violent. Once, she even read a news article about a man who was kidnapped and killed. His body was then chopped into pieces. But that wasn't the worst part. They had also skinned his face and sewn the skin onto a soccer ball. Ricky wasn't kidding when he said they had a tendency to be creative.

Finally, a voice from the back of the group of girls spoke up. It was Laura Ann.

"Me. I'll go first."

Ricky's evil grin once again broadened into a full smile when he saw who was making her way to the front of the group. "Didn't get enough the first time around?" he snickered. "You always were the group whore."

Amy and the other girls cringed at Ricky's words. Laura Ann, however, didn't seem to notice. She had entered into some sort of Zen place and was singularly focused on the task at hand. This was what the men wanted in exchange for her freedom, and as far as Laura Ann was concerned, it wasn't too high of a price to pay.

Stepping forward a few feet in front of the rest of the women, Laura Ann stared boldly into Ricky's eyes – a statement of defiance meant to declare her independence in spite of what she was about to do.

"I think," Ricky said mischievously, "that we'll put your expertise to good use." Glancing to his right at the other members of his kidnapping gang, Ricky motioned toward a boy standing near the doorway. Clearly uncomfortable to be in the room, he couldn't have been much older than twelve or thirteen. Turning to address Laura Ann again, Ricky said, "you're going to make Alejandro here a man."

Alejandro stepped nervously into the center of the room and stood next to Ricky, barely coming up to the older man's shoulder. "Take good care of this one," Ricky said, patting the young boy on the back. "He's Emiliano's little brother."

Amy and many of the other girls closed their eyes instead of watching the disgusting spectacle in front of them. Unfortunately, while they could block out the sights, they couldn't get rid of the sounds. The men in the room were clearly enjoying their front row seats to Laura Ann's 'expertise,' and Emiliano, the jefe, was obviously proud of himself for providing the means by which his little brother would, as Ricky put it, become a man. Amy very nearly threw up at the totality of everything happening just a few feet away from her, but more than anything what disgusted her most was the fact that these men thought kidnapping women and forcing one of them to perform sexual acts on a middle school-age child constituted 'brotherly love.' *This is so, so wrong on so many levels*, Amy thought to herself.

After Laura Ann's 'payment' to Alejandro was complete, she was taken away from the other girls and out of the room. Amy didn't hear any footsteps, so she assumed that they took Laura Ann back to the smaller room where Amy had first been held.

Tanner was the next of the Sorority Seventeen to step forward. Everyone had been surprised when Tanner decided to go on the trip. While a member of the sorority, she spent most of her time with either friends from high school or her fiancé, Matt, who she had been dating since freshman year. A pretty brunette with matching brown eyes and the kind of curves that made men drool, Tanner had told everybody she wanted to have one last hurrah with her Greek sisters, and they were happy to have her sweet-natured personality on the trip. Amy hadn't been expecting Tanner to be the next girl to go, but she couldn't really blame her for wanting to get it over with.

The men in the room continued to look on as their co-conspirator, another one that Amy didn't recognize as one of the usual guards, took his turn with Tanner. Unlike Alejandro, this second guy clearly knew what he wanted and how he wanted it done. Once again, Amy closed her eyes. She couldn't bring herself to watch it. The men in the room, however, were watching and cheering on the spectacle.

The cheering, hooting, and hollering continued and if anything got louder as the girls, one by one, made their in-kind ransom payments. Particularly difficult for Amy to hear was the ordeal of her good friend Caitlin. The two girls had become very close during their four years of college, and Amy knew that, like her, Caitlin was still a virgin. Until now, that is. The men's demands had gotten more and more bold as they went down the line, and the man who singled out Caitlin as 'his' was none other than The Enforcer. This time Amy did throw up at the sound of her friend's screams of pain, the heiress' tiny body simply unable to handle the force and anger and power of the large man stealing the last bit of her innocence that remained.

For Amy, the only thing worse than what was currently happening to Caitlin was the knowledge that it was her turn next. Caitlin was the sixteenth girl to step forward, and when she was finally carried into the other room – she was unable to walk after The Enforcer finished with her – Amy was the only hostage who remained. Just like her initial arrival in this God-forsaken building, Amy was once again alone with her captors. In the room with her were Ricky, the boss Emiliano, and four of the six regular guards. The Enforcer and the one guy they called Paquito had left, presumably to keep any eye on the other girls.

"How did I know you would be last, Rubia?" Ricky asked Amy, using the nickname he had given her because of her blonde hair. "I have always, how do you say, had a thing for tall, skinny blondes," he continued. "And you'll notice, I haven't had my turn yet. Which means," Ricky declared gleefully, his words slithering like a snake, "you're mine."

Amy shuddered at the thought. Ignoring Ricky and the other men, she closed her eyes and began to pray. For strength; for composure; for a future she didn't know if she would ever have.

"Ok, enough of that," Ricky said, knowing full well what Amy was doing. "Undress," he commanded. "I want all of you."

Amy slowly opened her eyes, their blazing emerald green color revealing the determination running deep into her soul. Standing up to her full height, Amy clenched her fists, gritted her teeth, and declared defiantly: "No."

THIRTY-TWO

"Jennifer Jones, here, reporting live from the Los Angeles airport as we await the arrival of the group of kidnapped American girls who were rescued less than forty-eight hours ago. For those of you who have somehow managed to remain unaware of this gripping story, a quick recap:

"Seventeen American girls, all but one recent college graduates and members of the same sorority, were kidnapped while on vacation in Acapulco, Mexico. A massive manhunt was quickly underway, with Mexican and American military and police searching to find the missing girls. Now authorities are being fairly tight-lipped about the whole situation, but sources say that the girls were released after a ransom payment was made; the transfer of money being arranged by the grandfather of one of the girls, billionaire investor Lawrence Van Oren. We're told Mr. Van Oren is here today, along with the families of the rest of the girls who should be arriving any minute now. One thing to note, of course, is that we're told that only sixteen girls are flying back today. One of the Sorority Seventeen, Amy Millhouse, is still missing and authorities continue to search for her. We will definitely keep you updated on any developments there.

"What? Okay, yes, yes, this is them. Here now for you live from LAX, the return of the Sorority Seventeen."

****

The wheels touching down on the black tarmac woke Caitlin from her medicinally-induced sleep. She was very groggy and very tired, but also very happy to be back on American soil. Caitlin waited in her seat while one of the nurses who had accompanied the girls on the flight brought a wheelchair down the wide aisle of the specially-designed medical transport plane. The petite brunette was still unable to walk without assistance, the rape by The Enforcer having done such severe damage that doctors said they didn't know if she would ever be able to have children. Caitlin had spoken with her parents and grandfather before the flight and knew that all three would be waiting for her in the airport terminal. The police had set up a conference room for the girls and their families so they could be reunited away from the cameras and the questions of the press. After the reunion, Miss Mitchell would be whisked away to Manhattan to begin the long road to recovery.

Caitlin's groggy thoughts turned to Amy, the one member of the group who wasn't on the plane. The girls didn't know what happened to their friend, aside from the fact that one of the kidnappers had commented about the "rubia" refusing to give the men what they wanted. "I guess she want to die" was what he said.

At first they all thought Amy was crazy. Chills ran up Caitlin's spine as she remembered Allison's words: "do what they want or die." In the end, though, the sorority sisters realized that their former president might have been on to something. Because Ricky changed the terms of the release. At first he said one time, one 'payment,' and then go free. But then, later, in the small room on the other side of the stairs in the basement, one payment turned into two, two to three, and for some girls three to four. Once the bad guys knew that the girls were willing to negotiate, they kept upping the price. Caitlin knew that the only reason she wasn't already having nightmares was because she was so heavily sedated. When the drugs stopped, though, the dreams would surely start.

****

Laura Ann was also in a wheelchair – almost all of the girls were – and as she made her way through the back hallways of the airport, away from the prying eyes of the media, Laura Ann was already counting down the minutes until she could have more pain medicine. Doctors in Chilpancingo had to do an emergency hysterectomy on Laura Ann, and the deep cut of the incision hurt like hell.

After what seemed like a lifetime, her wheelchair attendant finally made a wide, sweeping turn into the large conference room set up for the girls and their families. Laura Ann was shocked, truly shocked, to see her mom among the parents waiting for their daughters. The young woman had absolutely no idea how her mother had afforded the plane ticket, didn't want to begin to figure out where she was staying, although Laura Ann supposed the TV networks might have footed the bill. *Figures*, the daughter thought, *leeching money off of other people yet again.* Her mom wasn't exactly her favorite person in the world, and Laura Ann's experience in Mexico had taught her that she really didn't want to be like her mother anymore. She wanted respect. Stability. The white picket fence and the 2.4 kids.

Unable to turn around, Laura Ann raised her head back as much as she could and asked the middle-aged man pushing her wheelchair to take her over to where Caitlin and her family were. To earn respect you have to show respect, and Laura Ann knew that the tall, distinguished man in the corner deserved all the respect in the world. He was the reason she was here.

The tears began before Laura Ann even arrived in front of the Van Oren/Mitchell clan. She couldn't stop the flood, but she didn't care either. "Excuse me, Mr. Van Oren?"

Caitlin and her family stopped talking when they saw Laura Ann coming near. "Yes?" the grandfather answered.

Through her tears, Laura Ann spoke. "My name is Laura Ann Sanders. I just wanted to say thank you. For everything."

Lawrence had not expected any thanks. Indeed, if he had his way, no one would have known that he paid for the girls' release. But he appreciated the gesture by the young woman sitting in front of him; he knew it took a lot of maturity and composure on her part – far more than might be expected from someone so freshly removed from her kidnappers' control.

"You're very welcome, my dear. Although there's nothing to say thank you for. I'm just so glad you girls are back home." Leaning down, the billionaire investor embraced the daughter of a restaurant waitress in a big bear hug. Had there been any photographers in the room, it would've been the image of the year.

THIRTY-THREE

"Captured Americans Freed."

"16 of Sorority 17 Back on U.S. Soil."

"Free at Last!"

The headlines glared up at Josh Millhouse as he sat in his family's kitchen with newspapers from around the United States and the English-speaking world spread out across the table in front of him. Some of the papers had pictures of Amy's sorority sisters leaving the airport with their families; others showed images from the various press conferences held by American and Mexican authorities. The presidents of both countries had even released statements about how relieved they were that the girls had been set free. The news articles also contained detailed accounts of the young women's final hours before entering the protection of Mexican military forces in Chilpancingo, a city about an hour inland from Acapulco.

The whole world now knew about the kidnappers' ransom demands – financial and otherwise. The exact amount wasn't released, but everyone knew that Lawrence Van Oren had paid a fortune to obtain the girls' freedom. What he paid, though, paled in comparison to what the girls paid. Each of the sixteen acknowledged the sexual acts they were forced to perform in exchange for their freedom, but the news reports also revealed that the assaults didn't stop with that one 'payment.' Josh nearly vomited as he read a quote by one of his sister's friends, Brittany.

"The men took us into a smaller, separate room after 'our turn' was over. But there were more kidnappers waiting in that room. They said that the price had gone up. Literally, those were their exact words. Now that they knew we would do that stuff, we were going to have to do more. It's funny the things that come to mind in situations like this. My mind immediately flashed to a scene in the movie *Air Force One*. Harrison Ford gets the Russians to release the bad guy, and then the dude who hijacked the plane says something about how the president will be useful and get them more stuff now that they know he's willing to negotiate. We negotiated. And they got more stuff."

The 'stuff' that Brittany referenced was apparently the repeated rape of most, if not all, of the girls. Violent, brutal attacks. One girl, Laura Ann, was so badly assaulted that doctors in Chilpancingo had to do an emergency hysterectomy. Gynecological experts in the United States said it was too soon to tell if any of the other young women would have future reproductive problems. They were particularly worried about Van Oren's granddaughter, Caitlin. But, as the newspapers and television commentators were quick to point out, at least all sixteen were alive and back in the United States. The girls had been dropped off on the outskirts of Chilpancingo in the middle of the night, presumably to prevent the police from finding out where they had been held. The kidnappers then called Mr. Van Oren with their exact location, once they made their getaway. The young women were quickly located and taken to the nearest hospital for examination and treatment before being flown back to the United States. Fourteen days after their graduation trip began, those sixteen sorority sisters touched down at LAX to be greeted by their families and a swarm of media that was incredible even by Los Angeles standards.

****

Which only left Amy. Josh pushed aside the articles talking about the other girls and now focused on the ones about his sister.

"One American Still Missing."

"Sorority President Still Unaccounted For."

"Where is Amy Millhouse?"

That last headline asked the question that now haunted Josh, his parents, the authorities, and nearly everyone who had followed the spectacular kidnapping drama. Where was she?

The other girls knew why Amy hadn't been released with them. Some of their captors angrily complained when the "tall rubia" wouldn't cooperate, and then Ricky, the English speaker, gleefully told the young women that their "fearless leader" was a little too fearless and had "gotten hers." Ricky didn't specify what he meant, but it didn't take much imagination to figure it out. One British tabloid was particularly vulgar about it, printing a large picture of Amy along with the caption "the girl who wouldn't go down."

Everyone in the country and much of the world was now talking about Amy Millhouse. Debates over her decision to not make the extra, sexual ransom payment raged in all sectors of society – from religious to political to philosophical to even some asshole of a professor at Syracuse who used Amy's situation as an example in his class discussion of game theory. *Too soon, bro. Too soon*, Josh thought, shaking his head in disgust.

He and his parents had been so excited when they heard that Mr. Van Oren was contacted with the girls' location. All three Millhouses had cried tears of joy, thinking that the long nightmare would soon be over and their beloved Amy would be returning home. But then they got a second phone call, this time from an official at the State Department who had been assigned to serve as their liaison. There were only sixteen girls. Amy wasn't with the group.

****

The American and Mexican authorities currently had no idea where Amy was. The other girls had been blindfolded and driven around for hours before finally being dumped outside of Chilpancingo in an effort to keep the police from knowing where the holding house was located. So far, the scheme had worked. Because they had been in the basement of the house the entire time, the girls could not give authorities any kind of information that might be helpful in the search. They knew the kidnappers drove black SUVS, but so did a lot of other people. That was also a very common vehicle for drug cartels, and it was impossible to know which group might have been responsible, since many of the cars driven by the gang members were stolen anyway. A lot of times the *narcos* would claim responsibility for attacks as a way to threaten their enemies, but no one had claimed this kidnapping. Even those groups that expressly denied any involvement were still on the government's suspect list. It could have been anybody, and that was the problem.

So now the Millhouse family simply had to wait. They had been strongly discouraged from travelling to Mexico to search for Amy themselves. The American and Mexican authorities insisted that it would simply make matters worse, because security forces would have to be diverted from the search for Amy to the protection of the Millhouses and the various government officials who would invariably fly in to meet with them. Josh's parents were initially furious that they were being told not to go, but had eventually realized that the authorities were correct and they would be a distraction. Mr. and Mrs. Millhouse caused a ruckus about it again when the rest of the girls arrived home and Amy didn't, but once more they had reluctantly seen the logic in the government's arguments. Amy's family was also now very aware of exactly how dangerous it could be in territory controlled by the drug cartels, and the last thing anyone wanted was another kidnapping.

So they waited. And prayed. And ate the endless supply of food from their neighbors. And then waited some more. Josh knew it was killing his parents to not be able to do anything. It was killing him too. He felt so helpless; so useless. Several times he thought of sneaking out, hopping a flight to Mexico, and searching for Amy himself. One morning, Agent Canady had arrived early to find Josh packing up a duffel bag. But the FBI man talked him out of going, using the only kind of logic that he thought would work. "You don't know the territory or the language. If you go down there like this, you will only make matters worse than they already are."

Surely they'll have to find her soon. Somebody has to know where she is, Josh thought to himself as he gathered up the scattered newspapers, put them neatly in a pile on the counter, and went to rescue his mother from a mind-numbingly boring conversation with his visiting great-aunt Ethel.

THIRTY-FOUR

María Velazquez didn't want to go to work today. It was extremely hot, even for summertime, and she would much rather join some of her friends at a swimming hole they frequented just outside of town. But she knew she didn't have a choice. Her mother needed her help running their roadside fruit stand, and it was her responsibility to be there. *Deber. Responsibilidad. Familia. Duty. Responsibility. Family.* Those were the words that her older brother Fernando had drilled into her head for six years now, ever since their father abandoned them and reportedly went north to the United States to find a job. He left behind his wife and two children, and now it took all three of them working all day, every day just to make ends meet. So, unlike her friends, on this bright summer day fifteen-year-old María was going to work.

The *frutas y verduras* stand occupied all of her time in the summers, and she thought it was quite possibly the most boring job in the world. Sitting behind a makeshift table displaying samples of the fruits and vegetables they sold, María often daydreamed of going to a big city like Monterrey or even Los Angeles and becoming a famous actress or model. In her heart and in her head, though, she knew that would never happen. María knew she wasn't ugly, but she knew she wasn't particularly pretty either. She was of average height, average weight, and average looks, María grudgingly admitted. Consequently, she would probably live the rest of her life in the same countryside where she had been born, relying on the occasional rich tourist customer to provide some semblance of mystery and excitement in her life.

Those thoughts were still running through María's mind as she and her mother drove to where they set up their roadside stand. It was outside of town, at the intersection of the biggest roads that ran through the area. The family only had one car, which technically belonged to her brother. So, early every morning, the two Velazquez women loaded up the car with crates of fruits and vegetables and drove out to their spot. They then unloaded the car, and María, even though she didn't have an official driver's license yet, drove it back to their house so her brother could use it during the day. The teenage girl then hopped on a bicycle and rode the two miles or so back out to the stand. At the end of the day, Fernando drove out and picked them up.

As the small, battered sedan neared the crossroads and Señora Velazquez began to slow down, María noticed what looked like a body lying on the side of the road. While it didn't happen frequently, it wasn't completely uncommon for the local drug gangs to dump bodies on the side of this road. It was just far enough outside of town for no one to see them, although María knew they didn't really care about that. She had heard news reports of masked cartel members stopping traffic in busy cities in the middle of the day and dumping their victims in the road. She tried not to think about the ongoing war between the drug cartels and the Mexican military, but it was hard not to. More than anything, she just accepted it as a part of life.

Which was why she wasn't shocked to see the body beside the road. Especially in the summertime, because the *narcos* knew that the bodies would decompose pretty quickly. Either that or they would become food for scavenging birds and animals. María had taken an anatomy class in school this past year, which made her a lot less squeamish about dead bodies and a lot more interested in them. She would almost always approach the corpse to look at it, mostly to make sure she didn't recognize the person. If that happened, she would tell the family of the victim so they could come get their relative.

This girl definitely isn't from around here, María thought as she walked near the body. She had already helped her mother unload the car and would drive it back home soon, but not until she first got a look at this person. The victim, God help her, had long blonde hair and was very, very skinny. She also had large, nasty cuts and bruises all over her body. *They really messed her up badly*, María thought as she knelt down beside the young woman. *She hasn't been here long, either. Her skin isn't even sunburned yet. In fact, she's still really pale.*

Without stopping herself to ask why, María instinctively reached out and took hold of the woman's wrist, trying to feel for a pulse. "No, es imposible," María whispered anxiously, not believing what she had just felt. She quickly moved her fingers to the neck area to check for a pulse there. What she felt was confirmation of what the wrist had already told her.

"Mami! Ven aquí! Ven aquí!" Maria yelled hurriedly at her mother. She couldn't believe it. The roadside victim was still alive.

THIRTY-FIVE

Amy knew this feeling. She had felt this before, when she first drifted back to consciousness after being kidnapped. Except this time the pounding, bomb-fixing-to-explode pain in her head was much, much worse. And her body ached all over, like she had run head-on into a concrete wall. Actually, it was worse than a wall. Amy felt like she had been run over by a very large, very powerful truck. Every bone, every muscle, every fiber of her being hurt. Even her eyelashes hurt. Amy didn't even know that was possible. At least this time, as she was slowly awakening, Amy did not have to worry about keeping her eyes closed. They were swollen shut. Amy could only imagine what she looked like right now. If it was half as bad as she felt, she needed one of those signs that they flash at the beginning of television shows: 'warning, some images may be disturbing. Viewer discretion is advised.'

Without access to the use of her eyes, Amy tried to use her other senses to get a grasp of her surroundings. She had no idea what day it was, what time it was, or how long she had been here. She knew she wasn't dead, because she hurt too much to be in Heaven. And she also knew she wasn't still in the kidnapper's holding area because the smell was different. While her former location smelled like sweat, dirty men, and cigarettes, this place actually smelled fairly decent. Indeed, Amy caught a whiff of something cooking that resembled the pozole that she had learned to make in a Mexican culture class in college. Compared to the bug-infested mush that Amy had been served every day for weeks, the thought of a good corn stew made her mouth water and stomach rumble.

Amy could hear other people, two women, talking a short distance away. Across the room? In an adjoining room? She couldn't tell. But the sounds were somewhat muffled, so Amy guessed that they were in a different room or hallway. She was inside, she knew that much, because the sun wasn't beating down on her and she couldn't hear any of the tree rustlings or other sounds of nature that would indicate being outside. There was an occasional slight breeze, though, which felt glorious against Amy's battered body and led her to assume that there was a window open somewhere near the spot where she was lying on what felt like a coarse, possibly wool, blanket.

The voices near her got louder and defensive as a third person, a man, joined the conversation.

"¿Qué pasa aquí? ¿Quién es ella?" the male voice asked angrily, wanting to know what was going on and who Amy was.

"No es nada. No te preocupes."

"¿Quién es ella?" the man repeated, not willing to settle for the woman's dismissive answer for him not to worry about it.

There was a pause in the conversation, and what the man said next sent chills down Amy's spine. Well, not so much what he said as how he said it, asking in a snarling, menacing tone if Amy was the missing American girl. The women adamantly denied it, which didn't make much sense to Amy unless this man was one of her kidnappers. He didn't sound like any of them, but Amy hadn't heard all of the men talk for long enough to be able to identify all of their voices.

Again, Amy had never been more grateful for her Spanish language skills as she listened to the women try to convince the man that she wasn't the missing American girl. They told him she wasn't, that she was a visiting relative of a neighbor who had gotten mixed up with the wrong crowd. Around these parts, Amy presumed, that wasn't too difficult to do. The man's response provided mounds of clarity to the situation. Addressing one of the women as his mom, the man recounted how his father had left the family several years ago to try to find work in the United States but had never been heard from again. They hoped he was one of the hundreds of migrants who died on that arduous journey every year, since that was easier to accept than the thought of being abandoned. The disdain and hatred dripping from the young man's voice as he said the words "Estados Unidos" were clear. He hated Americans because his father had left the family to go to America.

"Si ella es la Americana secuestrada, me voy a informar a los secuestradores que ella está aquí." The man's final threat made Amy's head spin even more than it already was. It was bad enough that he knew who the kidnappers were . . . that meant that people had known where Amy and her friends were but didn't do anything about it. What was worse, though, was his declaration that if Amy was the kidnapped American girl, he would tell her kidnappers where she was.

THIRTY-SIX

Amy heard a door slam in the distance, and then a few minutes later someone entered her room. She could hear the person's footsteps and smell the food that accompanied her visitor; it was the stew that she had smelled earlier. Again, Amy's mouth began to water and her stomach growled loudly. The last full meal that Amy had eaten was dinner the night she arrived in Mexico, but even then she had just eaten a salad because she didn't want to feel bloated when she went out to the bar. *New life motto*, Amy thought to herself. *Always eat well – you never know when will be the next time you have a good meal.*

Amy heard something scrape loudly against the floor; it sounded like a chair against concrete or maybe hardwood floors. She could then feel the presence of someone next to her, and a slight squeaking noise accompanied by a soft thud indicated to Amy that the room's other occupant was now seated beside her cot. The other indication was the smell of the soup, which was now closer and stronger and oh so delicious. Amy had never been more excited at the prospect of food in her entire life.

A woman's voice cut into Amy's thoughts. She sounded young, but Amy couldn't pinpoint a good age range. The girl or woman was in that teenaged through late-twenties bracket where their voices all had pretty much the same level of depth and maturity.

"Hi," said the girl in heavily-accented English. "I have food for you."

Amy then felt a spoon touch her blistered bottom lip and realized that her companion was trying to feed her. Amy opened her mouth as much as possible and slowly swallowed the soup, careful not to choke on the liquid since she was lying flat on her back. The stew's mix of corn, pork, and other seasonings – Amy's nose had been correct, it was pozole – was quite possibly the best thing Amy had ever tasted. Even though the room she was in was a bit warm and stuffy, Amy didn't mind being served the hot soup. Every spoonful was like Christmas morning for the traumatized hostage survivor. Every drop served to warm not only her body but also her soul.

After a few minutes the spoonfuls stopped. "No more. Eat more and get sick," came the warning from Amy's hostess, who she desperately wanted to know more about. Amy heard the chair squeak again and tried to reach out her left arm to stop the woman from leaving, but Amy's arm wouldn't move. The searing pain in her shoulder and collarbone led Amy to believe that one or the other (or both) were broken. Panicked that she might lose this opportunity to find out where she was and what was going on, Amy mustered up all of her strength and managed to croak out one word.

"Wait."

The footsteps that had been getting farther away stopped and then started again, but this time they were coming back closer to Amy. Once more she heard the squeak-thud combination of a person sitting down in the bedside chair.

"Yes?" the same female voice asked.

"W-where a-am I?" whispered Amy, barely audible. After a short pause, just enough time to do a mental translation, the voice replied:

"Close to San José Tasajeras. Hour drive to Acapulco."

Acapulco, thought Amy. The haven for tourists that Amy and her friends had excitedly chosen over Cancún because some of them had never seen the Pacific Ocean. Well, to be accurate, the haven for tourists that Amy had chosen over Cancún because she had never seen the Pacific. The girls had narrowed it down to those two cities, and the vote was an 8-8 tie before Amy weighed in in favor of Acapulco. *The kidnappers didn't take us far then*, reasoned Amy, *if I am just an hour away from the city. We must have been right under the search party's noses the whole time.*

As Amy felt her voice beginning to return to her, the threat made by the man a little while ago popped back into her head. *I can't talk using my real voice. If I'm that close to Acapulco then these people will know what an American accent sounds like. I need a disguise. Canadian? Their accent is basically the same as the American one. No, it's too similar*, Amy reasoned. *The guy can say I am the American girl and I'm just claiming to be Canadian – which would be true. I need to distinguish myself. British. Done.* Amy mentally crossed her fingers and hoped these people wouldn't be able to tell a horrible imitation British accent from a real one.

"Who are you?" Amy asked, doing her best Kate Middleton impersonation.

"María," came the voice's reply. "I listen to English okay, but don't speak good." María paused, then continued, speaking slowly as she obviously tried to figure out what the correct English phrasing was. "Mami y me sell food by the road. We see you but you not dead, and carry you here, to our house."

Amy breathed a sigh of relief at María's story, happy that the young woman didn't appear to have any ties to her kidnappers. The man who had been in the house did, though, Amy was quick to remember. Wanting more details than the young woman's limited English speaking skills would be able to provide, and still not wanting to blow her cover as a fluent Spanish speaker, Amy thought of an idea.

Remembering that the girl said she understood English better than she could speak it, British-accented Amy said slowly, still trying to regain use of her scratchy throat:

"María, if I ask you something, can you answer yes or no if it is true or not?"

María seemed to quickly grasp the utility of this exercise and answered an affirmative,

"Sí. Yes."

A wave of excitement accompanied the flood of questions that entered Amy's mind. *What do I ask first? The guy could return at any point, and there's no way he would like for us to be talking a lot.* Question choice was critical. Amy's mind briefly travelled back to her high school history class and her teacher who loved to say that the questions someone asks reveal more about them than their answers ever will.

Another mental finger cross, and Amy began.

"Does anyone besides you, your mother, and the man I heard know that I am here?" Amy did her best to speak slowly and articulate her words fully, but it was hard with her face still so swollen.

"No," was María's reply.

Amy breathed a huge sigh of relief when María's answer finally came. The young woman was obviously doing two translations in her head: changing the question from English into Spanish, and then turning her answer from Spanish back into English. Even though the slow pace of conversation meant that Amy wouldn't be able to acquire as much information, she was just happy to have someone to talk to. Especially someone who seemed to care about Amy's well-being.

"Did you see any other bodies close to where you found me?"

"No." María's answer was almost a question, as she was clearly confused about why there would be more bodies nearby. *Maybe this girl really is the American that my brother has been talking about,* María thought. *She doesn't sound American though.* In María's opinion, the visitor sounded more like the princess that she had seen on the television in the town's general store. More likely than not, this woman was a backpacking tourist who got caught up in a bus attack. The *narcos* liked to stop transit buses in rural areas and rob and kill the passengers. People who ride those buses are almost exclusively Mexicans, but sometimes foreigners decide they want to see the 'real Mexico' and travel the country by bus. This woman was probably one of those unfortunate people, and she wanted to know if she had been dumped alongside the rest of the passengers. Whatever the reason for the question, María liked doing this. She really wanted to help this poor woman any way she could.

"I'm British," Amy lied. "From London. Is there any way you can take me to the Consulate in Acapulco?"

María paused, trying to think of how to answer the question in English. It needed more than a yes or no response.

"You too hurt now. Later, when you are better, we drive to Acapulco."

Okay, Amy thought. *That works. If these people are willing to take care of me, and if the guy – María's brother? – believes my British identity lie, then I can stay here a few days until I'm better.* Amy figured that her family probably all assumed that she was dead now anyway after she hadn't been released with the other girls. *A few days of a delay in getting to the city will be fine.*

THIRTY-SEVEN

A few days turned into well over a week as Amy's slow recovery revealed just how badly she had been beaten by her kidnappers. Amy knew in her mind that she had to be pretty messed up if the men had left her for dead, but the full impact of it didn't sink in until she saw herself in a mirror. She had been in the same room in the house for four days and María, getting annoyed by her guest's repeated questions about going to Acapulco, had borrowed her mother's handheld bathroom mirror and held it up in front of Amy's face.

Amy gasped in shock at what she saw. Her right eye was still almost completely swollen shut, but through her left eye she saw a face that was double its normal size and an ugly combination of black, purple, and blue. Streaks of red could also be seen where Amy's face was cut. In the midst of the brutal picture staring back at her, Amy was able to find a little bit of humor in how her lips looked. *If not for all the bruising, people would just think I had gotten a bad batch of collagen injected into my lips*, she thought, recalling what her older cousin had looked like one Thanksgiving a few years ago. The small amount of laughter that attempted to escape Amy's body, however, was quickly stifled by the sharp pain in her chest. Based on her troubled breathing, Amy guessed that several of her ribs were probably broken.

María also angled the mirror down some so Amy could see the cuts and bruises that made her body look more like an abstract art painting than part of a human being. What was most startling was the gash running diagonally from the middle of the left side of her collarbone all the way down to her right breast. At least a quarter of an inch wide and probably that deep as well, Amy knew that any hopes of one day wearing a strapless wedding dress were completely gone. *As if anyone would still want to marry me. Look at me*, Amy thought. *I'm a monster*.

****

After the episode with the mirror, Amy stopped asking about going to the British Consulate. Instead, she passed the time by thinking about her family and friends and eavesdropping on conversations between María and her family. She was able to find out through that eavesdropping and her other conversations with María that the male voice belonged to her brother, Fernando. He was a mechanic, which was why María had access to a car that was reliable enough to make the over two hour trip to Acapulco and back. Although he didn't like the idea at all, Fernando had agreed to let María and his mother drive Amy into the city as soon as she was healthy enough to travel. Fernando wasn't a fan of the two women travelling that far alone; neither did he like them using his car. If the *narcos* stopped the car and found Amy, a *gringa*, inside, they could not only kill his mother and sister but also trace the car back to him. Although he tried to remain as clean as possible, Fernando still made the strategic decision to stay on friendly terms with the area's drug gangs in an effort to not give them any reason to come after him – as if they needed one. The *narcos* could pick him as their next target just because they felt like it. But even with all of the risks involved in driving Amy to Acapulco, Fernando figured that it was a bigger risk to be hiding the blonde foreigner in his house, so he was willing to support any plan that got the girl out of there.

****

"Deen-ah," said the small voice of María's mother, the woman who had risked her life for these past two weeks to keep Amy safe, hidden, and on the road to recovery. Amy had managed to learn that the family's last name was Velazquez, and Señora Velazquez left the house for work fairly early each morning, not returning until late afternoon or early evening. From what she could gather from bits and pieces of overheard conversations, María usually went to work with her mother but had stopped doing so after they found the young blonde victim on the side of the road. María told Amy that she actually didn't mind staying in the house, because it was cooler in there than being out in the hot sun all day selling food at their roadside fruit and vegetable stand.

Señora Velazquez – Amy still didn't know the woman's first name, since María and her brother always called the older woman 'mami' or 'madre' – looked a lot like her daughter. Or, rather, her daughter looked a lot like her. They were both of medium height, probably somewhere between 5'4" and 5'6". They also had the same long, straight, jet black hair and big, round eyes the color of milk chocolate. Although both women were teetering on the border between healthy and overweight, they were still fairly well-proportioned and Amy knew that with a little help from a stylist, the Velazquez women could both go from ordinary to extraordinary. From drab to fab, as some of Amy's gay friends liked to say with all-too-stereotypical jazz hands flair. Add to the new wardrobe some properly applied makeup that emphasized the pretty brown eyes, and Amy could have a couple of Cinderellas on her hands. *I wonder if I could actually do that*, Amy thought. *After I get home and get healthy, maybe I could come back here to say thank you. Or even bring them up to the United States for a trip. Mom and I would have a ball taking them shopping.* Amy's thoughts of arranging an 'Extreme Makeover: Hero Addition' were interrupted by Señora Velazquez, as her host's announcement snapped the young woman back to reality.

"We go toomarroh," the woman said in her heavily accented English. She then left the room as quickly as she had entered it. Unlike her daughter, Señora Velazquez clearly had no interest in getting to know her guest.

As Amy ate the meal of rice and shredded chicken that had been prepared for her (her body could still only handle very simple, bland meals that were easy to both chew and digest), her thoughts drifted back to what the señora said. *Tomorrow. Tomorrow I'll leave here and go to Acapulco. Tomorrow I'll explain what happened and who I am to the British Consulate and they'll call the Americans. Tomorrow my family will find out I'm still alive. And maybe not tomorrow, but certainly in the next couple of days, I'll be going home.* A steady stream of tears began to fall down the young woman's face. Home. That word hung in the air and in Amy's mind like a beacon of hope. A shining reminder of a better place and a better time.

THIRTY-EIGHT

The sun rose early the next morning, strong and bright and scorching hot. The humidity was nearly unbearable, although Amy mused to herself that people who lived here would never have to worry about ironing their clothes or even sticking them in the bathroom with hot water running to steam out the wrinkles (which was Amy's preferred tactic). All one had to do in this sauna was hang the clothes outside for thirty seconds and they would be as straight as a board.

As she lie in the cot that she had grown accustomed to during her time in the Velazquez home, Amy went over the plan that she and María had worked out the night before.

Depending on road conditions and traffic around Acapulco, it would take them approximately an hour to an hour and a half to drive into the city and find the British Consulate. A few days earlier, María had gone to an internet café in town and looked up directions to the Consulate so they wouldn't have to stop and ask someone. Fernando, who still hadn't warmed up to Amy's presence in his family's home (but luckily had not told anyone about it either), was going to fill up the car with gas and bring it to the house between nine and nine-thirty in the morning. Sometime shortly before or after he arrived, María and her mother would have already helped hide Amy inside an emptied-out cornmeal sack. To ride like that in the back of the trunk all the way to Acapulco would definitely be uncomfortable and blazing hot, but the car had a busted-out taillight and a hole in the back bumper so she would at least have enough oxygen. It was simply too big of a risk for Amy to travel any other way. As a passenger in the back seat she could be easily spotted by passersby, and even riding in the trunk but not inside the sack would also be too dangerous because of the roadblocks and checkpoints that the *narcos* commonly set up on the roads leading into Acapulco, both as a show of force and an efficient way to capture and kill members of rival cartels. If the two Velazquez women were stopped, their car would undoubtedly be searched and Amy would be discovered. Since they didn't know who was involved in the kidnapping and who wasn't, hiding Amy and passing her off as a sack of cornmeal was really the only viable solution they could see. Amy thought the idea sounded more than a little bit crazy, but she knew full well what *los narcos* were capable of and she wanted to follow the safest plan possible, even if it was going to be highly uncomfortable and likely also highly painful. After all, after close to a month of hell, what were a few more hours?

Following what seemed like forever, Señora Velazquez finally came into the small room that had become Amy's and began helping her sit up. Even after twelve days of rest and healing, Amy was still incredibly weak and extremely sore. Once seated upright, the older woman then placed Amy's right arm over her shoulder and her arm around Amy's waist and gently lifted the young American to her feet. This action had become ritual, as either Señora Velazquez or María would then help Amy shuffle herself down the hall to the small house's one bathroom. Six months ago – heck, six weeks ago – Amy would have found the whole exercise extremely humiliating. She had always been modest when it came to things like nudity (something her sorority sisters constantly teased her about) and was also fiercely proud of her independence, so the thought of having someone help you dress, undress, bathe, and even go to the bathroom would have been too much for the old Amy to handle. She always joked that she could have never been a duchess or princess or anything like that 'back in the day,' because they had ladies maids to help them in and out of their clothes. The new Amy, however, was well past the point of caring about such things. She needed help and they gave it to her. Amy figured that when you've faced seemingly imminent death head-on, trivialities like bathroom assistance become just that: trivial.

María was waiting when Amy and the girl's mother made the approximately ten foot journey back down the hallway. The young Mexican girl with flowing black hair and striking chocolate-colored eyes looked nervous, and rightly so. Hiding Amy in their house was one thing, but travelling a good distance through drug gang-controlled territory and into a bustling city – where the discovery of decapitated bodies in street gutters was not uncommon – was an entirely different matter.

As she stood in the middle of the room, María held in her hand the massive cornmeal sack that would be Amy's disguise for the next several hours. It reminded Amy of the big, light brown bags that she used to use at summer camp for the potato sack races. *In fact,* Amy thought, *that's exactly what they looked like.* The only difference was that the contents of this sack had been corn instead of potatoes.

The three women heard a car pull up outside, and a quick glance out the window confirmed that it was Fernando. As the young man parked and came inside the house, Amy did her best to come up with the words to thank her two caregivers. The group had to say their goodbyes now, since there would be no time for such things once they arrived in Acapulco. Amy was simply going to be dropped off, in the sack, at the front gates of the British Consulate so María and her mother wouldn't have to be questioned by police. Amy gave the best smile she could, her face muscles straining against bruises and possible broken bones, and said "thank you" to each of the two women.

"You saved my life – literally. I don't know how I'll ever be able to repay you," Amy continued, her voice cracking as tears welled in her eyes. "Thank you. Thank you. Gracias," she concluded, keeping her wits about her enough to remember to say her thank you's with a British accent. She trusted the two women standing before her, but the man leaning against the doorway, their brother and son, she did not trust. Amy had kept up her British accented English-only charade for this long, and the desire to properly thank María and her mother in a language they could fully understand was outweighed by the risk of angering Fernando and bringing a crushing end to Amy's now-within-reach dream of returning home.

"Time to go," came the harsh, heavily-accented command from the hallway. The two Mexican women helped Amy ease herself back down onto the cot and then carefully folded her skinny frame into the sack: first one leg, then the other; then Amy's torso, arms, and head until she was balled up in a fetal position. They tied the bag securely closed with a small rope, but were careful to leave a hole in the top of the bag. They had also cut several small air holes in the light brown sack, since the last thing any of them wanted was for Amy to suffocate in the trunk of the car. Fernando then helped his mother and sister pick up their precious cargo and carry it down the short hallway and out of the house. He had backed the car up to the front door and left the trunk open, so it only took the three of them a few steps on the dirt and gravel driveway before they arrived at the car and carefully placed the sack in the trunk. They then loaded a few small crates of fruits and vegetables into the back with Amy, along with another cornmeal sack that had a freshly slaughtered pig inside of it. The crates and extra sack would provide María and her mother with a cover story for why they were going into the city. If they were unfortunate enough to be stopped en route, they could tell people that they were going to Acapulco to sell the items at one of the open-air markets.

Once the trunk had been loaded nearly full with Amy and the other cargo, María and her mother wished the young woman good luck and then walked around the side of the small four-door sedan and climbed inside. Señora Velazquez would be driving, since the fifteen-year-old Maria had yet to get her driver's license. Fernando remained standing behind the car until the engine was started and his mother signaled that they were ready to leave.

"Que Dios te bendiga," Amy heard Fernando say softly as he shut the lid of the trunk. They were the first words the young man had spoken to her, and Amy had to believe that he didn't know that she knew what he said. Despite his gruff exterior, despite the threats and seeming dislike of his houseguest, Fernando's first – and last – words to Amy were to wish her well. Oddly enough, Fernando's message comforted Amy as she felt the car start to move and her journey to Acapulco began. It was going to be a long ride; an hour and a half that was sure to feel like a lifetime.

THIRTY-NINE

Why are we stopped? Has it really already been an hour and a half? I thought they said we shouldn't have any traffic until we get close to Acapulco. Thoughts raced through Amy's mind as she lied in the trunk of the car. Although she had enough fresh air, it was still extremely stuffy inside the cornmeal sack and the heat was nearly unbearable. Not to mention the fact that there seemed to be more potholes in this one area than there were in all of New York City. Amy's bruised and battered body felt every bump in the road, and her extreme weight loss over the past several weeks meant that any cushioning or shock absorption capability was gone. And now, they were stopped. Or, more accurately at this moment, they were slowly creeping forward. Amy strained to listen to what was going on outside. She certainly couldn't hear the typical sounds associated with the hustle and bustle of a city. *Oh no*, Amy thought as she audibly gasped in fear. *A checkpoint.*

María and Señora Velazquez had warned her that this might happen. Members of competing drug cartels would establish roadblocks along highways in an effort to show their dominance of the area, scare people into submission, or often rob them of their possessions. Amy knew full well the reputation of these checkpoints, with the road blocked off and heavily-armed men searching the cars. Her cab driver on her first night in Mexico had told her and the other passengers in her car about them, thinking that the trap set by their kidnappers had only been a narco roadblock. More fear gripped Amy as she remembered the cab driver's words: "Don't worry. They only bother the locals. They leave the tourists alone." *They only bother the locals. Shit*, Amy thought as she heard loud voices and footsteps approaching the vehicle. *María and her mother are locals. Am I really going to make it this far just to die in the trunk of a car on the side of the road, less than an hour away from safety?*

All such thoughts ceased, however, and Amy instantly froze when she heard a man outside the car tell Señora Velazquez to unlock the trunk. Amy knew she couldn't move, couldn't breathe, couldn't even blink until they closed the trunk again. Her life, and the lives of the two women who had so kindly taken her in and nursed her back from the brink of death, depended on it.

The lid of the trunk squeaked as it opened to reveal several crates of fresh fruit and vegetables, a tattered brown blanket, and two large and lumpy cornmeal sacks – one containing Amy and the other a decoy containing the pig to be sold at the market.

As the men began what sounded like rummaging through the crates to pick out the best pieces of fruit and vegetables for themselves, Amy remained motionless and prayed like she had never prayed before that the highly armed, highly dangerous men inches away from her couldn't hear her heart pounding through her chest.

From the front of the vehicle, near the driver's door, came the declaration that María and Señora Velazquez were clean and good to go. No weapons had been found in the car, and the two ladies didn't match the descriptions of anyone on the cartel's hit list. Amy would've breathed a sigh of relief, but the trunk was still open and she knew she wasn't in the clear yet.

"Jamón y harina de maiz," one of the trunk inspectors said, laughing. "La vida en el campo es un asco," he declared, and Amy could hear many men laughing as their partner in crime at once both condemned and made fun of people who lived in the countryside. What happened next, though, took Amy completely by surprise.

First she heard a slashing noise near her feet, accompanied by more laughter and snide remarks about people from rural Mexico's small towns.

Then came the pain.

Sharp, intense, searing pain ripping into her left thigh with surgical precision. Amy thought her teeth might crack under the pressure of her gritting them together to keep from screaming. Immediately after the gash to her thigh came the one to her stomach, on her right side just below her ribs. Tears began flowing from her eyes as this latest round of pain was simply too much for the tortured young woman to bear. Amazingly, though, she still somehow managed not to scream.

"Vale, vale, vamos," came instructions from the front of the car. "Hay más coches." The men finally slammed the trunk shut again, still laughing as they walked past the driver-side door and told Señora Velazquez that they had left a surprise in the trunk, and good luck selling the meat at the market now.

The car then began to move again, but even after it was well clear of earshot of the roadblock, María and her mother still heard no noise coming from the trunk. "You okay?" When no reply came, the two women feared the worst. They had seen one man wiping blood off of his knife as he walked away from the trunk, and they knew that the young woman hiding in the cornmeal sack had likely been mistaken for another pig and stabbed. It was too dangerous, however, for them to stop and check on her. They simply had to keep going and hopefully get to the British Consulate before it was too late.

FORTY

Jamie Echols was bored, but that was nothing new. When he volunteered two years ago for an overseas posting with the Foreign and Commonwealth Office, he had imagined being sent somewhere exotic and having a modern-day, real-life James Bond type job. He certainly received the exotic part – Acapulco, Mexico – but to say that his job description was less than exciting was the understatement of the century. Jamie worked front-gate security at the British Consulate. Which meant, basically, that he sat under an umbrella all day in full uniform in the blazing hot sun while locals and a few tourists bustled by. He would've rather taken a job watching paint dry.

It was late morning and Jamie had so far counted sixteen motorcycles and nine police cars…a game he played every day to keep his mind at least somewhat occupied. *Only an hour more until my break for lunch*, he thought. As his mind started to drift to what kind of food he would eat for lunch that day, a speeding car caught his attention and broke his train of thought. Cars usually drove slower than that on the road that ran in front of the Consulate, since it was narrower than most and a bit away from the usual tourist routes. The car was also clearly very old and very dirty – signs that whoever was driving had come in from one of the more rural areas surrounding the resort city.

Jamie's thoughts, however, went from *finally something out of the ordinary* straight to *WTF!* when the speeding car came to a screeching halt directly in front of the Consulate's gates. Jamie grabbed the government-issue rifle lying on the ground beside him and ran over to the six-foot wrought-iron fence. The driver and passenger, both women, had jumped out seemingly before the car even made a complete stop and were now around the back of the vehicle, attempting to lift what looked like a sack of wheat or corn out of the trunk. An alarm went off in Jamie's head when he saw that the sack was soaked with what looked like blood, with bits of the dark red liquid dripping down onto the road and sidewalk.

The first thing Jamie had been taught in his job training was to never open the gate unless and until the person on the other side displayed proper identification and he had checked inside to make sure the person had an appointment. However, Jamie was seriously considering breaking that cardinal rule as the two women carefully but quickly placed the human body-shaped, blood-soaked sack on the ground next to the gate and ran back to their car. As the younger of the two women scrambled back inside the passenger side of the vehicle, she looked at Jamie but pointed to the sack and said in a heavy accent, "Help. British woman. Help." She then slammed the door shut and the car sped off, leaving as quickly as it had arrived.

Holy shit, thought Jamie. *They just left a body outside the gate!* He quickly radioed inside for help and began to unlock the various chains on the Consulate's gate. As other security officers ran outside and provided backup – in case this was all a setup of some sort – Jamie slung his rifle over his shoulder and pulled open the large gate. He then quickly went over to the sack and carefully cut a hole in it with his pocketknife. He knew this could all be a trap; that the women driving the car could have simply sped around the corner and were now waiting to detonate a bomb inside the bag, with the blood as a distraction. But something deep in his gut told Jamie that it wasn't a trap. And even if it was, he didn't like the kind of man he would have to be to let a person bleed to death whilst he waited on a bomb squad to arrive and investigate the 'suspicious package.'

What he saw when he opened the once brown, now red bag, though, was definitely not a trap.

"Someone phone for a doctor! Hurry!" Jamie yelled as he tore open the rest of the sack as quickly has his hands and knife would let him. The car's passenger had been telling the truth. Inside the bag was a woman, malnourished, badly beaten, and covered in blood. Another consular official, upon seeing the body, ran outside the gate and helped Jamie pick up the woman. Once inside the fence, yet another worker came over and the three men carefully transported the skeleton of a person inside the Consulate building.

FORTY-ONE

Alistair Bailey was a semi-retired desk officer at the British Consulate in Acapulco, but he had originally been trained as a trauma surgeon and served in Her Majesty's Armed Forces in that capacity. He had taken the Consulate position several years earlier after his wife died as a way to live near the beach but still stay somewhat busy. He wasn't the kind to just sit around in retirement…he needed something to do. Working at the Consulate suited him well, and the consular workers liked having 'Dr. Ali' there; mainly because he could dispense medical advice for head colds and other minor ailments and was certified to administer government-mandated vaccines.

Dr. Ali was busy reading through the latest tourist incident report – the usual summary of drunken teenagers on holiday – when he heard large amounts of yelling and commotion outside. As he rose from the chair behind his desk, a young receptionist burst into his office and said, breathlessly, "Dr. Ali, quickly! A woman is injured!"

The doctor-turned-diplomat followed the receptionist out onto the second floor landing of the Consulate and saw three security guards carrying a woman, bruised, bloodied, and beaten, into the building's entryway. From the landing, he couldn't tell if the person inside the limp body was even still alive. Dr. Ali hurriedly made his way down the sweeping, curved staircase and called below for the men to take the poor woman into the conference room located just to the left of the front door.

"Lie her down on the table – carefully!" he instructed. As Alistair crossed the marble floor of the foyer, he turned to the receptionist who had followed him down the stairs. "Get me my bag from my office, lots of clean towels, and a bucket of water. And call an ambulance."

Dr. Ali entered the conference room, with the Consul and the medicine bag-carrying receptionist following shortly behind him. Having reverted back to full trauma surgeon mode, Alistair quickly put on a pair of latex gloves and went to work. A wave of relief rushed over him when he found a pulse and saw that the woman was still breathing. *Probably not for long*, he thought. He then began instructing the security guards who had carried her inside to take clean towels and apply pressure to her wounds to stop the bleeding, which they had determined was coming from two large gashes – most likely stab wounds – in her left thigh and the right side of her abdomen.

Dr. Ali kept an eye on the woman as he stepped back, took off his gloves, and called the emergency room at Santa Lucía Hospital. He had made a point over the years to get to know several of the doctors and nurses at the hospital, mainly so they wouldn't cause a fuss when he took vaccination clients away from them. Luckily, an English-speaking nurse was on duty when Alistair called, and he proceeded to explain the situation.

"We have a woman here at the Consulate who is in very bad shape. I believe she's been stabbed," Alistair began. "She's lost a lot of blood and will need a transfusion. I don't know anything about her except she looks fairly young and someone said she's British."

Shortly after he finished his phone conversation, the ambulance arrived from the hospital, which was located just down the street. Dr. Ali went with the girl in the ambulance to the hospital, while Jamie and the other two men who had carried the woman inside and were now covered in blood stayed behind. The Consul and several other security guards followed the ambulance in a separate car. If this young woman was indeed a British citizen, as the person who dropped her off had claimed, the Consul was determined to give her twenty-four-hour security protection to make sure whoever had attacked her did not return.

****

Nearly ten hours after the car had dropped Amy off in front of the Consulate, she finally came out of surgery and was moved into a private recovery room. Waiting anxiously the whole time was Dr. Ali, who still had on the same blood-stained clothes from earlier that day. Seated beside him was a representative of the American Consulate since, while the claim was that she was British, the patient fit the profile of the one remaining missing member of the kidnapped sorority girl group. So far the two consulates and the hospital had been able to keep the media in the dark about the whole situation, but if – or rather, when – word got out that Amy Millhouse might be at Santa Lucía, the place would turn into a zoo. Discrete preparations had already begun to be made for the arrival of the Millhouse family, who had been contacted by the U.S. State Department and informed that they were needed in Acapulco for help identifying a patient who might be their daughter.

FORTY-TWO

Jack Millhouse's heart hadn't stopped racing since they got the call that Amy might be alive and in a hospital in Acapulco. He hadn't wanted his daughter to vacation in Mexico; he had told her not to go. A part of him, though, had swelled with pride when she stood in the family kitchen during Christmas break of her senior year of college and declared that she was an adult and was going on the trip with her friends whether her parents liked it or not. Amy had his spirit, his strong will, and he secretly loved when she put it on display. Now, though, he wished that she had a little less of that fire and a little more of her mother's calm, placid temperament. The stories being told by the girls who had already returned home – of the torture they had all endured, of Amy's stubborn defiance – were horrifying. He knew Amy was fully grown, an adult woman, but the image of those sick bastards even laying a finger on his little girl filled him with rage and made him nauseous all at the same time. And now, knowing that the stubborn, prideful streak that Amy had inherited from him might have gotten her killed was more than Jack could handle.

****

As the private chartered jet that the State Department had sent for the Millhouses descended from the Mexican sky and Acapulco's high rises and pristine beaches came into view, Linda Millhouse glanced over at her husband of twenty-eight years. His hands gripped the armrests of his seat so tightly that she could see his veins. The hair at the base of his neck and by his temples was wet with sweat. His usually blue eyes, the same color as Amy's, had once again changed color with his emotions and had been the same eerie, storm-cloud gray for the past three and a half weeks, ever since the police had first knocked on the Millhouse's front door. Linda was just as worried as her husband, but it wasn't in her nature to let it show in public like Jack was now. Still waters run deep, and Linda's good Southern mother taught her to be a good Southern mother as well . . . loving, caring, doting, but also strong and a steady presence for her husband and children to rely on. She would, however, undoubtedly break down and cry when they reached their hotel room that night, especially if it turned out that Amy wasn't the girl in the hospital. But right now, with a government official seated across the aisle, Linda was the epitome of a steel magnolia.

The State Department worker who had sat silently in his chair for the whole flight now leaned across the aisle to Mr. and Mrs. Millhouse, his forward posture betraying the intensity of his impending message.

"Things are going to move quickly once we land," he began, his voice deep and serious. "Remember, the goal is to not only find your daughter but also keep the press out of this as long as possible. The more people who know you're here, the bigger security concern it becomes. Particularly if the young woman in the hospital is not Miss Millhouse. If the kidnappers still have her, we don't want them knowing you're in-country and then having them do something desperate."

Husband and wife nodded their heads affirmatively and in unison. They didn't want to do anything that could possibly put their daughter in more danger. They continued listening intently as the man went on with his instructions.

"As you have been briefed, the girl we believe could be your daughter was dropped off at the British Consulate and then taken to the local hospital, where she has been in surgery ever since. The Brits are working closely with us on this and have sent a car from their consulate to the airport. As far as anyone at the airport knows, you two are simply some very important British citizens flying in. The car will take you to a back entrance of the hospital. Acapulco police believe the Jane Doe in the hospital is a British tourist, and you guys are her family." The gray-suited man paused briefly to let the information sink in with his captive audience, then continued: "we'll need to take you to her room immediately to attempt to identify her. And I need to warn you; from the reports I've gotten, she's been injured very badly. She has also apparently been in surgery for a long time. There is a chance that, even if it is your daughter, you won't be able to recognize her at first."

The Millhouses nodded again, although pain and worry were etched across both of their faces and set deep into their eyes. "Did you bring her birth certificate?" the man then asked.

Linda quickly shook her head yes and began fumbling through her purse to find the document.

"Good," came the agent's reply. "You don't have to get it out now. We just want to try to match the fingerprints on your daughter's birth certificate to our Jane Doe."

Again the parents nodded, seemingly incapable of speaking and instead bracing themselves for the onslaught of action and emotion that would follow the plane's landing. Jack knew that this would be the most emotionally draining day of his life. If the girl was Amy, as he hoped and prayed like he had never hoped and prayed before, then the upcoming hours and days would be full of joy and relief but also worry over her recovery. No one had told him or his wife what exactly this mystery girl's injuries were, but he did know that she was unconscious when she was dropped off at the Consulate and therefore unable to tell anyone who she was. If it wasn't Amy, though . . . he couldn't bear to think of the level of disappointment and continued fear that would grip him. And he had already decided, now that he was in Mexico, he wasn't leaving without his daughter.

****

As soon as the plane came to a stop on the tarmac, the Millhouse's government escort went to work. On his cell phone, he appeared to be checking in with the hospital while his VIPs gathered their belongings and made their way through the small cabin to the plane's door. The agent's surprised exclamation of "really?!" caught their attention, and there was a slight smile and shine in his eyes when he turned to Jack and Linda to announce that the young woman had survived surgery. All parties involved knew it was touch and go with the patient, and making it out of surgery alive was obviously great news for everyone.

As they exited the Gulfstream jet, the attractive American couple could have been more easily mistaken for L. L. Bean catalogue models than for the tortured souls that they were. Jack Millhouse wore his standard non-work outfit: a brightly-colored golf shirt (today's choice was green, for luck) that tucked neatly into his khaki chino pants, with a brown leather belt matching his boat shoes. Linda, for her part, had chosen a light-weight, flowing skirt that hit right at her knees and whose simple floral pattern went perfectly with her white blouse and stylish brown sandals. The shoes weren't particularly comfortable, but she had chosen to wear them because Amy always laughed and said they looked like 'Jerusalem cruisers' – her term for shoes Jesus would have worn.

From a distance, Jack and Linda looked immaculate. Up close, though, one could see that these were not your ordinary wealthy tourists jetting in for a holiday. Worry lines creased their faces, blood-shot eyes betrayed their many sleepless nights, and fidgeting hands and feet demonstrated that this airport tarmac was the last place in the world that they wanted to be at the moment.

FORTY-THREE

"So it was you?" The therapist's question jolted Amy out of the zombie-like trance she had settled into every day for the past several weeks while recounting what had happened to her in Mexico. "It was you?" Susan Vilsek repeated. "The girl in the hospital?"

"Yes," Amy said as she nodded. "It was me. My parents could tell it was me as soon as they entered the room and saw me. They said I was so bruised and beat up, though, that my mom fainted and my dad threw up. But I have seen a few pictures, and you can't blame them for that. The older bruises, the ones from the kidnappers, had started to heal and were that ugly puke green and yellow color, and they were mixed with the fresh blue and purple bruises from the trip in to Acapulco. From being in the back of the car in the trunk on those unpaved roads and then from being dropped on the sidewalk in front of the Consulate."

"And from the attack at the checkpoint," Dr. Vilsek offered gently.

"Yes, from that too," Amy replied softly but curtly.

The therapist marveled at the young woman sitting across from her in what had become their everyday positions: Dr. Vilsek in her high-backed leather chair and Amy on the window seat, facing sideways so as to be perpendicular to her therapist. Lying on the seat beside Amy was her family's pet dog, Gus. A big, cuddly Labrador Retriever whose fur was such a dark brown that it sometimes looked black, Gus had become a fairly frequent visitor to Dr. Vilsek's office ever since the therapist suggested bringing the dog along one day. Susan Vilsek was well-aware of the medical research surrounding the healing and comforting powers of animals, especially for trauma victims, and she could easily see how much more relaxed Amy was on days when Gus tagged along.

The young woman hadn't been seeing her therapist for all that long compared to other patients and yet she had made incredible progress, partly thanks to Gus but mostly due to Amy's willingness to talk through everything about her traumatizing experience. Dr. Vilsek now knew what had happened in Mexico. Every gory, painful, nausea-inducing detail had been laid out before her by the young woman unfortunate enough to have experienced it all firsthand. And Amy had been correct when she warned Dr. Vilsek that, once she heard the story, she would never be able to forget it. Susan had treated hundreds of patients during her career, many of whom had gone through unspeakable tragedy. But Amy's experience wasn't just unspeakable. It was unthinkable and worse, unforgettable. And yet there she was, once again dressed to her preppy best and looking like she was ready to take on the world.

"So what happened after your parents identified you?" Dr. Vilsek asked. She knew most of the details of Amy's return to the United States, having read about it in newspapers and magazines both at the time it happened and then again when Amy became her patient. Nonetheless, she knew it was important for Amy to tell the whole story.

"Well, as you can imagine, I was pretty banged up. I had been in surgery for almost half a day, and my heart stopped twice on the operating table. When the surgeons finally finished repairing the damage from the stab wounds, they put me in a medically-induced coma to allow my body to heal some on its own. They kept me in the coma for seventy-two hours and then woke me up. I had to stay in the hospital in Acapulco for another twenty-four hours before they finally let us leave."

"Did you go to Los Angeles like the other girls?"

"No, I flew on an ambulance-like plane from Acapulco to a military hospital in San Antonio. The government figured that keeping me on a military base was the best way to keep all the over-zealous press away, since they could restrict access more easily. The State Department had kind of taken possession of me in Mexico and I guess they felt some sort of duty to still protect me even once I was back in the United States."

"How long were you in San Antonio?" the therapist asked.

"Five days. That's how long it took for the doctors to feel comfortable enough with me flying home. I was pretty jacked up, if you hadn't already figured that out," Amy commented, with a slightly defensive smile. Susan Vilsek had gotten used to that smile. Her patient would flash her pearly whites in order to mask the traces of pain that would otherwise be visible on her face. It was a nice tool to have, but was also an easy tell for anybody who took the time to figure it out.

"I want to go back for a second, Amy. To something you said a minute ago," Dr. Vilsek began, treading carefully because she could sense that Amy was in a particularly vulnerable spot today.

"Okay," replied Amy, who by now was used to her therapist changing topics quickly in their conversations.

"You said your heart stopped beating twice while you were on the operating table. I know some people who that has happened to remember parts of the experience. Do you?"

Susan Vilsek's patient slowly turned her gaze from the window to the hands in her lap and just sat there, staring downward, for what seemed like an eternity. When she finally looked up at Dr. Vilsek, there were tears in her eyes. "No one has ever asked me about that before," Amy began slowly, petting Gus on the head as she spoke. "But I do. It was like I was in a dream, but everything seemed so real. I really did see a bright light, just like people talk about. And I was slowly moving towards that light, like I was on a moving sidewalk or something."

"Did that happen both times? Did you see the light twice?" Dr. Vilsek asked, fascinated by Amy's revelations.

"Yes, but it was different the second time. The first time was the moving sidewalk – like I was a robot on a conveyor belt and I couldn't move or look around or anything. I was just slowly but steadily going towards the bright light."

"And the second time?"

"The light was there again. Almost like it was at the end of a tunnel. But I could move around this time." Amy paused her story as the tears that had been streaming down her face increased in their intensity and she began to sob.

Dr. Vilsek handed her a tissue from the box on her desk, then gently prodded, "what else happened that second time, Amy?"

The patient took a minute or two to compose herself, blowing her nose and next drying her eyes with a fresh tissue. She then continued, "I was being pulled in two directions. One way was towards the light . . . it seemed so easy to just keep going that way. The other direction was definitely going against the grain; it was hard to even look back that way." Amy's tears began once again, and Dr. Vilsek gave her another tissue before urging her to continue the story. "B-behind me," Amy said, struggling to make out the words between her sobbing, "w-was my f-family. My mom and dad, and my brother J-joshie. They were all there, at the other end of the tunnel, smiling and w-waving and asking me to come home."

"And that's the way you chose to go?" Dr. Vilsek asked, assuming that Amy had chosen the direction of her family.

"That's just it," Amy replied, the pain and anguish on her face almost too much for Dr. Vilsek to bear. "I didn't choose them. I was standing there, in the middle of the road or path or whatever it was, and I would look to the right and see the beautiful bright light and then look to the left and see my family. But I couldn't make up my mind. After all I had been through, how could I have not chosen to go home?"

Dr. Vilsek watched as her patient then completely broke down, sobbing and crying uncontrollably in the big window seat across from where the therapist was sitting. The big brown dog beside her crept closer to his owner, putting his head in her lap as a gesture of love and support. *Poor girl*, Susan thought. *She sincerely blames herself for that. Blames herself for a hallucination she had while she was lying on an operating table, medically dead.* "Shhh, Amy, it's okay. You weren't making an actual choice. The doctors were the ones who revived you. What you saw was all in your head. It was just a dream."

Amy stopped crying then and looked up at Dr. Vilsek, her cheeks red and swollen and her eyes still filled with water. Her words, though, cut Dr. Vilsek to her very core. "Was it?"

FORTY-FOUR

Dr. Vilsek had ended her last therapy session with Amy with the question of the girl's visions of a bright light still unanswered, and the good doctor wasn't exactly thrilled about broaching the subject again when Amy arrived in her office this afternoon. Life after death and reports of "bright lights" by people who died and were then brought back to life by doctors were highly controversial topics, and it was a general subject matter that Susan tried to avoid. She personally believed it was nothing more than a hallucination – just like she had told Amy yesterday. But many people disagreed with her, including the therapist's own father, who talked about seeing "a light at the end of a tunnel" when he nearly died in surgery following a car crash decades earlier. Knowing how important Amy's religious beliefs were to her, Dr. Vilsek did not want to challenge her on this specific issue. She didn't think it was particularly relevant to Amy's healing process, so she just added it to the list of things on which she and her patient would have to agree to disagree.

There was one part of the story, though, that Dr. Vilsek couldn't get out of her mind. A loose end that she wanted Amy to tie up for her. And it was with that loose end that the two women began their therapy session that afternoon.

"Amy, I know yesterday was a hard day for you. We talked about some pretty deep emotions and some things that you hadn't told anybody about before." Amy nodded her head in agreement, and Dr. Vilsek continued: "I just have one question for you about what you told me yesterday, and then we can move on, if you're ready."

"Okay," Amy said. "Shoot."

"You've told me about how you were left for dead on the side of the road by your kidnappers. Then the two women nursed you back to health, somewhat, in their house, only to have you be stabbed twice while hiding in the back of their car."

"Yes…" Amy replied, not sure where her therapist was going with this.

"An eleven hour surgery, a medically induced coma…how in the world did a baby survive all of that?"

Oh. That's the question, Amy thought, caught off-guard by Dr. Vilsek's sudden reference to her baby. It had been over a month since her therapist had mentioned the infant that Amy gave up for adoption. "You mean how did a baby survive this?" Amy asked, lifting up her light blue, women's cut golf shirt to reveal an ugly three-inch scar on the right side of her upper torso, near her rib cage. "Or the blood loss from this?" she added, pulling her shirt back down before shimmying her khaki shorts farther up her left thigh to show her therapist the nearly identical scar on that leg. They were nasty, scraggly marks that gave Susan Vilsek a sudden insight into why the young woman never wore shorts that went above mid-thigh and reacted curiously the one time Dr. Vilsek casually asked if Amy had gotten her bathing suit shopping done for that year.

As if sensing what Dr. Vilsek was thinking, Amy undid the two buttons at the top of her shirt and slid the fabric apart. "I guess you haven't seen this one either, have you?" she then asked, referencing the large scar running diagonal from Amy's collarbone down across her chest. Susan couldn't help but gasp, since this mark made the ones on her patient's stomach and thigh look like paper cuts. "The other two actually did more damage; those are the stab wounds from the trunk. This one just looks the worst. It must have been the handiwork of the kidnappers, because I don't remember it happening but I had it on me when I got to the Velazquez's house." Amy spoke with a surprising level of ease about the three disfiguring scars that served as daily reminders of her kidnappers' brutality and her harrowing journey from María's home to the British Consulate in Acapulco.

Returning her shirt and shorts to their original positions, Amy finally addressed Dr. Vilsek's original question. "To be honest, I don't know how the baby survived. The doctors don't either. I lost a lot of blood; nearly died twice…it was an incredible amount of stress to put on a fully grown body, let alone an itty-bitty, newly-formed embryo. But she made it. Maybe that was another reason why I never even considered having an abortion. If the tiny little human growing inside of me had survived so much already, she was clearly meant to be born. God had a plan for her, for sure. He had to, for her to make it through all of that."

Dr. Vilsek nodded her head in understanding, still amazed by the medical miracle that enabled Amy to not miscarry. Many, many women had lost their pregnancies after experiencing much less trauma than Amy did. Susan also couldn't help but notice Amy's constant use of "she" when talking about the baby she gave up for adoption. Even though Amy had never even held the child and had no idea where she was or how she was doing, the little girl was still very much a part of Amy's psyche and life.

For the second time that day, Amy could tell by the look in her therapist's eyes what she was thinking. "Yes, to answer your question. I still think about her every day. I suppose I always will. I try not to; I try to ignore it and think about other things. Maybe in the future, if I'm lucky enough to have more children, then I'll think about her less. But I doubt it."

Dr. Vilsek's thoughts quickly shifted to her own two children, and she understood exactly what Amy meant. "I know you will. It's a mom thing. We can't help it," she said, smiling reassuringly at the young woman seated across from her. "And on that note, how about we change subjects?"

Amy nodded her head in approval at the idea. She was ready to move onto something else, and she hoped the new topic would be a little less on the depressing side. "What did you have in mind?"

FORTY-FIVE

"Well, I've been wondering about something," Dr. Vilsek said as she opened the new topic of conversation. "What happened to the men that kidnapped you? I don't remember seeing much about that in the newspapers."

Amy breathed a mental sigh of relief after hearing Dr. Vilsek's question. This was definitely an easier subject to tackle than the last one had been. "Yeah, the media kind of lost interest in the story once I got home. There was a lot more coverage of the arrest and trial by the Mexican media and other Spanish-language outlets, but I guess the American newspapers and TV shows figured that the dramatic part was over. And it was, for the most part. Especially once they found the kidnappers, the trial against them was pretty straightforward."

"How did they find the kidnappers?" Dr. Vilsek asked, unaware of the conclusion to her patient's harrowing ordeal.

"A tipster," Amy replied. "A couple of weeks after I went home, the police in Acapulco got an anonymous letter about who the 'Sorority Seventeen' kidnappers were and where they were hiding out. We still don't know who sent in that information, but whoever it was obviously had serious ties to the group because he knew the names of all the members of the kidnapping gang and exactly where they were. It just goes to show how cocky they all were. They were still hanging around the same area and openly associating with each other. Ricky told me that they would never get caught, and they all obviously believed that."

"So an insider gave them away? That must have been a really risky move on the part of whoever turned them in," Dr. Vilsek commented.

"Yeah, it was. Very dangerous. The prosecutors and police speculated that it might have been a former associate of theirs, or a former accomplice or something like that. Someone who had worked with them on previous kidnappings but thought that this one crossed the line. Which is very possible. My theory has always been that it was someone in a bank. With the enormous cash ransom payment the group received, they had to have an insider at a bank somewhere helping to launder the money. Or even just helping to convert it all into Mexican pesos instead of $100 U.S. bills. But, like I said, that's just my theory."

"Interesting," Dr. Vilsek replied, still curious. "So what happened next? After the police got the tip?"

"They found them. Arrested them. Apparently it was a huge operation, with Federal Police and army personnel and helicopters flying overhead. Again, with all of the publicity surrounding our kidnapping, the government was really eager to solve this case. Nineteen men in the kidnapping gang were arrested in one sweep. Two of them were shot in a brief firefight at the beginning, but from what I heard and read about it, they realized pretty quickly that they were surrounded and should surrender. Luckily none of the police officers or soldiers was injured."

"Surrender doesn't seem like a word that would be in the vocabulary of men like them."

"You're right, it normally probably wouldn't be. But I guess they figured that they could escape from whatever prison they were put in so it wouldn't be that big of a deal. I don't think they realized what kind of punishment was waiting for them."

"And the two who were shot – did they survive?"

"Oh yeah. Surface wounds," Amy responded. "They were fine." Amy paused her storytelling for a moment to look out the bay window beside her. By this point, having talked with the young woman five days a week, every week, for almost three months, Dr. Vilsek had a pretty good idea of what Amy was thinking about. 'They were fine,' Amy said. The kidnappers who wreaked havoc on the lives of Amy and her friends were physically no worse for the wear. *That must be so frustrating*, Dr. Vilsek thought. *After all of the pain and suffering that she went through…to know that the men responsible escaped with only 'surface wounds.'*

"Was that all of them? Were they put in jail?" Dr. Vilsek asked, her questions running together as she tried to get her patient to continue the story. "You mentioned something about a trial?"

"We don't know if it was all of them. We never saw all of the men at the same time . . . they were always switching who was guarding us and stuff like that. But I know they got the leaders of the group and at least most of the men. The prosecutor in charge told me it was the biggest yet easiest case she ever tried. A slam dunk, in her words. The police in Acapulco and the surrounding parts of Guerrero worked tirelessly with the federal police to build an airtight case against the kidnapping gang, and their efforts paid off. The FBI even sent agents down to help in the investigation, since our forensic science is pretty much the best. The reports I read were like something straight out of the TV show *CSI*. The shells from the taxi driver executions were matched to the guns found in the house where we were held. Once they had possession of the kidnappers' SUVs, they could match the tire tread marks from the kidnapping location to those vehicles. Passengers on our initial flight identified Ricky. All seventeen of us gave sworn statements about what happened. And, luckily, the evidence against the men was so extensive that none of us had to actually go to Mexico and testify."

"It really was a slam dunk," Dr. Vilsek commented, amazed by the level of skill and efficiency shown by the authorities in charge of the investigation and trial. "What was the sentence? I assume they were convicted."

"Oh yeah, all of them. They tied everything together on Mexico's version of conspiracy grounds, so the whole group was found guilty of the four taxi driver murders, kidnapping, forced imprisonment, sexual assault, extortion . . . you name it, they were guilty of it."

"Wow."

"Wow, is right," Amy agreed. "They all received life sentences and a spot in Mexico's supermax prison."

"Were you pleased with the outcome of the trial?" Dr. Vilsek asked, curious to know Amy's reaction to that crucial chapter in the story of her kidnapping.

"As pleased as I could be. Mexico doesn't have the death penalty, so they got the harshest punishment possible." Amy paused, fidgeting with the thin silver bracelet on her wrist. "I heard, though, that a lot of people in Mexico want the government to reinstate the death penalty. Especially for kidnappers who kill their victims," Amy paused again, this time to shift her gaze from her bracelet to the bay window. "Maybe they will. It wouldn't do anything to change my case, but I don't think a little more deterrence would hurt anybody."

Dr. Vilsek took Amy's comments on the death penalty in stride – after nearly three months of therapy, she was used to the young woman making statements that might be deemed politically controversial. But as Susan told Amy at the very beginning of their therapy sessions, this office was the girl's safe space. A bubble, if you will, where Amy was the top priority and no thoughts or statements needed to be censored for political correctness. That was Dr. Vilsek's policy with all of her patients, and even though she disagreed with many of Amy's political preferences, this was neither the time nor the place to discuss that.

The therapist was about to bring up a suggestion that she knew Amy would be resistant to when the soft knock of her assistant Christine's hand alerted them that the next patient had arrived. "Okay, I guess that will have to be all for today," Dr. Vilsek stated. "I'll see you again on Monday," she added as both she and Amy rose from their chairs and walked towards the office door.

"See you Monday," Amy replied.

FORTY-SIX

Monday morning dawned bleak and gray, and by the time Amy Millhouse arrived at Dr. Vilsek's office for her 3pm appointment, it was pouring down rain. Amy shook out her umbrella as best she could under the short overhang outside the front door before going inside. She then placed the umbrella in a plastic bin and took off her stylish red raincoat, placing it on a hook by the door.

"She's ready for you," Christine called from her reception desk further inside the renovated house. "You can go on in."

"Thanks, Christine," Amy replied. She had gotten to know Dr. Vilsek's assistant fairly well over the past few months and liked the older woman very much. She always seemed to be in a good mood but also managed to not be annoying about it, which Amy figured had to be difficult given the kind of environment in which she worked.

Amy crossed through the now-familiar foyer and knocked once on Dr. Vilsek's office door. She then entered the room and immediately took a seat in what had become 'her' chair. Dr. Vilsek smiled as the young woman entered the office, put down the papers she was reading, and walked around her large, cherry wood desk to sit in her customary spot. Amy could tell by the look on her therapist's face that she already had a topic picked out for today's session. Wasting no time, Dr. Vilsek jumped right in, skipping over even her usual small-talk questions about Amy's weekend and the weather.

"So, I know we have talked some about this, but today and probably for the rest of this week I'd really like to return to the end of your time in the basement. Walk me through it. I want to understand why exactly you wouldn't do what they asked, when freedom – and your life – was being offered in exchange."

Not wasting any time today, are we? Amy thought to herself. She had known this line of questioning was coming; she just hadn't known exactly when it would hit. *Today, I guess*, Amy mused. She didn't expect her therapist to understand her reasoning surrounding what she did, or rather, didn't do in the basement where she was held. No one could, really, unless they had been in the same situation. It wasn't really an academic, pro- and con-weighing exercise that had brought Amy to the conclusion that she wouldn't do what the kidnappers wanted and make what they referred to as the 'extra ransom payment.' It was more of a gut reaction; an instinctive decision. But Amy knew that Dr. Vilsek would want more of an explanation than that, and she felt she owed it to the woman to try and spell out her reasoning.

"Well," Amy began, "like I've said before, I knew right away what my answer would be. But I guess, when looking back, I know it sounds silly or stupid or whatever, but I kind of thought of it like I would be negotiating with terrorists. Actually, it was exactly like negotiating with terrorists. Not the current kind, who just want death and destruction. The old kind, who would hijack planes and hold people hostage in order to get their buddies out of jail. I felt like, if I did that, then where would it stop? Ricky promised that it would be a one-time thing, but what reason did I have to believe him? And it turns out I was right, since they assaulted the other girls again before they finally let them go." Amy looked over at Dr. Vilsek to make sure her therapist didn't appear to have any questions, then continued: "I know, logically, that there was no real difference between Mr. Van Oren paying the money and the girls consenting to the sex. They're both ransom payments – just in different currencies. I mean, I get that *up here*," Amy said, gesturing towards her head. "In my mind, I know that now. But at the time it was different."

"How so?" Susan asked.

"I've actually thought a lot about why it was different, and I still don't really know. It's kind of hypocritical of me to expect my family to pay but refuse to pay myself. I mean, the way I thought of it, if my family wanted to pay money to get me released, okay. In fact, yes, please do! But I wasn't going to give those macho pigs the satisfaction of, well, satisfaction. Plus, that's just not the way things are done. Ransom payments are cash. Unmarked bills in duffel bags shoved in lockers at bus stations. The kidnappers were breaking the code of thieves; the custom of expectations."

"Was all of that really running through your head while you and the other girls were discussing it? When Ricky and the other men left you in the room to talk about what they were asking you to do?" questioned Dr. Vilsek.

"No," Amy replied. "The 'negotiating with terrorists' thing was, but it didn't even cross my mind that it was basically just another form of ransom payment. I was raised to believe that the body is precious and sacred, and the kidnappers were asking me to pay a price that I wouldn't accept. I couldn't accept."

Dr. Vilsek continued to press the issue, partly to help Amy reach a full realization of the root causes for her actions and partly because she was genuinely intrigued by what made this young woman tick.

"I read in the newspaper that all of you girls were told that if you, umm, did what they asked, that you would be set free; but if you didn't then they would kill you. So you're saying that the price was too steep not only for your freedom but also for your life?"

Amy turned her head away from the bay window and looked directly at Dr. Vilsek, almost challenging the older woman with the fierceness of her gaze. "That question assumes I'm afraid to die."

"Explain that to me," Dr. Vilsek pressed.

Amy took a deep breath, then continued: "Being kidnapped was horrible. It's a terrible, horrible, no good very bad thing that I wouldn't wish on my worst enemy. But it was my duty to stand up for what I believe in. It's easy to say 'this is what I believe' in the comfort of your living room or Bible study or whatever. But when there's a gun to your head? When your life is on the line, do you believe it enough to die for it? Like that student at Columbine who was asked if she believed in God right before she was shot." Amy sighed heavily. "Look, I don't expect you to understand it. Nobody does. Well, my parents might, but they don't like to think about what actually happened to me there. The 'do this or you'll die' argument doesn't work on me because I'm not afraid to die. I've been right with God since I was a little girl and I know where I'm going when my time on Earth is over. So I'm not afraid of getting there a little earlier than people might have wanted or expected."

After all they had been through together in their therapy sessions – all of the tears and the fears and the uncertainty – Dr. Vilsek couldn't help but smile a little bit at the strength of conviction with which her patient spoke about her faith. It wasn't a faith or religion that Susan shared with Amy, but she admired the young woman for it nonetheless.

Maybe that was the biggest difference between this Amy and the one who had walked into Dr. Vilsek's office three months ago.

Back then, Amy looked like she wanted nothing more than to crawl into a hole and hide . . . disappear from the world. But now? Now the young Miss Millhouse looked strong – defiant, almost – and capable of handling anything that came her way. That was good, the therapist concluded. And that also meant that Amy might finally be ready to do the one thing that the public still wanted and expected from her: an interview.

FORTY-SEVEN

Dr. Vilsek knew that bringing up the idea of an interview would be difficult. Amy had repeatedly mentioned that her parents didn't like the idea, mainly because they were worried that it would be too painful for their daughter. But the therapist believed, and got the impression that her patient did as well, that a wide-ranging interview could provide a measure of closure for Amy. While her emotional, mental, and even physical healing would continue for years to come, a public expression of her reflections on the dramatic series of events could provide a sense of empowerment and calming strength.

Bearing all of that in mind, Dr. Vilsek adopted a reserved, quiet tone before beginning to broach the sensitive subject.

"Amy, I've been thinking a lot about your progress. I first want to say that you've made incredible advances since beginning therapy with me."

At the girl's half smile and brief nod of acknowledgment, Susan Vilsek continued: "I think it's time for you to start considering an interview. I know you've received inquiries from multiple networks."

"Yes, from every network actually," Amy replied. "I even got a call from producers at ESPN wanting to do a '30 for 30' about me," she continued with a smile.

"ESPN?" Dr. Vilsek questioned. "The sports channel ESPN?"

"Yeah," Amy said, laughing as she spoke. "They said I'm the most famous former cheerleader in America."

"Well, I suppose that might be true," her therapist mused, her mind drifting back to a picture of Amy that had been aired frequently on TV while the young woman was missing. A senior in high school when the photo was taken, Amy looked as American as apple pie, smiling in her bright red cheerleading uniform with the sun shining down on her blonde hair and summer-tanned skin. That, along with her official college graduation photo, were widely reported to be her parents' favorite pictures of their daughter and the two they had chosen to release to the press.

Coming back to the present, Dr. Vilsek pressed the interview topic. "Well, what do you think?"

"About an interview?" Amy questioned. "Honestly, I don't know. I guess it could be a good thing, you know? To kind of signal to the country that I'm okay and bring the intense part of my healing to a close." After a brief pause, Amy added with a grin, "not that I'm trying to get rid of you or anything."

That gentle teasing and the wit and confidence that inspired it told the good doctor everything she needed to know about her patient's recovery. The Amy Millhouse who first came to her office didn't joke like that. She didn't tease people, and she definitely didn't tease with an impish grin that revealed the personality behind the girl who had been the most popular person in school her whole life. This Amy was closer to the old Amy – maybe as close as she would ever get, given how much the young woman had been through.

After receiving a mock scolding look and a wink from her trusted therapist, Amy came to an abrupt conclusion about the interview idea.

"I'll do it," she declared. "But on my terms. I decide when; I decide where. I decide what questions they get to ask," Amy continued, laying out her demands as if she were positioned across the negotiating table from network executives rather than sitting cross-legged in a large, plush chair inside a posh townhome-turned-office building.

"That all sounds good to me," Dr. Vilsek said in agreement. "I also think you're ready to cut back on the therapy sessions."

That last statement startled the young blonde patient. Coming to Susan Vilsek's office every weekday afternoon at 3pm had become an integral part of her routine; indeed, it was often the only thing she had scheduled to do in any given day (or sometimes week). Now that she had emerged from the trance-like state that consumed her for so long, Amy couldn't imagine what her life would be like without daily meetings with the woman who had chipped away at the zombie exterior and eventually helped slay Amy's kidnapping dragons.

Sensing Amy's panic, Dr. Vilsek quickly interjected: "Don't worry. I was only talking about reducing the number of days. Not stopping our sessions altogether." Her patient breathed a visible sigh of relief as Dr. Vilsek continued: "You're ready. You've come so far. The Amy Millhouse sitting in front of me right now is not the same Amy Millhouse who first came here almost three months ago.

You're stronger. More confident. But again, I'm not saying to go cold turkey. You're better, but you're not better."

Amy smiled at that last comment, as it reminded her of the Yogi Berra quotes that her dad loved to recite. *It's déjà vu all over again. When you come to a fork in the road, take it.* "Okay," she said with conviction, placing her hands firmly down on either side of her and sitting up straight for added effect. "That settles it, then. I'm doing an interview, and we'll cut back on my sessions."

"Agreed," Dr. Vilsek replied. "You're ready for both."

FORTY-EIGHT

Amy never imagined how detailed the contract for her TV interview would be. Or how much control over the process she would have. The Millhouse family had discretely put out inquiries to the major broadcast networks to see if any of them would be interested in an interview on Amy's terms, and the one Amy eventually chose was so thrilled to land the primetime exclusive that they had given Amy basically everything she wanted. One of the partners at her dad's firm negotiated on Amy's behalf, and he and the network's lawyers literally talked about every detail in the world. When would it be? Where would it be? How long? How many questions? Would they be chosen in advance, impromptu, or a mixture of the two? Formal or informal dress? Would they be seated or walking somewhere? Amy insisted on at least part of it being seated. She had always hated that clichéd interview walk down some grassy field or dirt road. Amy had spent the better part of the last year in a trauma-induced fog, but she was better now and wanted to be taken seriously – not viewed as a pitiful crime victim. She was a strong, serious survivor and it would be a strong, serious interview. If for no other reason than to prove to any of her kidnappers who might be watching that they no longer had any hold over her. And to prove that to herself as well. Amy had also wanted a female reporter, and even though the network's star had pitched a fit that he got passed over, they agreed.

Her final request was the toughest thing to sell, not to the network – they loved the idea – but to her family and the U.S. and Mexican state departments. Amy wanted to go back to Mexico. To retrace the path she took while kidnapped and after being released. When Amy first suggested the idea to Dr. Vilsek, her therapist had balked for many of the same reasons that Mr. and Mrs. Millhouse and the two governments had. It would be a big risk to allow Amy back in the country . . . if, God forbid, something happened to Amy again, the public relations nightmare would never end. But Dr. Vilsek soon saw the same value in the trip that Amy saw. It would be the ultimate closure. A re-affirmation that she had come to terms with what happened to her. Dr. Vilsek even helped convince Amy's parents that this would be good for their daughter and for them as well, since it would help them better understand their daughter's experience and the pain it caused.

Amy couldn't really blame the network for promoting the event as much as it had, although she did wish they had waited until the air date was a little closer to start running their "The Amy Millhouse Exclusive: Terror in Mexico" ads. A month of that, in increasing frequency, only served to put Amy, her family, and her sorority sisters back in the limelight. The other girls had done a group interview about six months ago, but at that point Amy was noticeably pregnant and still in no mental condition to even consider speaking to the media. She had talked with each of the other kidnapping victims before agreeing to do her own interview…making sure they were okay with it. Some of the girls were hesitant, but in the end they all understood that Amy deserved a chance to tell her story just as they had.

Those conversations were actually the only time she had spoken to the other girls since Mexico. Dr. Vilsek said that tragedy either brings people together or tears them apart, and Amy simply couldn't imagine ever talking with the girls without being constantly reminded of what happened to them during those terrifying days in Mexico. She assumed that her sorority sisters felt the same way, since they hadn't made any attempts to reach out either. In fact, after watching the group interview several times and talking to the girls on the phone, Amy got the idea that some of them still blamed her for what happened. Katie, the girl with asthma, was quick to point out in the group interview that it had been Amy who cast the deciding vote on whether the group went to Acapulco or Cancún. And just as she had when they were still locked up in the basement's holding room, Allison made sure everyone knew that Amy told the kidnappers "name your price" regarding the ransom amount. Allison was probably the most bitter about the whole event, and definitely the least forgiving. But Dr. Vilsek had worked hard with Amy to help her realize that each victim responds to trauma differently, and Amy was not the one at fault in the situation. Neither was Laura Ann, although Amy could tell that the girls also blamed her for what happened since she was so chatty with Ricky during the flight. Amy just simply had to accept that the people she went through that harrowing experience with weren't going to be around anymore. It was a tough realization to come to, that she had lost almost all of her best friends and that some people out there would always blame her for the kidnapping, but it was a necessary realization nonetheless. Necessary for her recovery.

****

And so here we are, Amy thought as she arrived at the airport in her hometown for the trip to Mexico. She suddenly felt very uncomfortable and began to regret this whole idea, since it was impossible to avoid the stares of fellow air travelers as they tried to figure out who the family was with a camera crew following them everywhere. Her parents and brother were also making the journey, something that was at once both comforting and embarrassing to Amy. It was one thing for her family to hear stories of what had happened. But to actually retrace the steps was entirely different. Amy wasn't looking forward to taking her father and brother to the room where she was gang-raped. Just the thought of it was . . . awkward. *Oh well*, Amy thought. *It's not like they don't know what happened.*

The reporter chosen for the interview, Lynn Patterson, sat down beside Amy in the gate terminal area as the cameras continued to roll. Lynn was just shy of sixty years old, but, thanks to the magic help of cosmetic surgery and hair dye, didn't have to admit her true age to anyone. She was dressed today in a pair of stylish yet comfortable beige slacks and a green silk shirt, with a navy blue pashmina scarf tying the outfit together. Her dark brown hair contrasted beautifully with her hazel eyes, and Amy could tell that Ms. Patterson was the kind of woman who would have had no shortage of eligible suitors over the years.

"So, this is actually the exact same gate that you flew out of last time," the veteran, award-winning reporter began.

"Yes," Amy answered with a nod, still trying to get comfortable with the production crew all around her.

"Is it bringing back memories?" Lynn continued in a very calm, easy-going manner that Amy appreciated.

"Yes ma'am, definitely."

The reporter smiled at Amy's use of "ma'am" and issued a gentle reminder: "You don't have to call me ma'am. Just think of me as a really curious friend."

Amy joined Lynn in smiling as she replied, "Sorry, force of habit. I'll work on it."

The young woman paused and looked around, eventually returning to Ms. Patterson's original question. "It is bringing back memories. The airline said this flight, from here to Acapulco, almost always leaves from this gate. But yes ma' – but yeah, we were all so happy. So excited about the trip and so, so naïve. I know we must have been annoying the crap out of everybody in the gate area because we were giggling and laughing and talking way too loudly about being tan, getting drunk, and finding hot guys." Amy paused, a shadow passing over her face. "We sure did make it easy on Ricky to find his prey."

Just as the reporter was about to ask who Ricky was, their flight began boarding. An eerie sensation washed over Amy as she handed the smiling gate attendant her ticket and then began walking down the gangway to the plane. It was a strange kind of déjà vu – one that Amy knew she might as well get used to for the next four days. *That's the whole point, right?* Amy pondered to herself. *This whole thing is a forced déjà vu.*

****

Once seated on the plane – the network had bought out the entire first class cabin to make filming easier – the reporter's questions began again. Amy couldn't help but notice that her parents and brother were seated as closely as possible to her. They wanted to hear the whole story too.

"You mentioned before boarding that you and your group of friends made it easy for Ricky to find his prey," Lynn stated, picking up where she left off. "Who is Ricky?"

Amy exhaled deeply before answering. *This is it. No turning back*, she thought. She had agreed to tell her whole story to the public, and the story undeniably began with Ricky.

"Ricky, if that was even his real name, was the scout for the kidnappers. He was straight from central casting. Tall, dark, handsome, well-dressed, and well-spoken. He spoke fluent English with only a slight hint of an accent – enough to make him sound sexy but not enough to make it difficult to understand him," Amy added with a slight, yet jaded, smile. "His job was to fly from the U.S. to Mexico and pick out kidnapping targets on the plane. He got paid a flat rate per person, so when he saw our group he got dollar signs in his eyes."

"That's what you assume?" Lynn asked.

"No. He told me," Amy replied. "He was quite proud of himself for managing to trap as big of a group as we were, and one day he bragged about it to us. $1,000 per girl. A finder's fee, if you will."

"Wow," was the only response Lynn could come up with. She was a seasoned reporter and had extensive experience with exclusive interviews, but she could already tell that this story was going to go beyond anything she had been expecting.

"So tell me about the flight," Lynn continued. "Was it like the airport, happy and excited?"

"Somewhat," Amy replied. "A couple of the girls, one in particular, talked to Ricky during most of the flight. Well, gushed over him would be more appropriate. He really was very handsome. Other girls watched movies or read magazines. I listened to music at first, read a little bit from a book that my aunt had given me at graduation, and then took a nap for the rest of the flight. It was pretty uneventful, to tell the truth. The calm before the storm, I guess."

FORTY-NINE

There weren't many questions to ask during the rest of the flight, and once they arrived at the Acapulco airport everyone busied themselves picking up their luggage and finding their way to the cars that would take them to their hotel. The lack of questioning didn't stop the camera crew from stalking Amy's every move, though, trying to capture on film the emotions of the journey. Amy asked, at one point, if there had to be a camera recording her at all times, even for the hours in the air during which Amy fiddled with a crossword puzzle and watched an in-flight movie that she thought was just a little too risqué for the eyes and ears of the many children on the flight. *Yes*, the production crew had replied. They would film everything and then mine through all of the footage to find anything that might be used in commercial promos or as filler material for the voice-over parts of the interview.

Amy didn't know exactly why, but she was surprised by how big of an operation the whole thing was. It reminded her of the iceberg example that Dr. Vilsek used one day in therapy when Mr. and Mrs. Millhouse had joined their daughter for a progress report of sorts.

"The emotions you're seeing in Amy are, to use a common metaphor, just the tip of the iceberg. There are parts of what she has been through and what she is feeling that are so far beneath the surface that you'll never see them, but that doesn't mean that they aren't there. It doesn't help matters that Amy likes to push as much as possible under the metaphorical water so as not to be a bother. But that just means that there is even more lurking beneath the surface. Or behind the scenes, if you like that comparison better."

A primetime interview has a lot more going on behind the scenes than I ever would've thought, mused Amy just as the plane touched down and the flight attendant issued a very peppy "¡Bienvenidos a México!" over the loudspeaker.

****

The first difference that Amy noticed after disembarking the plane was the security. Publicity from Amy and her sorority sisters' kidnapping had caused a huge downturn in foreign tourism in the area, and Mexico's government wanted to make absolutely sure that the Millhouse family's trip went off without a hitch. Consequently, a disproportionately large and heavily-armed security team would be accompanying the American group for the duration of their visit, and all travel routes would be cleared ahead of time. They would take no chances of running into a cartel checkpoint. In the security briefing Amy received prior to leaving the United States, she learned that the major drug gangs were reportedly calling off the dogs during Amy's trip as well. The brutal kidnapping of the Sorority Seventeen had galvanized opposition to the *narcos* from even those who had previously been willing to look the other way. The drug lords knew that if anything happened to the Millhouses or their film crew, all the threats and bribery in the world wouldn't be able to stop the fury of the Mexican and, God forbid, American militaries.

The hotel where they were staying was much nicer than the one the girls had booked on their economy budgets. Amy, her brother, and their parents all had separate rooms with king size beds and spectacular views of the ocean. After Amy unpacked her insanely large suitcase – her mother had insisted she bring way too many clothes because "you're going to be on national television, you need to look your absolute best!" – Amy slid open the glass door in her room and stepped out onto the small balcony outside. She leaned slightly against the chest-high white railing and breathed in deeply, closing her eyes and letting the warm ocean breeze wash over her.

Amy heard a noise behind her and turned her head to see the reporter, Lynn, and a cameraman joining her on the balcony. They had been setting up the small sitting room in Amy's suite as a possible interview space, but the seasoned reporter in Ms. Patterson knew that shots of Amy with the Pacific Ocean in the background were too good to pass up.

"You look like something's on your mind," Lynn said, hoping her pretty blonde interviewee would be in a talkative mood.

Amy gave a slight, haunting smile which came across as more sad than happy before turning back to face the ocean once again. "It's just that this is the one part of Acapulco that I desperately wanted to see during the other trip but didn't get to. Our hotel wasn't directly on the beach, so I didn't get to see the water last time. This is the first time I've seen the Pacific Ocean…did you know that? My family always went to the Florida panhandle in the Gulf of Mexico for vacation. One time we took a Caribbean cruise, but I've never seen the Pacific before. It's beautiful."

"Yes, you're right, it is," Lynn agreed, joining Amy at the railing.

Amy paused, because the rest of that story wasn't something that she was particularly proud of and still wrestled with guilt over. But being there in Acapulco again made all of the memories and emotions come rushing back, and they needed an outlet. Taking a deep breath, Amy continued: "I chose the Pacific. Did the other girls tell you that?" Amy asked, knowing that the network had conducted off-camera background interviews with a couple of her sorority sisters who were willing to talk about it again.

"No, they didn't, but I remember hearing something about it in the interview that the rest of the group did a while back," Lynn replied truthfully.

"That's right," Amy answered, nodding her head. "Katie told y'all. Well, anyway, the other girls were in charge of planning the trip. I was too busy with the annual graduation ball and pre-recruitment stuff to have much time to help plan, but they were split on where we should go. Half wanted to go to Cancún, and half wanted Acapulco. Since the group was an odd number, I had to break the tie. And since I had never seen the Pacific, I chose Acapulco." Amy's voice dropped to a barely audible whisper as she added, "everything would be so different if I had only chosen Cancún."

For the first time in her career as a reporter, tears filled Lynn Patterson's eyes as she listened to the story of the young woman standing beside her. Lynn had come into this interview expecting that sadness, anger, pain, and maybe even a little bit of fear would be part of "The Amy Millhouse Exclusive: Terror in Mexico." But this, this *guilt*, was not an emotion she was expecting Amy to display.

She blames herself for what happened, thought Lynn, stunned by that realization. "It's not your fault, Amy," Lynn said instinctively.

The young woman tried to shrug off the emotions cascading down on her. "I know, don't worry about me. Just a little lingering survivor's guilt," Amy said, as if it was a head cold.

"But everyone in your group survived," Lynn responded, not understanding where the survivor's guilt would come from.

"We did, yes. But we were so lucky. So, so lucky. Kidnappings like mine happen all too often in Mexico, and we were only held captive for two weeks. That's nothing. Some people are missing for months before they're set free. Others are never seen again. Even for the families that can afford the ransom payments, it's not unheard of for the kidnappers to not hold up their end of the bargain. For us to be there for such a relatively short period of time and to be let go after the first ransom payment . . ." Amy's voice trailed off as the full meaning of her words, including those left unsaid, became clear to the reporter standing beside her. *She was very lucky, indeed*, Lynn thought.

FIFTY

The next morning dawned bright and beautiful, and Amy couldn't help but smile as she strode in her pink pajamas from her bed to the balcony's sliding glass door and opened it, instantly filling her hotel suite with a warm salt air. *This is the vacation I wanted*, Amy thought to herself, completely relaxed and content. But that moment didn't last long as she heard a knock at the door and knew it would be the hair and makeup stylist arriving to get Amy ready for the morning shoot. Today would begin with a visit to the site where the actual abduction occurred, followed by a break for lunch and then a round of question prep and practice at the hotel that afternoon. Lynn and her crew wanted to be able to devote a full day to the holding house – that was tomorrow.

While Amy's hair was being meticulously ironed and straightened to combat the humidity outside, she ate the deliciously fresh grapefruit that was ordered for her breakfast – even though Amy really wanted to eat whatever combination of breakfast meat and pancakes that the person across the hall had ordered. It smelled like Heaven, but Amy had heard her mother's voice in her head as she filled out the room service menu the night before: *The camera adds ten pounds, you know. You don't want to look bloated. Plus you know maple syrup doesn't always agree with your stomach.* And while the young woman knew her mother was right, she still chafed at Linda Millhouse's somewhat overbearing manner. Like a cross between a beauty pageant mom and the character Marie from the TV show 'Everybody Loves Raymond,' except toned down a few notches.

After her makeup was finished, Amy slipped into the breezy, pale blue halter dress that she and the stylist had agreed on and touched up the outfit with her favorite pearl earrings and stylish white sandals. Amy knew the shoes would probably get dirty when they visited the roadside kidnapping location, but Labor Day was rapidly approaching and Amy didn't want to have to wait until next Easter to wear the shoes again.

****

Now that she looked the part, the young woman went downstairs to the hotel lobby to join the others. Normally Amy always felt bad about being late or keeping people waiting, but she knew the group today couldn't really go anywhere without the subject of the interview – her – so she didn't feel quite as bad.

As Amy and her family and Lynn and her crew walked outside to the caravan of heavily-fortified SUVs that would carry them around town that day, Amy couldn't help admiring how polished her brother and parents looked. Her mother was wearing baby pink linen capris with a white blouse and matching white sandals, her makeup spotless as usual and her hair perfectly coifed. Amy knew the stylist hadn't done any of it, either; her mother would've insisted on doing it herself. Her father and brother, in true Southern gentleman style, were dressed nearly identically yet managed to pull it off without a hitch – their matching stone-colored chino shorts and boat shoes complemented by red and green golf shirts from Polo and Brooks Brothers, respectively. *It truly is remarkable*, thought Amy, *how much Joshie resembles Daddy. Even though he desperately wants to be independent.*

Amy's thoughts about family matters quickly ceased once their cars started moving. Her body's reaction to the movement was instantaneous, as if she had developed some sort of muscular reflex to warn her of the danger of this particular road running through the outskirts of town. The young woman was sitting beside her father in the back bench seat of the SUV and, sensing the tension in his daughter's frame, Jack Millhouse grabbed hold of Amy's hand and held it tightly. He was looking out the window to his left but nonetheless kept talking to Amy, reassuring her in a way that only he had always been able to do.

"It's going to be fine. We'll be there with you the whole time. Your mother, Josh, and I will be there. You're safe now, darlin'. You're protected. It's going to be fine."

FIFTY-ONE

And it was. The visit to the kidnapping location went smoothly and uneventfully, and Amy surprised even herself by how calm and collected she remained while telling Lynn and the cameras what happened in that spot. Her composure was particularly impressive given that she had received permission from the Mexican authorities to reveal details of the kidnapping that previously were kept secret.

"And over there," Amy pointed with her manicured index finger to a spot about ten yards away, "is where they executed the cab drivers. The girls who saw it said it was one of the most horrific parts of the entire experience, second only to the sexual abuse."

Amy paused, her eyes and head angled down as she moved the dirt around with her toes. "They said it was like watching an old grainy World War II movie shown in high school, with the bad guys lining up their victims and then forcing them to kneel on the ground with their hands tied behind their backs. Except in the video the camera always cuts away at the last minute to show the stone-faced shooter instead of the victim's brains being blown out." Amy stopped for a moment, the next sentence catching in her throat: "the camera doesn't cut away in real life."

It took a moment for that statement to sink in before Lynn continued with her next question. "And you didn't see that execution happen?"

"No, like I said, I was knocked unconscious at that point. So I didn't see the lineup or the shootings. Luckily for all of us, the kidnappers waited until after we left before they finished off the taxi drivers."

"Finished off?" the reporter asked, not understanding the meaning of the term.

"Cruelty is the name of the game for these guys. It's not enough to just kill people. No, they have to also decapitate them and then use the various body parts to intimidate people. Nothing says 'pay us the money or else' like a bag full of severed heads left near a home or office."

The reporter shook her head in disgust. "I've read news reports about that happening, but it still seems so outrageous. I can't believe people actually do that to each other."

"Yet they do," Amy responded. She then walked over to the spot where the police report said the men were executed. Amy had pored over those reports – obsessed over them, really – wanting to know exactly what had happened while she was unconscious. She wasn't quite sure if she bought the whole idea of repressed memories, that some memories are so bad that our brain basically wipes them from our conscious memory. Some of the other girls were reportedly dealing with that. Regardless, Amy's problem wasn't repressed memories. It was that she literally had been unconscious for the first several hours of her time as a hostage. The police reports were a godsend – an answer to the questions that her sorority sisters didn't want to talk about while they were in the basement. And Amy knew she was lucky, because such detailed reports were definitely uncommon in cartel-related murders and kidnappings. The high profile nature of Amy's ordeal was what ensured the detailed police investigation and reporting.

As Amy stood over the execution spot, she wrapped her arms around her chest and got chills, even though the late-morning heat of the Mexican summer was nearing oppressive levels. Amy knew not to feel guilty; she and Dr. Vilsek had spent countless sessions talking through the guilt that overwhelmed the young woman when she got back to the United States. But even though her head knew she had nothing to be guilty about – she was a victim, just like her sorority sisters and the taxi drivers – her heart couldn't help but hurt for the men who died where she now stood. Yes, they were all victims; but these men weren't even the targets . . . they were collateral damage, unlucky enough to be working that night and driving the Sorority Seventeen.

Amy snorted in disgust as the 'Sorority Seventeen' moniker came to mind. It amazed her how many different labels the girls were given by the media. Anything that rhymed or had alliteration in it was the media's favorite as they reported on every tiny detail of the kidnapping. Amy knew the press had a job to do; she even really enjoyed her journalism class in college. It was the over-reporting that got to her. The paparazzi camping out at her parents' house and following them everywhere they went. The blog 'reporters,' if you can call them that, trying to gain access to the girls' private medical records to see if any of them had a drug problem that could have instigated the kidnapping. Amy had even watched recorded clips from national news broadcasts in which total stoners from the university lied and said Amy's sorority was full of girls hooked on cocaine. "Some people will say anything to get on television," had been Mrs. Millhouse's response to Amy's outrage at those stories. Amy knew her mother was right, but it still pissed her off that the TV stations would air the clips. *Oh well*, Amy thought as she could feel herself starting to get worked up inside. *That's water under the bridge now.*

She then turned around and walked over to rejoin her family and Lynn the reporter. "Are we ready to go?" Amy asked, and the others nodded their heads affirmatively. This first stop on the 'kidnapping tour,' as Josh was calling it, had been very productive, and Amy was confident that the rest of the trip would also be a success.

FIFTY-TWO

"What do you remember most about the building where you were held?" asked Lynn. She was sitting beside Amy in the middle row of their SUV as it drove away from the hustle and bustle of Acapulco into the Mexican 'campo,' or countryside. Amy and her family had enjoyed a wonderful breakfast at the hotel, and now the caravan of cars was headed out to the rural part of the state of Guerrero for the day. Dressed in her favorite navy blue chino shorts that stopped mid-thigh and a stylish white blouse that managed to cover the scar on her chest, Amy was prepared for the hot weather that she would inevitably face that day. What she wasn't prepared for, and couldn't prepare for, were the emotions that would accompany her return to the hacienda that had served as her kidnappers' home base. The young woman knew that today would be the hardest part of both the trip and the overall interview.

"The smell," replied Amy to the reporter's question. "Or rather, I should say, the stench. Sweaty, dirty men; sweaty, dirty female hostages; cigarette smoke; and of course the nauseating smell of human excrement and vomit since we didn't have access to a bathroom or even a toilet." Amy paused as the memory of that unforgettable combination of horrible smells flooded her mind and immediately made her feel sick to her stomach. "I'll never forget that smell," Amy declared. "In fact, about a month ago I went by my old high school to say hello to my favorite teachers. One of them was a conditioning coach, and as soon as I walked into the school's weight room I immediately had to turn around and leave it. I ran outside and threw up. The strong stench of sweat was too much for me."

Lynn paused, letting Amy's words hang in the air for dramatic effect, before continuing with her questioning. "What did you think about most while you were being held by the *narcos*?" She liked the way the word '*narcos*' sounded, and also liked that it was the term popularly used by the Mexican public to refer to members of the drug cartels.

"What did I think about most? Home," Amy answered without hesitation. "My family," she added, glancing over at her parents and brother who were listening intently to the interview. Having not wanted to pry or to interfere with Amy's recovery, neither Amy's parents nor Josh had asked her questions like the ones that Lynn was asking now. The Millhouses were hearing these details for the first time.

"It's amazing how clear things become when you're put in a situation like the one I was in. Before, I had thought about maybe living abroad one day, and also thought I was a pretty independent person." Amy issued a short laughing sound that was choked off by the tears beginning to well in her eyes and throat. "I couldn't have been more wrong." Gesturing towards her family, she continued: "I need them. Maybe not always in a financial sense – especially since Teach for America was nice enough to allow me to defer my start date by two years – but definitely in an emotional and almost spiritual sense. I need to be around them. Even when I went away to college, I still saw my family for home football games and went home at least once during each semester. I feed off of them – their energy, their love," Amy said through the tears that were flowing steadily now.

"So to answer your question, I thought about home. My family. But I also thought about if the kidnappers were going to contact our families, and then later what the result of the contact had been. If we would be released. Or rescued. When that might happen. How." Amy let out another short laugh. "Believe me, every possible Rambo-style, SWAT team, Navy Seal rescue scenario was played out in my head." The slight smile disappeared and Amy's voice got softer as she added, "every possible bad ending also went through my mind. Prolonged death from illness caused by the mush they fed us or the deplorable sanitary conditions we were kept in. Straight up execution like what happened to the taxi drivers. Lifetime servitude to the kidnappers. Sold into slavery. I even had a dream one night, well, more like a nightmare, that they sold us into slavery. Human trafficking as it's called now, as if a new label makes it any less horrible. I was bought by a couple who lived near my hometown and rescued one day when a guest in the couple's home recognized me."

"Wow," declared the reporter.

"I know. Tell me about it," responded Amy, shaking her head as she remembered waking up in the middle of the night in a cold sweat after having that dream.

Lynn Patterson continued with her seemingly endless stream of questions. "Did you ever imagine that your time as a hostage would end like it did?"

Amy's voice got quiet and the people listening could almost hear the pain in her words when she answered. "No. Never. Of all the crazy endings I thought of, the way it actually went down never crossed my mind."

As Amy responded to that question, their caravan began to slow and the SUVs pulled off the street and onto the long, curving driveway that led to the former home base for the upstart drug and kidnapping gang that had taken Amy and her friends. Amy had learned from the numerous reports she read about Mexico after returning home that it was fairly common for the cartels to use houses like this one for their headquarters, training sites, or, all too often, burial grounds for their victims. Many farmers had abandoned their homes due to the drug wars, which left the *narcos* with plenty of locations from which to choose. The one that Amy's kidnappers had chosen was set far back off the road and, as Amy saw for the first time, actually looked like a very nice house, with its pretty exterior masking the very ugly things that happened inside. Like so many ranch homes in Mexico and the southwestern United States, Amy saw that this building was one story and had a somewhat sprawling, L-shaped layout, with a slightly slanted red tile roof settled on top of the stucco walls. Amy could tell that with a little bit of TLC this place could actually transform into a beautiful piece of property. *A beautiful piece of property with a haunted past*, she thought.

Amy's mental examination of the building was cut short by the sounds of her fellow travelers unbuckling their seat belts and exiting the cars.

Here we go, thought Amy. *The moment I've been dreading. Dr. Vilsek was right, this is the hardest part. Reliving it all. But it's time to face the demons. Time to move on.* Taking a deep, determined breath, Amy opened her car door and stepped boldly into the bright Mexican sun.

FIFTY-THREE

It was a strange experience for Amy Millhouse to actually be standing in front of the building where she had been held prisoner. Like some strange variation of déjà vu, since she knew she had been there before but didn't have any recollection of it at all. While part of the security team and camera crew went inside to set things up, Amy stood a few feet away from where the cars were parked with her hands on her slender hips and the steel blue color of her eyes once again matching her outfit and betraying her determined state of mind. During some of her therapy sessions, Dr. Vilsek had encouraged Amy to bring along the family's pet Labrador Retriever to help comfort the young woman so she could fully recount what happened to her. But there was no sweet, lovable, huggable Gus alongside Amy today. It was her versus her past; versus what happened inside the large, compound-like house approximately ten yards in front of her. Amy suddenly had the strange sensation that she had become a cage fighter, like she was about to enter the ring against her most dangerous, most hated opponent.

The interview's executive producer instructed a cameraman to zoom in directly on Amy's face as she took in her surroundings. When one of the security officers came outside and gave the all-clear, the camera continued to focus on Amy as the entire group of people entered through a large car port and then a side door of the house.

The property now belonged to the government of Guerrero, the state in western Mexico which was home to Acapulco and its surrounding areas. The Guerrero government's stated goal was to spruce up the house and hopefully sell it, so there was fresh paint on the walls and everything looked like it had been power-washed with bleach. But despite the government cleaning crew's best efforts, Amy could still smell the old smells. Maybe it was her mind playing tricks on her, since no one else seemed to notice. Maybe, for Amy, her brain would always associate this house with those smells and those smells with this house. Just like when she had gone into her old high school weight room and her mind instantly returned to the kidnapping. But to Amy, even as members of her family were commenting on how clean and nice the house looked – "it smells like a Febreeze factory exploded in here," commented Josh – it still smelled the same. Dirty, sweaty men. Marijuana. Cigarettes. Human waste. Mold. Fear. Amy could still smell the fear.

"You don't remember this part of the house, do you honey?" asked Mrs. Millhouse, interrupting her daughter's thoughts.

"No ma'am," replied Amy. "If I've been in this room before, I don't remember it," she continued as she looked around what appeared to be a kitchen area. There weren't any appliances in the house right now since it would be too big of a temptation for looters, but there was a sink and Amy could clearly see where a stove and refrigerator would go. *So this is where they prepared our mush*, Amy thought. *Actually, probably not. They wouldn't want the real food they were eating to be near whatever they fed us.*

"What are you thinking about?" Lynn asked. She could see the wheels in her interview subject's brain turning rapidly, and was hoping to get some more material for the television special.

"Right now? I'm thinking about how they probably ate fairly good meals in this kitchen. Then would go outside and pour dog food into a bowl, mix it with a little water, and give it to us as our 'food.'" Amy made air quotes with her fingers as she said the word food.

"Do you really think they fed you dog food? I know one of the other girls said in her interview that they fed you all some form of oatmeal."

"I don't know," replied Amy, shrugging her shoulders and shaking her head. "Whatever it was, it was not fit for human consumption. I wouldn't feed it to our dog, either."

Lynn nodded in understanding. "On that note, are you ready to go downstairs to the basement?"

"As ready as I'll ever be," stated Amy.

****

The stairs leading down to the basement were in a hallway just off the kitchen area. For dramatic effect, the producer had Amy open the door leading to the stairs, even though there was already a cameraman at the bottom of the stairs, waiting to record Amy's reaction as she entered the basement.

The wooden boards squeaked with each step as Amy made her way down. The smell was more pronounced now, and the others travelling down the stairs with Amy also noticed the stench. There were no windows on this level of the house, so the smells had escaped into the walls instead. No amount of bleach or air freshener could ever remove that now. *Good luck selling this place with it smelling this bad*, Amy thought.

The ability to think sarcastic thoughts ended as Amy reached the basement floor. When her stylish Toms-clad feet touched the cool concrete, she froze, almost causing a pile-up on the stairs as her family and the interview crew and security team behind her also had to abruptly stop. This wasn't some sort of cognitive trick like upstairs, knowing she'd been there before but not remembering it. Amy remembered the basement. Vividly. There were only two rooms down here. To her right was the smaller of the two, the one where the kidnappers had held her until she regained consciousness after the abduction. To her left . . . Amy shuddered. To her left was the room that gave her nightmares. Where she spent two terrifying weeks, not knowing if she would ever make it out of there alive. Where she stood as her friends, one by one, performed sexual acts on the kidnappers, some of them so heinous they would only be seen on the most outrageous versions of hard core pornography. Where she herself refused to agree to do such things, and when she refused, where the men took what they wanted without her consent.

"So this is where the Sorority Seventeen were held," said Lynn, who had made her way down the stairs and was now standing beside Amy. When the noticeably nervous and traumatized young woman nodded her head in agreement, Lynn continued, "why don't you walk us around, Amy. Tell us about the room and what it was like when you were down here."

****

Amy took a deep breath and then began telling the story everyone had been waiting to hear. "Well, for starters, there are two rooms, not just one," Amy clarified as she turned to her right and entered the smaller room. "This is where they took me at first. I don't know what they used this room for the rest of the time, but when they first brought us to the house I was put in here because I was still unconscious. I guess maybe they thought I might die and didn't want the other girls freaking out too much if that happened." Amy glanced at her mother as she mentioned dying and saw the older woman grimace. She knew that this whole trip was really hard on her family, especially her mom. "I dunno," Amy stated. "But I was in here until I woke up."

"And you were unconscious from the initial abduction?" asked Lynn, trying to refresh her memory.

"Yeah. Like I said before, I tried to fight back when they were kidnapping us from the taxi cabs, and my head met the butt end of an AK," Amy commented, referring to the short-hand nickname for an AK-47, the machine gun of choice for many cartel members. "Or maybe it was the business end of a baseball bat. I don't know. Whatever it was, it knocked me out cold for several hours. When I finally came to, they moved me over into the other room."

"Let's go there now, if you're ready to," suggested Lynn.

"Okay, like I said, I don't remember much about this room," agreed Amy.

"Oh, before we leave," said Lynn, stopping in her tracks. "It was in this room that you decided on a key strategy for getting information from the kidnappers, right? Tell us about that."

Amy nodded her head as she began to speak. She and Lynn had spent part of their car ride this morning off-camera, going over some of the questions that would be asked while in the house, and Amy's choice to hide her Spanish skills was one of them. "When I was first regaining consciousness, my head hurt so bad that my initial thought was that I had a wicked hangover," Amy said with a slight laugh. "But then almost immediately I started remembering the taxi drivers and the roadblock and the kidnapping. I also quickly realized that the other people in the room were speaking Spanish. I majored in Spanish in college, and was about as close to fluent as I could get as a non-native speaker." Amy paused, replaying the event in her mind, before she continued with her story. "I don't know how I was able to think so quickly on my feet – figuratively, of course; literally I was still lying on the floor with my eyes closed at that point – but I decided that it was in my best interest if the men in the room, whoever they might be, didn't know that I spoke Spanish. That way they would feel comfortable speaking freely amongst themselves and I might be able to get some inside information."

"So you never once spoke to them in Spanish?" asked Lynn.

"Never. In fact, there were even a couple of times when they told me to do something, be quiet or sit down or something like that, and I purposely did the opposite to make them think that I didn't understand the Spanish command."

"That's pretty smart," said Lynn admiringly.

"Thanks," Amy replied with a shrug of her shoulders. "Like I said, I don't know how I was coherent enough to come up with the idea. Divine intervention, I guess." She then started walking towards the stairs and the other room, signaling to everyone that she was ready to move on.

FIFTY-FOUR

The large room to the left of the stairs didn't immediately come across as a typical 'holding room'; at least not how Hollywood would have designed one. But, then again, touch-up work had been done on this room too. Power-washed walls managed to remove a good portion of the water and mold stains, and a fresh coat of white paint also helped. The power-washer had obviously also been directed at the concrete floor, and Amy could now see no traces of the blood stains that had once decorated the gray ground. It was also impossible to tell which corner had been used by the girls as a toilet area, even though Amy knew exactly which one it was. The wooden boards in the ceiling were also new, making the basement of this house actually look respectable.

"Hey Dad," Amy called out.

"Yes darlin'?" answered Jack Millhouse as he strode over to stand next to his daughter.

"What's that legal term where when you're selling a house you don't have to tell the buyers if bad stuff happened in it?"

"*Caveat emptor*," replied Jack. "Buyer beware." A slight smile crossed his lips as he remembered that Amy always loved to hear her father's Halloween story about caveat emptor. It was a fairly famous law case, actually, where the people buying a house didn't know it was haunted by ghosts. As a little girl, Amy always liked when her father told that story on Halloween.

"That's it. *Caveat emptor*. I wonder if they have that sort of rule here," Amy mused. The pleasant memories in Jack's mind immediately faded as she said that, aware that his daughter was wondering if the people selling this house would have to disclose what had happened to her here. If Jack had his way, they would've already destroyed the building. He was of half a mind to buy the place himself and tear it down, but he knew that the asking price was far too steep for his pocketbook. The house was set on several dozen acres and really was the perfect spot for a ranch home or a country house for someone living in Acapulco or Chilpancingo, a city Jack had never heard of before the kidnapping but was now well-versed on. Unfortunately, everything that made this house a great getaway spot – large lot, secluded, close but not too close to the city – had also made it a great hideout spot.

"I don't know sweetie," Jack said as he finally answered his daughter. "I'd have to look up Mexican property law."

"Oh, no need," Amy responded. "I was just wondering."

By this time, Lynn and the main cameraman had made their way through the group and were standing in front of Amy and her father. Everyone was still closer to the stairs than the far wall, though – maybe about one-third of the way into the room.

"So this is where you spent most of your time," Lynn stated.

"Yep," Amy affirmed, shaking her head in agreement while at the same time pursing her lips together in a straight line – an action that her family knew meant she wasn't happy with what Lynn had just said. Amy knew the reporter meant well and probably hadn't thought anything of it, but there were certainly better ways to phrase that statement. 'Where you spent your time' made it seem like there was a choice to be somewhere else. It put the room in too positive a light, Amy thought. She didn't say anything, though. For the most part, Lynn was doing a wonderful job and was generally very sensitive to Amy's emotions.

"This is where we were held hostage," Amy clarified. "The worst twelve days of my life."

"I know everybody is curious about this room and what happened here, so why don't I just let you talk? Say what you want to about it and don't say what you don't want to," Lynn suggested.

"Okay, we can do that," came Amy's reply. She then paused, wondering where best to begin. As with Dr. Vilsek several months earlier in therapy, Amy chose to start at the very beginning . . . a very good place to start.

****

"The far corner on the left is where we were kept. All seventeen of us huddled close together. The guards set it up that way so they could easily keep an eye on us, but to be honest we didn't mind. There was a sense of relative safety in numbers, and there were times when the men were over on this side of the room that we could whisper to each other."

"So for twelve whole days, all seventeen of you had to stay in that corner?" Lynn asked to clarify.

"Yep. We sat on the concrete floor, no blankets or cushioning of any kind. We squeezed up next to each other to sleep in a kind of a dominoes formation, with each girl's head resting on the legs of another girl."

"A makeshift pillow," Lynn commented.

"Yeah. It took the other girls a couple of hours on the first night to get that system figured out, but they had it down to a science by the time I joined them in this room."

"They say some of the best inventions are created out of necessity," said Lynn.

"Exactly," responded Amy. "It wasn't a particularly comfortable sleeping arrangement, but it was better than nothing."

"What about a bathroom? How did the kidnappers handle that?" Lynn asked.

"That was in the other corner," Amy answered as she started to walk into the center of the room. "Over there, on the right," she continued, pointing her finger toward the corresponding corner. "The kidnappers put a big pot over there, which we had to use as a toilet. They only emptied it out once a day, if we were lucky, and with seventeen girls using that one pot, I'm sure you can imagine how bad it smelled in here. Plus sometimes the pot would, umm, fill up, so we just had to go on the floor."

Everyone in the room made a face when Amy told that part of her story, trying not to imagine what it would be like to live with the constant smell of human waste.

"If you needed to go to the bathroom," Amy went on, "you had to raise your hand and ask permission. We weren't allowed to talk, so sometimes it took a while for the men guarding us to look up from their card game."

"What if you had to go really bad?" asked Josh, curious about this part of the story.

"That happened a couple of times," Amy answered, looking over at her brother. "You just had to decide how much longer you could hold it. You always had the option of calling out to get their attention, but we understood that we would be punished for doing that."

"Punished?" asked Jack Millhouse, joining in the conversation.

"Pistol-whipped," was Amy's reply. The group of people in the room with her cringed, but the use of a handgun to violently slap whichever girl had talked was such a common occurrence during her time as a hostage that Amy hardly gave it any thought. "Of course, if The Enforcer was in the room, he used his favorite big nightstick instead of a gun."

"The Enforcer," Lynn interrupted. "The other girls talked about him too. What was he like?"

"Mean," Amy said. "As mean as a snake. All of the kidnappers were comfortable using violence, but The Enforcer actually seemed to enjoy it. He was big, probably 6'4" and over 250 pounds, and brute force was very obviously his life's currency. He got this wicked gleam in his eyes right before he hit us. I think he liked hearing us scream in pain; liked seeing blood splatter and bruises swell on our faces."

"Nice guy," Josh said sarcastically.

"Oh yeah. Mr. Congeniality for sure," Amy replied. She then walked over to the corner where she and her sorority sisters had sat huddled for just shy of two weeks nearly a year and a half ago. Amy turned to face the other side of the room, trying to find the right angle to help her remember exactly where 'her spot' had been. A couple shuffle-steps to her left and she was there. Even without closing her eyes, Amy could see the run-down, dirty table where the men on guard duty would sit while playing cards.

What she did next surprised everyone in the room. Amy kneeled and then sat down in literally the exact same spot where her kidnappers had placed her. You could have heard a pin drop in the room, as everyone stood motionless to see what Amy would do next. She seemed to be staring at the ground beneath where she sat, looking for something.

Eventually Lynn walked over and knelt down next to the young Miss Millhouse. "What are you looking at, Amy?"

"This," Amy said as she gently ran her fingers over the concrete immediately next to her. There were tears in the young woman's eyes as she continued: "these marks. One scratch for each day I spent here."

FIFTY-FIVE

Lynn joined Amy in looking at the spot on the floor where there were dash marks, barely visible now even when one knew exactly where to find them. The cameraman zoomed in on the markings, and then slowly panned back to show the pain and anguish on Amy's face and in her eyes.

"I was a Spanish major in college," Amy began, and Lynn wondered where she was going with this story, "but I've always had a soft spot for good poetry. T.S. Eliot is one of my favorites." Amy ran her hand along the concrete floor again, picking up dirt and dust as her palm brushed the ground. She then turned her hand over and rubbed the gray matter between her fingers. "I will show you fear in a handful of dust," she said pensively.

"Eliot?" Lynn asked.

Amy nodded her head affirmatively. "It's from 'The Waste Land.' That's what this room is to me. Fear. More than the smells, more than the images, even more than the pain. What I remember most, truly, is the fear. My fear. The fear of my friends. And that's what this room still is now: fear in a handful of dust." Amy looked again at the dirt in her hand, holding it up to the light coming from the center of the room. "I'm still afraid. Afraid that the life I once knew and the innocence I once had can never return. It died here. Like the line they say at funerals – ashes to ashes, dust to dust."

"Do you think you'll ever be able to think about this room, this house, even this country of Mexico without feeling that fear?" asked Lynn.

"This room? No. This house? All I remember about this house is this room and the one across the hall, so no. But Mexico? Sure, I think so. Not right now. Not yet. But this is a beautiful country with wonderful people." Amy laughed at the look of surprise on Lynn's face as she said that. "Obviously they're not all wonderful people. But I'd be willing to say the majority of them probably are. Every time I get angry and bitter and want to blame what happened to me on Mexico or Mexicans in general, I stop and think about everybody who went out of their way to try to find me, help me, capture the kidnappers, etcetera. The doctors and nurses who operated on me at the hospital. The government officials who found, arrested, prosecuted, and convicted the men responsible for this. Everyone who helped arrange this interview. And, above all else, the incredible people who found me left for dead on the side of the road and took me into their home. They kept me safe and nursed me back to health, and then at great risk to themselves and their family drove me into Acapulco. They didn't have to do any of that. But they did. They are wonderful people. And they represent the Mexico that I want to think of and remember."

In that moment, for one of the first times in her career, Lynn couldn't think of another question to ask. Amy's moving tribute to the people who had saved her seemed a fitting conclusion to their time in the basement, since the young woman and the network had already negotiated that she wouldn't directly discuss the rape during the interview. It had already been covered extensively in news reports, and Amy was adamant about not going into the details of that part of her kidnapping. She was still extremely worried, even to the point of slight paranoia, that someone would find out about her pregnancy. She could easily imagine Lynn making some off-hand comment about how Amy and the other girls were lucky they didn't get pregnant, and then Amy's response would somehow betray her secret.

Lynn Patterson, of course, didn't know the full reason behind her interview subject not wanting to talk about the rape. She just knew that the topic was contractually off-limits, and she also knew that right now was the right moment to call a wrap to this portion of the interview. She suggested as much to Amy, who readily agreed. The group then made their way back up the basement stairs and out of the house. Amy was the last person to climb back into a waiting SUV, as she turned around for one final look at the house where her world had changed forever. Dr. Vilsek had been right – this visit was exactly the closure that Amy needed. And the young woman knew, without a doubt, that she would never return here again.

FIFTY-SIX

"I want to start by saying thank you to both you and your family for agreeing to do this interview," Lynn began. They had returned to Acapulco in the late afternoon of the day before after finishing the tour of the house where the Sorority Seventeen were hidden, and Amy and her family spent a relaxing evening having dinner at the hotel and then walking along the beach. Amy and Josh had also stayed up late that night in her hotel room, laughing and talking about everything and nothing, just like they used to do as kids. It was the first time in years that she and her brother had spent time together like that, and Amy was reminded how lucky she was to have such a great brother like Josh.

The happy luster of the night before had faded, though, and Amy and Lynn were now seated in a small conference room in the hotel that was set up for a sit-down interview. Even though Amy had already touched on some very emotional subjects during her return trips to the kidnapping site and the house where she was held, she knew that the topics of conversation in today's portion of the interview would be the most difficult. Lynn Patterson was known as a hard-hitter in the world of journalism, and a person she interviewed seldom made it through the experience without crying. Knowing that, Amy had braced herself for an onslaught and was pleasantly surprised when Lynn didn't jump right in with the tough questions. Amy listened as the reporter finished her introductory statement: "You certainly didn't have to open yourself up like this for the world to see and hear your story, but I know that I for one am glad you did."

Amy knew the woman sitting across from her meant what she said. She could tell that the veteran reporter had been deeply moved by Amy's experiences. "You're welcome," Amy responded. "And thank you for giving me the opportunity to tell my story. As I think I alluded to before, coming here to Mexico, visiting the sites where it happened, and telling people what I went through has been a significant part of my healing process." Amy paused, remembering to speak more slowly and try to not ramble. "I've been in therapy for a while now and this is definitely part of the closure that my therapist and I have talked about."

"Before we return to your specific story," Lynn replied, "I want to briefly mention the public awareness campaign that you and some other victims of the drug war here have started. Tell us a little bit about that."

Amy nodded her head in acknowledgment of the subject, again happy that her interviewer had opened with a softball question. "Yeah, sure. Well, it is a group of us that were all in a sense 'collateral damage' from the war going on here. By that I mean that we were all innocent bystanders who got swept up in the violence in one way or another. Before it used to mostly be bad guys killing bad guys, but now victims are really picked indiscriminately. And it is a war. The president of Mexico declared war on the drug cartels in 2006, and the national military has been fighting them ever since. The number of people who have died continues to grow, and the number of *desaparecidos* is just incredibly high."

"Desaparecidos?" Lynn interrupted, confused by the word.

"Oh, sorry. Literally, it means missing people. I guess a better word might be *perdidos* – the lost. *Desaparecidos* has a more specific meaning. But that's neither here nor there. What I'm trying to say, inarticulately, is that a lot of people have died and a lot more have gone missing."

Lynn nodded her head to signal that she understood Amy's explanation, and then the young woman went on: "So, basically, this group that I'm a part of is trying to make the world more aware of what's going on in Mexico. Especially non-Spanish speaking countries. A lot of times I'll read an article online in Spanish that's talking about violence in Mexico, and then I'll go to that news outlet's English-language website to try to find the same article, but it's not there. I think that a lot of people in the United States in particular have closed their eyes to what is going on south of the border. They've been starting to pay a little more attention in the last couple of years, and there's definitely more awareness now because of what happened to my sorority sisters and me, but I think more can and should be done."

"An awareness campaign, I see. And a noble cause, certainly," Lynn declared.

"We're trying," Amy agreed.

The reporter then glanced down at the notepad in her lap, looking for her next topic of discussion. Amy sat patiently across from her, her jeans-clad legs crossed at the ankles and her perfectly manicured hands resting softly in her lap. Today Amy was wearing her favorite pale pink Oxford shirt with a matching pink headband and her always present pearl necklace and earrings. Despite her mother's objections to her decision to wear jeans, everyone else in the room thought the young Miss Millhouse looked every ounce of the well-bred, well-educated Southern woman that she was.

After a short mental deliberation of which direction the interview should take, Lynn looked up from her notepad and resumed her questions for Amy.

"Now, you've given us a sort of guided tour of where you were taken while you were kidnapped and missing," Lynn began. Amy nodded her head in agreement, and the reporter continued, "but there's one place we didn't go. One location where you spent a significant amount of time that we didn't see."

"That's true," Amy replied softly.

"I know the answer, but for the sake of the cameras, why don't you tell us where we didn't go."

"Well, to do that I'll have to fill in the rest of the story," Amy explained. "We left for Acapulco on a Thursday. It was a beautiful Southern summer morning, and still early enough in the season to not be too hot. We had a layover in Mexico City, but luckily we didn't have to change planes. Or, I guess, depending on how you look at it, unluckily we didn't have to change planes."

"How do you mean?" asked Lynn.

"If we had switched planes then maybe we would have somehow lost Ricky in the shuffle. Probably not, though. Regardless, that doesn't matter now. Our plane landed in Acapulco early that evening, and we went straight from the airport to the hotel." Amy took a sip of water from the glass on the small table in front of her, then continued. "There were seventeen of us, as you know, so we had four hotel rooms. Three rooms with four people and one with five. It was cramped, but we figured it was worth it to save money but still stay in a fairly nice hotel. We spent that first night unpacking and the girls in my room with me – Caitlin, Sophie, and Tanner – and I ate dinner in one of the hotel restaurants. I only ate a small salad. I remember that because I was kicking myself for it later on. I had been worried that I would feel bloated or look like I had a belly both when we went out that night and the next day in my bathing suit at the beach, so I purposely didn't eat much. But then all the kidnappers fed us was that garbage, so the first couple of days after we were kidnapped I was really wishing I had ordered a steak or something at the hotel that night. Just so I could have a little more food in the reserve tank, you know?"

Lynn nodded in agreement. "You never know which meal might be your last."

"Exactly," Amy replied. "Exactly."

"So you had dinner and unpacked, and then what?" the reporter asked, helping the conversation along.

"Just before eleven o'clock that night, we left the hotel for the bar that Ricky told us about. Like I explained yesterday and the day before, we never made it to the bar. We were kidnapped from our taxis and taken to the *hacienda* that served as the gang's home base. I'm sure I'm repeating some things I've already said during the trip, but I figure it's best to just run through it all again quickly." Amy brushed a stray strand of hair behind her ear before moving on to the next part of the story.

"All seventeen of us were kept in the basement for twelve days. At first we were so scared by what was happening that we weren't really able to feel anything else. A few days in, though, we all got pretty down in the dumps as we started to realize that we could be held prisoner there for a really long time. But then, towards the end, our spirits improved a good deal because we knew that the kidnappers had contacted our families and that a ransom payment was being arranged. So we were still scared, for sure, but at least we had more hope then."

Amy paused, waiting as if to see if the woman sitting across from her in the well-tailored navy pantsuit had any questions. When Lynn didn't say anything, Amy began again.

"Day Twelve was the last day when we were all there together. The day that has received so much press coverage. When the *narcos* demanded the extra ransom payment, as they called it." Amy swallowed hard and the features on her face began to crinkle up, a sign that her closely-watching family members knew meant that she was trying not to cry. "If you don't mind," Amy said as she reached for a tissue from the box that had been set out before the interview began, "I'd rather not rehash the details of what happened then. I think y'all in the media have covered it enough. Everybody knows what came next. And everybody knows I refused to do it."

"Yes, that sequence of events has been well-documented," Lynn said gently. She could tell that the cool, calm demeanor of her interview subject was beginning to crack, and Lynn didn't want the girl to break down before they reached the even tougher questions. "What happened after that, though? After the rest of the girls were taken away and eventually set free?"

Amy smoothed her hands down her thighs and took a deep breath, trying to retain her composure. "I don't know exactly how long they kept me in the house after everybody else left. Everything that happened between the time the other girls went away and the time I was rescued is a blur. But we do know from police interviews with the kidnappers that it was hours, not days. What I also know, though, and this is getting back to your original question about where we didn't visit, is that after the men had done enough to, in their eyes, sufficiently punish me for refusing to cooperate, they took me to an area in the same general vicinity of the house and left my body on the side of the road. The investigators figure that the kidnappers either thought I was already dead or that I was close enough to dead that I wouldn't survive. And if not for the people who rescued me, I probably wouldn't have made it."

Lynn's eyebrows quirked upwards at the way Amy phrased that last sentence. "That's the second time you've used the word 'rescued.' Why is that?"

"Because that's what happened," Amy replied steadfastly. "I was rescued. Some people – I don't want to say who or be any more specific than that – but some people found me in a ditch by the road. They told me that they originally thought I was dead, and only got close to me to check to see if they knew who I was. They said that sometimes they recognized the faces of the corpses that the *narcos* leave scattered in roadside ditches or playing fields or wherever else they feel like. If the people, the ones who found me, recognize the dead person then they try to contact the family members and let them know so they can go get the body."

"That just seems unreal to me," Lynn said, shocked by the underlying brutality of the situation that Amy was describing. "To have death, and not just death, but murder, be so common."

"Unfortunately, it is all too real," Amy stated somberly. She then quickly shook her head from side to side, as if to bring her back to the task at hand of recounting her experience. "When the people who found me, who rescued me, realized that I was still alive, they amazingly took me back to their home."

"Why 'amazingly'?" Lynn asked, curious.

"Because it was so dangerous for them to do so. They had no idea who I was or who was responsible for putting me in the condition I was in. Taking me in was very risky for them. My attackers could have found out that I was still alive and in these people's home and come back to finish the job. And punish the good people for interfering."

"I see," the reporter responded. "So these people, these rescuers, took you in and nursed you back to health?"

"That's exactly what they did," Amy said reverently. The respect and appreciation she felt for her saviors was evident in the way she spoke about them. "They clothed me, fed me, and nursed me back from the brink of death. But, probably most importantly, they hid me. At this point in time, my kidnappers were still at large. Armed and dangerous. But these incredible people kept my existence hidden from everyone, even their next door neighbors. Hidden and safe."

"Do you ever wish they hadn't kept your presence there a secret? I mean, if they had told someone that they found you then you might have made it home sooner."

It was a valid question, and one that Amy hadn't thought about before. She furrowed her brow for a moment, considering the idea, before reaching a conclusion. "No. In theory, your question makes perfect sense. If they had told people I was there, then the police and the State Department and my family might have found out where I was a good two weeks earlier than they did. But there are several reasons why I don't think it would've worked that way in practice. To begin with, by the time they got me off the road and to their house, I was in no condition to go anywhere. I was drifting in and out of consciousness, had lost a good bit of blood, and there's no telling how many broken bones I had. Even if the best doctors in the world had suddenly appeared in the room next to me, they almost assuredly would've said they couldn't move me anywhere. I was in really bad shape, but I was stable. My body just needed time to heal itself.

"The second reason why I'm glad they kept me secret was that it would've spelled death and destruction for all of us if they hadn't. Like I said, my kidnappers hadn't been arrested yet. And there were plenty of other drug gangs and just generally bad people around who would have wanted to either kill me or make another ransom demand for my return. Not to mention punishing my rescuers for trying to help me." Amy paused, trying to figure out the best way to articulate her reasoning. "Look, it's easy to sit here now and second guess. To use 20/20 hindsight and say this or that should have been done differently. But the people who took care of me knew the situation. They knew the environment we were in and the best way for all of us to survive it. So I don't doubt their decisions at all."

The reporter across from Amy nodded her head and smiled, impressed by the young woman's defense of the people who saved her life.

"Now, it will have been lost on no one that you keep referring to the people who found you and took you in as 'them' or 'they,' with no gender or numerical descriptors at all. Why is that?"

"Well," Amy began, "it corresponds to why we didn't visit their house during this trip. I want to protect them. And not just in the way that most people probably mean when giving interviews. I definitely want to protect their privacy, but I also want to protect their lives. Literally. I don't know what friends and family of my kidnappers are still out there, or if they might try to seek revenge on the people who helped me. Don't get me wrong, part of me would love for the whole world to know all about these heroes. Because that's what they are. They're my heroes. They gave so much and risked so much for a complete stranger, without ever asking for anything in return. I owe them everything. *Everything*."

"So you want to keep them safe just like they kept you safe," Lynn said, finishing Amy's thoughts for her.

"Yes. Most definitely."

"I'm sure they appreciate that," Lynn replied. "And with that," she said, turning to face the camera beside her, "we're going to take a short commercial break. When we come back, you'll hear more of my conversation with Amy Millhouse."

FIFTY-SEVEN

There hadn't actually been a commercial break. It was just something that the producer wrote into the script so when the primetime special aired they would be able to insert commercials. In reality, in the hotel conference room in Mexico, Lynn and Amy had a quick touch up of their makeup before the cameras started rolling again.

"And we're back here in Acapulco with kidnapping victim Amy Millhouse. Or rather, I should say, kidnapping survivor." Amy gave a brief half-smile at Lynn's survivor comment before the seasoned reporter continued with her speech. "Amy, you've just finished telling us about the people who found you left for dead on the side of the road and nursed you back to health. They also took you back to the city we're in now after you had recovered enough to travel, did they not?"

"They did," Amy said, nodding in agreement. "I was in their house for twelve days, which is funny – not 'ha ha' funny, but coincidentally funny – since I was also in the kidnappers' basement for twelve days. But, after my time recovering, the people drove me to Acapulco."

"It wasn't your typical trip, though, was it?" Lynn asked, pushing the conversation toward Amy's ride in the trunk of the Velazquez's car.

"No, it wasn't. As I explained earlier, we were all worried that I would be discovered. We didn't know who were the good guys and who were the bad guys, so for safety's sake we had to assume everybody was bad. To that end, when the time came for me to leave and return to Acapulco, my rescuers decided that the safest way to get me from their house to the city was in the trunk of their car."

"The trunk," Lynn repeated, half-statement and half-question.

"Yes, the trunk. They cut air holes in an emptied-out cornmeal sack, and I rode inside that sack in the trunk of the car."

"Why the sack?" Lynn asked curiously.

"Roadblocks are one of the favorite tools of the cartels to demonstrate their control over a territory and instill fear in the citizenry. It's also a great way to find their rivals and kill them. I read about this one guy whose job it was to pull members of rival drug gangs from buses and kill them. He said he killed at least seventy-five people. Think about that. One of America's most famous serial killers, Ted Bundy, confessed to somewhere around forty murders. This guy who targeted buses killed nearly double that number. It's insane." Amy shook her head in disgust. "You'll remember I told you that on my first night in Mexico, the taxi drivers thought that the kidnappers were just another cartel checkpoint. Driving into Acapulco, we knew that if our car got stopped and they saw me, it might set off all kinds of red flags. Again, we couldn't trust anyone. So I stayed in the sack to make sure no one would see me, even if they opened the trunk to check for drugs or weapons or money."

"And you did hit a roadblock along the way."

"Yes, we did." Amy took a deep breath and sighed, not liking this part of the story. "I was in the trunk, in the cornmeal sack, along with some crates of fruits and vegetables and another sack that had a dead pig in it. The cover story for why my rescuers were driving into the city was to sell the items at one of the markets. But the cartel members who stopped the car had other plans for the things in the trunk. They made a lot of snide, derogatory comments about people who lived in the countryside, and they stole some of the fruit from the baskets. Then, for seemingly no other reason than to be mean, they decided to make it where the pigs couldn't be sold at market."

"But you were one of those 'pigs,'" Lynn commented.

"I was," Amy said with a sigh. "They stabbed the other sack first. I was absolutely petrified at that point, trying so hard to stay still and not breathe and not scream. And then they stabbed the bag I was curled up in. They got me twice, once in the left thigh and once on the right side of my torso, just below my ribs."

"And you didn't scream? Cry out or anything?"

"Amazingly, by the grace of God, no. I seriously thought my teeth were going to shatter because I was gritting them together so hard to keep from making any noises. But the pain was so sudden and so acute that I passed out shortly after I was stabbed. A miracle of sorts, I guess. If I was unconscious then I couldn't scream in pain."

Lynn couldn't help but let out a small laugh. "I think that's the first time I've heard anyone say they were glad that they passed out."

Amy smiled, recognizing the humor in her statement. "Yeah, well, opportunistic lack of consciousness appears to be a recurring theme during my experience here." Lynn knew without asking that the young woman was referring to not witnessing the execution of the taxi drivers and being knocked out during part of her rape. "But anyway," Amy then said, returning to the storyline, "after we made it through the roadblock or checkpoint or whatever you want to call it, the people in the car with me drove, as my grandmother would say, like a bat out of hell, trying to get to the British Consulate as quickly as possible."

"Why British?" Lynn asked.

"That was the drop-off point," Amy responded, before realizing that she had skipped something. "Oh, sorry, I forgot a part of the story. Just as the people who rescued me didn't know who they could trust, I personally didn't know if I could completely trust them. Maybe these people who found me were okay with me being a generic victim, but if they found out who I really was then their position might change." Amy paused, and she hoped that the cameras pointed her direction wouldn't be able to reveal the fact that she wasn't telling the whole truth. She didn't want to tell them exactly why she pretended to be British, because that might reveal too much about María and her mother. After all, how many families in that rural part of the state of Guerrero hated America because their husband and father abandoned them to travel north to the States? *Maybe a lot, actually*, Amy thought. But she didn't want to risk it. The people who she felt deserved to know the whole truth already knew it, and she didn't owe it to Lynn Patterson, the TV network, or the audience watching to reveal every tiny detail.

When Lynn's expression didn't change and Amy saw no signs that the other woman suspected she was getting less than the whole story, Amy went on. "So I told them I was British. I figured there might be a lot of reasons why people could hate America, especially in a country with such a long and complicated history with the United States. But, as far as I knew, nobody in this region had any real reason to dislike somebody from Great Britain. So I did my best Kate Middleton impersonation and told them I was from London. And they bought it."

So they took you to the British Consulate, thinking it represented your home country," Lynn reasoned.

"Precisely. They dropped me off at the front gates of the Consulate and drove away." Amy then took a deep breath, sitting back all the way in her chair and crossing her slender legs. "Things were pretty straightforward from then. The people at the Consulate called an ambulance and took me to the hospital, where a team of very talented doctors operated on me to fix the damage from the stab wounds and re-set some of the bones that the kidnappers had broken. In fact, after we finish this interview, my family and I are having dinner with some people from the Consulate and the hospital. I want to see them all again and say a proper thank you."

"And, just to fill in the rest," the reporter added, "your family came down to Acapulco and stayed with you until you were stable enough to fly back to the United States."

"And the rest, as they say, is history," Amy said with a slight grin.

"One more question, before we take another break." After Amy nodded her head in agreement, Lynn asked "do you ever wonder what happened to the kidnappers? They're in jail, right?"

"Yes, they're in jail," Amy responded, skipping over the first question to reach the second, easier one. "Nineteen of them were sentenced to life in Mexico's supermax prison."

"Nineteen? That seems like a lot."

"We don't really know how many men were involved in the actual kidnapping, since they were never all in the same room with us at once. But all of the key players were caught and convicted."

"That must be difficult for you to know that some of the kidnappers are still running free," Lynn commented.

Amy shrugged her shoulders as she responded "it is. Sometimes. I try not to think about it. And it helps that I know the worst ones are behind bars. The ones I really hated. The ones who did the most damage."

"How were they caught? Do you know?" the reporter asked.

"No," Amy shook her head. "I don't."

It was a lie. The truth of the matter was that Amy did know how the men were caught. A couple of weeks earlier, right after she decided to do the interview, after she had already told Dr. Vilsek that she didn't know who the tipster was, Amy received a letter in the mail from one of the kidnappers. Ángel. Amy could still see the note in her mind. It began with him saying that he hoped she could understand his writing, since he used a free internet translator to help him write in English. There was then a profuse apology, and Ángel telling her that he wouldn't even ask for her forgiveness because he knew he wasn't worthy of it. He explained that he had never wanted to join Emiliano's gang – he was the cousin of one of the other men (Paquito) and earned some extra money driving him around from time to time. He was a driver on the night that the girls were abducted, and said that if he had known what was going to happen he never would have taken the job. Ángel apologized again, and said he had tried to make life in the basement a little bit more bearable for the girls. His letter declared that he knew his motivations and his actions didn't excuse what he had done – he was just as guilty as the rest of the men – but he hoped that one day Amy could find it in her heart to maybe not forgive him but at least not hate him.

He explained that after all of the girls were finally released and the other members of Emiliano's gang relaxed a little bit, Ángel and Davíd made a run for it. They took the money that they were given for their role in the kidnapping – it wasn't much, since Emiliano didn't deem them 'key players' – and escaped under cover of darkness. They travelled north for six weeks, steering clear of main roads and areas known for being strongholds of Emiliano's former cartel. They only stopped long enough to sleep and eat, and on one occasion to mail a letter. They sent the anonymous note to the American Consulate in Acapulco, detailing who had been involved in the kidnapping and where they could be found. Ángel told Amy that he had made sure to include facts about her time in the basement that only an insider could know, so that the police would believe it.

The letter then went on to say that the two young men had made it across the border and were living or, rather, hiding in the United States. There was no return address, but the letter was postmarked from a town just south of Tucson, Arizona. Amy was not a fan of illegal immigration in any way, but a part of her was glad that the two had made it safely across the border. In her mind, they were more like refugees than illegal immigrants. And they probably had a decent case to make for refugee status, given the contents of Ángel's letter. He was Paquito's cousin – their fathers were brothers – so Ángel's father was safe for the time being. But Emiliano had Ángel's mother killed, along with his mother's sister and her children. All as retribution for Ángel's betrayal. Davíd had gotten off easily . . . the only family he had left was a murderous father and the uncle who sold him into cartel slavery, so their deaths were actually more of a bonus for Davíd.

Amy hoped that Ángel and Davíd were doing well wherever they were in the United States, and genuinely hoped they wouldn't be caught and deported back to Mexico, because she knew that they would be dead men walking down there. They might be dead men walking in America too, depending on how many contacts Emiliano still had with his former cartel. But at least they had a chance of surviving in the U.S. It was ridiculous, Amy acknowledged, to wish well upon any of the men involved in her kidnapping. Perhaps it was Stockholm Syndrome or something like that, but those two weren't kidnappers in her mind. They were Ángel and his friend Davíd, the only two men who had been even remotely nice to her while she was held hostage. She hadn't forgiven them for participating in the kidnapping – Amy felt certain that she never would. But, after reading the letter, she could now understand their actions a little bit better. We all make decisions that we think are a good idea at the time or don't think will be that big of a deal, and then they end up changing the entire trajectory of our lives. It didn't excuse what Ángel and Davíd had done, and it certainly didn't lessen the impact on their victims, but there it was anyway.

Amy had a pretty good idea what Dr. Vilsek would say if she told her all of that, which was why she hadn't told her. And why she had just told a bold-faced lie to Lynn Patterson. The official story was that she didn't know how the kidnappers were caught, and she was sticking to it.

Oblivious to the thoughts running through Amy's head, Lynn simply accepted the young woman's answer, nodded her head, and smiled. "We're going to take another quick break, but stick around because when we return I'll have some tough questions for Amy here to answer."

FIFTY-EIGHT

The award-winning journalist wasn't lying when she said she had tough questions planned. She also didn't waste any time, jumping right in as soon as the 'commercial break' ended.

"You've said previously that one of your favorite authors is T.S. Eliot. You even quoted him while we were in the basement of the house where you were held." Lynn paused and Amy nodded her head in agreement. "I'm also a fan of Eliot. One of his quotes that I find most intriguing is 'you do not know what hope is until you have lost it.' While you were held captive, did you ever lose hope?"

Amy's first reaction to the question was a smile – a defensive mechanism meant to give her time to formulate an answer in her mind and to shield her actual emotions. "Not wasting any time getting to the tough questions, are we?" Amy asked as she issued a short, nervous laugh. "To answer your question: yes and no. Were there times when I thought I'd never see my family again? That I'd die right there in that God-forsaken basement? Yes. But," she added, "I never lost the big hope – the hope that, when it was all said and done, things would work out for the best. Whether that was safe and sound with my family back home or watching down on them from Heaven, I never lost hope that I would be okay."

"That's a fairly broad description of 'okay,'" Lynn responded. "Most people wouldn't include dying as things working out for the best."

"I know," was Amy's only reply. Left unsaid, though, was the ending to the sentence that everyone who knew Amy or had gotten to know her while watching the interview already acknowledged: she wasn't like most people.

"Now you've already admitted to going through a lot of therapy to help you deal with the emotions of what you experienced here," Lynn continued, changing the subject slightly. Amy nodded her head in agreement. "Taking that into account, and just your own personal reflections, how do you think you made it through that time? Again, a lot of people would have cracked. A lot of people would have lost the big hope, as you put it. But you seem to be well-adjusted, composed, poised for success in the future. How do you think you did it?"

Amy knew going into the interview that she would be asked some variation of this question. In some ways it was easy to answer, since she could revert to answers contrived from hours of therapy and countless self-improvement and empowerment books that Dr. Vilsek had recommended to her. But, on the other hand, it was the hardest question to answer. Because it required her to reflect deep into her own soul about what made her tick. For that was really what Lynn was asking. 'How are you different? What makes you strong enough to rejoin the public world when so many who have experienced what you have experienced cannot?'

Taking a deep breath, Amy began her explanation of herself to the world. "I think it is several things. I think a not insignificant part of it is the two periods of time that I was unconscious. Like I said earlier, opportunistic lack of consciousness was a recurring theme. So I can't remember the taxi driver execution, I didn't see one of the girls get raped as a warning to the rest of us to behave, and I was knocked out for the most gruesome parts of the gang rape. Because while I know what happened, I don't have to deal with the tiny details of it lingering in my mind. I don't close my eyes and see those things happening. So that helps," Amy said with a sigh. "I've also had a few therapists suggest that I'm stress-resistant. Studies have shown that some people are just wired differently in that they can handle stress better than others. Maybe that's me . . . I don't know."

"Do you think you're stress-resistant?" interrupted Lynn.

"I don't know. Six months ago I would've said no. Actually, to be honest, six months ago I would've stared off into space when you asked me anything. So my family, the people who have been with me during this entire recovery process, would probably say no. But maybe one part of being stress-resistant is the ability to bounce back . . . I've been to the dark place but I was able to come back out of it. I dunno," Amy said as she sighed, then reached out and took another sip of water from the glass on the small table in front of her. Placing the glass back down, Amy continued, "I do know one thing for sure. I never would've survived what happened if not for my faith."

The tone in Amy's voice shifted, and she now spoke with a passion and conviction that had been lacking in her previous, matter-of-fact statements. "Prayer, faith, and hope are a package deal for me. And they got me through my time in Mexico. But with faith also comes duty. And I had a duty to live according to the principles of my faith, which meant not giving in to the kidnappers' demands. Don't get me wrong," Amy said, holding up her hands in front of her, "I don't blame the other girls for doing what they did. They were offered freedom and they made the deal. A lot of people, probably most people, would also make the deal. But I couldn't. And I know that the same religious convictions that gave me the courage to make it through that time also gave me the courage to say no."

The reporter sitting across from Amy simply nodded her head, amazed once again by the poise and inner strength and, yes, conviction of the young woman in front of her. Lynn didn't want to ask this next question, but she knew she had to.

"Does that mean you were ready to die? I mean, what I'm asking is, when the men came back into the room and the girls began to line up and do what they did, knowing that you were going to say no, did you think you would make it out of there alive?"

Amy paused, breathing deeply as she contemplated what Lynn had just asked her. Unlike the previous question, she hadn't prepared for this one ahead of time. Amy squirmed in her seat and readjusted her shirt, trying to stall a little bit.

"Was I ready to die?" Amy repeated Lynn's first version of the question, still stalling. "No. I think a bigger question that goes hand in hand with that is if I was afraid to die. And to answer that I'd say that there is a difference between not wanting something to happen and being afraid of it." The pretty blonde woman then took another deep breath before tackling the bear in front of her. "Did I think I would make it out alive? I don't know. No, that's not true. I thought that the odds were that I would die. I knew that. As each girl stepped forward and the sick bastards – oh, sorry . . . the bad guys – did what they did, getting closer and closer to my turn, I prayed a sort of Last Rites prayer. I closed my eyes and crossed myself and asked God to please protect me, but if that wasn't in the cards then thank You for a great life on Earth and please let St. Peter know that I'm on my way and my name is in the Book."

The final words of Amy's answer caught in her throat and when she looked around she saw that she wasn't the only one affected by her statement. There wasn't a dry eye in the room, with her mother the most visibly affected, sobbing nearly uncontrollably as Amy's also tearful father held his wife closely, partly to comfort her and partly to help her remain standing. Amy knew this part of the interview was harder on her parents than it was on her – she had said or thought all of these things before, but it was her parents' first exposure to the true depths of their daughter's pain.

As Lynn wiped tears from her eyes, using a tissue from the box that was supposed to have been for Amy, all that the supposedly tough, seasoned reporter could bring herself to say was: "thank you, Amy. Thank you for sharing with us and letting us hopefully learn from your experiences."

Lynn then turned to directly face the camera beside her. "Ladies and gentlemen, I hope you realize what an incredible interview you have just witnessed. I've been in this business a long time; I've interviewed kings and dictators, business magnates and beauty queens. But this young woman, this Amy Millhouse, is special. I count myself lucky to have spent these past several days with her, and to have brought her story to you. God Bless Amy and her family, and God Bless you all. From Acapulco, Mexico, I'm Lynn Patterson. Goodnight."

EPILOGUE

FIFTY-NINE

The headline above her picture on the front cover of *Time* magazine was a bit much for Amy's liking. "Amy Murphy – Superwoman" was the caption chosen by the magazine's editors that had sent her publicity team into a frenzy, fielding calls from around the country and the world asking if the first term governor was implicitly announcing her bid for the presidency. "No, we didn't pick the headline, the magazine did" had been the standard answer given, but excitement still hung in the air of the Governor's Mansion as everyone from the Chief of Staff to the newspaper delivery boy sensed that the mansion's current occupant might one day soon be living in a much more visible, much more white executive house.

Twenty years after the broadcast of her exclusive interview had earned Amy rave reviews and Lynn Patterson an Emmy Award, few people consistently remembered that 'Amy Murphy, political star' had once been 'Amy Millhouse, kidnapping victim.' Her well-laid plans to be a stay-at-home mom also went by the wayside a long time ago when Amy was first elected as president of the Parent Teacher Association at her children's school. From there she quickly moved to school board member, county commission CEO, state senator, and now governor. Her rise through the political ranks was as seamless as it was unexpected, with no one in the political establishment of the state having any idea who she was ten years earlier.

****

At first glance, and certainly now in the glossy pages of the magazine feature, Amy's life appeared to be perfect. She had been married for over sixteen years to a man named Paul Murphy whose Black Irish features contrasted beautifully with Amy's blonde hair and whose height – 6'3" when standing upright – made Amy feel less self-conscious about being tall herself. Amy's mother often commented about how Paul was 'a good man' – the ultimate compliment in her very Southern sub-culture. It was easier to earn the label of 'good husband,' 'good father,' or even 'good person.'

But to be consistently named a 'good man' encompassed the husband, father, and person categories plus a little something extra that tied all of the other components together. No one could quite put a finger on it, but knew it when they saw it.

In Paul's case, the X-factor was probably the way he handled the still-delicate memories of what had happened to Amy in Mexico. Paul knew what the public knew and what Amy and her family had told him over the years, which included the pregnancy and the baby she had given up for adoption. Amy could still vividly remember when she told Paul the whole story. They were married on a Saturday night and went straight from the reception to the airport to catch their honeymoon flight to the Cayman Islands. The next day, after a long and lazy morning, Paul had walked down the street from the hotel to a little store that sold sunscreen, since they had forgotten to pack theirs. When he returned to their hotel room, all smiles and talking about what a beautiful day it was, Amy was sitting on the bed with tears streaming down her face. She then proceeded to tell him about the pregnancy and the adoption, stopping seemingly every five seconds to apologize again for not telling him sooner. He had taken it all in, held her close while she cried, and told her he would always love her, no matter what happened in the past or the future. They were the exact words Amy had needed to hear and were delivered in exactly the right fashion. And, to Paul's credit and Amy's relief, they had never mentioned it again.

The couple's three sons were featured prominently in the magazine article, with their handsome features leading several online gossip columnists to dub the Murphy's "America's New Camelot," a reference to the title formerly reserved for the Kennedy family. The boys all looked like miniature versions of their father, with dark brown, nearly black wavy hair and beautiful, caramel-colored eyes.

Paul, Jr., 13, was a stereotypical oldest child and overachiever. Paul, Jr. was also the athlete of the group and loved playing baseball and basketball. In fact, any sport involving throwing, catching, or shooting was sure to catch Paul, Jr.'s attention. He had even started playing little league lacrosse recently, a sport which Amy and her husband knew little about but that he seemed to enjoy and be a natural. Paul, Jr. didn't have his parent's academic talents, but always managed a solid B average on his report cards. He was a bright kid, but sports and his friends were simply much more interesting than school. His parents could only imagine how it would be once girls entered the picture. They managed to keep their oldest son on track academically by threatening to bench him in games if he didn't put enough focus and effort into his studies.

LJ, short for "Little Jack," was named after Amy's father. At eleven years old he was already taller than his older brother, which irked Paul, Jr. to no end. Unlike his athletic older brother, however, LJ preferred music and was the lead guitarist in a band that he and his friends started. He had also inherited his mother's strong religious convictions and was looking forward to entering middle school the next year so he would be old enough to join their church's worship band. LJ's friends called him "Rev," and Amy had a sneaking suspicion that her middle son would end up being a preacher one day.

Graham, at age eight, was the youngest of the boys and definitely relished the attention that came with being the baby of the family. He was also a fascinating combination of his parents, having inherited his mother's serious, reflective side and his father's innate curiosity and knack for computers. Paul hoped that one day his youngest boy might want to take over the family private investigations business, but Amy was quick to caution her husband not to place too much pressure on Graham. She knew all too well what it was like to grow up with a father who was very open about his desire to have his child take over the family business, and she didn't want Graham to feel like his career options were limited in any way. The boy's serious nature and interest in computers led many outside observers to place him in the 'nerd' category, but luckily he was blessed with his father's linebacker build and two older brothers who never hesitated to defend the youngest member of the Murphy clan.

Amy loved her family dearly and considered herself very blessed to have such a wonderful husband and three happy, healthy sons. Amy joked that she was outnumbered by all the men in the house, and just last year when the family got a Saint Bernard puppy from a local breeder, Amy laughed and told people that they had to get a girl dog to balance out the hormone levels in their home. The boys thought it was funny; Paul a little less so, since he knew when Amy made the joke that she was thinking about the daughter she had and gave away.

Just last night, hours before the *Time* story hit the newsstands, Amy had dreamt about Mexico. She hadn't had a dream like that in nearly ten years – a vivid, nightmarish re-creation of the time she spent as a hostage in that basement outside of Acapulco. Amy was shaking and covered in sweat when she woke up in the middle of the night, and she wasn't able to get back to sleep for well over an hour. The dream was so sudden, so unexpected, so *real* that Amy had seriously considered calling up her old therapist, Dr. Vilsek, to talk about it. She didn't make the call, though, because she knew that the publicity from the magazine cover would bring ever-heightening scrutiny to what she did and the people she interacted with. The last thing she wanted was for someone to hack into her phone records, discover the call to Dr. Vilsek, and publish a story about how Governor Murphy was mentally or emotionally unstable. Amy didn't make a secret of her past, but she didn't advertise it either. She knew, however, that a story about her resuming therapy would be seen as a weakness that her political opponents could exploit.

****

Amy was still glancing through the magazine article that morning when an aide came into her well-appointed office in the Governor's Mansion and told her that everyone was assembled downstairs for the reception. Amy's office was recognizing and honoring the women's soccer team from a local college that had just won its first-ever conference championship. The newly-minted Governor Murphy quickly found that events like these were some of her favorite parts of being the state's chief executive, since they provided a needed respite from the serious, often tedious work of running one of the nation's fastest-growing states.

Amy nodded her head in acknowledgment of the staff member's announcement and slowly rose from behind her desk, careful to not step on the oversized Saint Bernard sleeping at her feet. Dressed in a crisp, neatly tailored gray pantsuit and red blouse, the tall, slender woman who was now in her early forties looked every inch of the powerful, capable politician that the magazine article portrayed her to be. Her favorite stylist ensured that Amy's shoulder-length blonde hair had not turned gray, and Amy was unashamed to admit that she received occasional Botox injections in order to smooth out the wrinkles around her eyes. She knew full well the double standard regarding youth and appearance that applied to men and women in politics, and the image consultant that Amy had hired during her gubernatorial campaign was considered the best in the business. She quickly ran a lint brush over her suit to remove any lingering dog hair and then walked toward the door.

The governor's four-inch Christian Louboutin heels click-clacked loudly on the hardwood flooring of the Governor's Mansion as she made her way down the main stairs and through the foyer to the large and ornate first-floor living room that was often used for receptions like the one today. Even though she enjoyed these events, Amy had a very busy afternoon scheduled and her mind was focused on several meetings taking place later that day, including budget negotiations with members of the state legislature and essentially a sales pitch to a corporation that was considering bringing a textile factory and 800 jobs to the state. Amy had campaigned on fiscal responsibility and economic growth, and she knew that persuading this company to relocate would be key in helping her state continue its best-in-the-nation economic performance.

She was admittedly distracted, then, as she walked into the room full of 18- to 22-year-old soccer players, their coaches, and representatives from the university. Amy took her place in the center of the group for a picture, and then stayed put as the photographer began taking individual pictures with the governor and each player and coach. Amy smiled politely and shook hands with each girl, even posing in silly positions with the goofier, more outgoing players. All the while, however, Amy's mind was still more attuned to her meetings that afternoon than the people she was surrounded by now. Over the years, through motherhood and her various other political offices, Amy had gotten very good at feigning happiness and interest while simultaneously doing mental problem-solving. One of the boys would be telling a story about his friends, and Amy would listen enough to retain the important details while at the same time planning out that week's dinner menu. Or a staffer would recount the details of his conversation with a reporter while Amy decided how best to address an issue that would come up in her next meeting. More than intelligence, experience, or any other skill, Amy was convinced that multi-tasking was the most important tool in a politician's toolbox. Now, as Amy continued to 'say cheese!' for pictures and shake hands with her visitors, she silently practiced her miniature speech on why her state would be the best location for the company's new factory.

One of the girls waiting for her picture stepped up next to Governor Murphy and asked if they could both 'do a thumbs up' in the photo. Amy was happy to oblige, but as she turned her head and glanced down the line of players waiting to get their picture taken, all of the multi-tasking in Amy's head immediately stopped. The room seemed to go quiet as well, and the only thing Amy could see or hear was the tall blonde girl still in line, three spots away from her turn. Amy tried to focus on the remaining pictures, making a thumbs up sign with the one girl and asking the name and position of the next two, but all the while she couldn't help glancing sideways at the young woman who was slowly moving closer. Even before the object of the governor's attention stepped up next to her for a picture, Amy knew who she was. The handshake they shared simply confirmed it: the young woman standing beside Amy was her daughter.

SIXTY

Amy tried valiantly to hide the feelings of complete shock that were coursing through her mind and body. *Oh my God*, she kept thinking as she turned to face the cameraman for the picture with this miniature version of herself. The resemblance was truly uncanny: the same blonde hair, the same blue eyes. The same tall and lanky build. The girl's complexion was a shade or two darker than Amy's, but aside from that they were the same person. And everyone in the room could see it.

Amy laughed to try and diffuse some of the tension in her mind. People in the room who were paying attention and noticed the similarities between the two women were more amused than anything else, since they had no reason to suspect what Amy was convinced was the truth. *They don't know anything*, Amy reminded herself. *Calm down. Deep breaths. Calm down.*

Trying to take control of the situation, Amy laughed again and broke the ice: "Well, they say everybody has a twin out there somewhere!"

The room filled with laughter at her remark, but on the inside Amy was still shaking. It was her. This beautiful, confident woman who introduced herself as the team captain, Megan Hunter. This was the same girl that Amy had given birth to twenty-one years earlier. It didn't matter that Amy had never seen her baby before the doctor took her away. Instinctively, at the deepest gut level, Amy just knew.

****

When the individual pictures were finally finished and the small reception began, Governor Murphy headed over to where Megan was standing. She kept telling herself to take deep breaths and remain calm, but that was nearly impossible given the rush of emotions she was feeling. Amy had never wanted to meet her daughter. She didn't want to disrupt the girl's life in any way, and, when Amy was completely honest with herself, she admitted that she also didn't want to have to deal with the emotional impact that reliving that part of her life would cause. But now that the young woman was here, in her house, those feelings couldn't be avoided. Surprise at meeting the girl. — Excitement. — Sadness. — Guilt that she'd missed so much of the young woman's life. — Pain at the memories of the kidnapping that necessarily accompanied any thought of her daughter. — Parental protectiveness about not letting this Megan Hunter find out the truth about her biological father, whichever kidnapper he was.

There was also the tiniest twinge of uncertainty that maybe it wasn't really her. It couldn't be. Could it? But more than anything, Amy just wanted to talk to her. Stand near her. Soak up every second of this extremely rare and completely unexpected opportunity.

Amy wanted to ask this girl, this Megan, *her* Megan, a million questions, but she knew she had to play it cool. She needed to deliver a performance worthy of an Academy Award in order to convince everyone that she didn't care anything about this girl beyond thinking it was quirky and interesting that they looked so much alike. After all, only seven people in the world knew about that first pregnancy of Amy's. Her parents and her brother, since they had been there to nurse her through the ordeal. Paul, her husband. Dr. Vilsek, of course, and her trusted OB-GYN. The same doctor who had delivered the baby girl twenty-one years ago and driven her to a fire station an hour away was the one who delivered Amy's three sons. Those six people, plus Amy, knew her deepest, darkest secret. No one else, not even her long-time chief of staff, Dan, who she otherwise trusted with her life. And that's the way it needed to stay.

Like any public figure facing a tough press conference or any parent who has had a rough day and then must pretend nothing is wrong around the kids, Amy took a deep breath, flashed her patented smile, and walked up to Megan, placing her hand lightly on the girl's shoulder and declaring jovially, "so there you are, long lost twin!"

SIXTY-ONE

The room filled with laughter once again and Amy felt a rush of relief that the hurricane of emotions inside her didn't appear to be showing on the outside. It was a skill she had mastered following the kidnapping – masking her emotions to spare her parents the pain. Dr. Vilsek had helped cure Amy of that tendency to repress, but the skill remained and was extremely useful today.

Amy didn't notice that her husband had slipped quietly into the back of the room and was watching her intently. Paul Murphy was Amy's first and only love, her husband of sixteen years who had swept her off her feet after he first saw her in her father's office. Amy was there to have lunch with her dad, something they tried to do at least once a month, and Paul was in the office meeting with one of Mr. Millhouse's partners about his company's contract with the firm. A naturally curious person, Paul had put that and his internet and computer skills to good use by starting his own private investigation company. He usually worked with local police departments and prosecutors' offices, but he was starting to branch out into defense-side work as well. Paul had seen the striking blonde enter the reception area through a window in the partner's office and proceeded to lose all train of thought, causing the partner he was meeting with to laugh and say "that's Amy, Jack Millhouse's daughter. I'm pretty sure she's single, in case you were wondering."

Paul just shook his head and turned his attention back to the meeting, but when he was still thinking about her three days later, he got up the nerve to call the law firm in search of Amy's phone number. The attorney he was working with didn't have it, but the firm's long-serving, grandmotherly receptionist did and had been more than happy to help set up Amy with 'that nice young investigator boy.' Paul called Amy the same afternoon, asked her out to dinner for that Friday night, and they were married less than a year later. Ever since Amy had been elected governor, Paul had turned over management of his now-thriving investigations business to the company's vice president and spent his days helping raise the couple's children and crusading on a wide variety of issues, namely fatherhood and men's health.

One of Paul's aides had come into his office and told him that he needed to drop by the soccer team reception because there was a girl on the team that looked exactly like the governor. Paul had initially brushed off the aide, dismissing it without thought, but then stopped the young man as he was about to exit the room. "Which team did you say it was? High school?"

"No, college. Conference champions."

The thought that instantly jumped into Paul's head wasn't a particularly pleasant one. What if this girl was his wife's daughter? The one she had given up for adoption? What if people figured it out and Amy's secret was uncovered? *The timing fits*, thought Paul, *since the girl would be in college by now. But in college in this state? And in the Governor's Mansion right now?* Paul tried not to let his face reveal his thoughts.

"Hmm, yeah, maybe I'll go check it out," Paul said nonchalantly as he rose from his chair and walked over to the coat rack to put on his suit jacket. "You said she looks just like my wife?"

"Identical," came the aide's reply.

As Paul made the short walk from his second floor office to the first floor reception area, he couldn't shake the feeling that this look-alike that the house and office staffs were buzzing about was in fact his wife's long-lost daughter. It had never bothered him that Amy had another child that she had given up for adoption – he could hardly blame her for being raped, after all. In fact, he rarely ever thought about it. Every once in a while someone would remark about them only having sons, and Paul could hear the slightest twinge in Amy's voice as she laughed politely and said "yep, just me and my boys."

Amy had told him about the rape and the baby while on their honeymoon. Not exactly a romantic topic, but his wife, the ever-cautious daughter of a lawyer, didn't want to tell him her deepest, darkest secret until after they were officially married. And he understood that. He also understood her decision to give up the baby for adoption and to never tell anyone about it – even though, on the rare occasions when he did think about the child, it bothered him just in the slightest that there were some details from the kidnapping that Amy still wouldn't share with him. She said they weren't important, and the few times he had actually pressed her about it, Amy had emphatically declared that she couldn't 'go there again,' before bursting into tears.

****

When Paul arrived in the large reception room, the group had just finished taking their individual pictures. He watched as his wife began to cross the room and followed her gaze to the tall blonde chatting happily with a few of her coaches and teammates. The resemblance between Amy and the girl was indeed striking – Paul could see why it had caused such a stir with the staff. Same height; same build. The younger woman's skin was a few shades darker than Amy's, but that was undoubtedly due to the darker features of the kidnappers. Paul shuddered at that thought. It made him physically ill to think of his wonderful, beautiful wife being violated in that way by those men.

Paul continued to watch as Amy, the proud, accomplished governor, strode across the room. He saw the momentary pause, barely visible even to her husband of sixteen years. Paul always said that if Amy had wanted to, she could've been an incredible actress. And she was giving an Oscar-worthy performance right now. As Amy finally arrived near the young woman, Paul began to cross the room. He knew Amy needed someone there, by her side, sending her strength and encouragement. He couldn't hear what Amy's opening line was to the group, but it was obviously funny since they all broke up in laughter.

Paul casually took his place beside his wife, laying a comforting hand on the small of Amy's back and kissing her cheek before turning to face the group, careful to avoid looking first at the girl who, close up, was a dead ringer for Amy.

"Hey darlin'," Amy said with a smile. "Everyone, this is my husband, Paul. Honey, these are some members of the Lady Wolverines' soccer team from Calumet College."

Paul went around the half circle of people, right to left, shaking hands with each of them but all the while keeping his hand on Amy's back, a gesture of support that he knew from experience she appreciated. After what seemed like a lifetime, he finally turned to the girl standing on the other side of Amy. "Hi there. You must be the new body double that the state patrol hired."

As the group laughed at her husband's remark on the obvious resemblance between the governor and the co-ed, Amy couldn't help but think how lucky she was to be married to Paul. She was more grateful than words could express for his presence at that moment, since people's focus would now at least be somewhat split between her and her husband, making it easier for Amy to hide her nerves.

Megan Hunter smiled as she shook the First Gentleman's hand and jokingly replied, "yes sir, that's me."

Paul then continued his efforts to keep attention on himself and off of his nervous wife. "It really is remarkable, the resemblance between you two."

The girl, having no reason to suspect anything beyond a quirky coincidence, and being somewhat used to the comparison from images of the governor on the news, merely nodded her head and smiled some more. Her parents had never told her she was adopted, and her blonde hair matched that of her father before he went prematurely bald, so she didn't think anything of the similarities between her and Amy Murphy. Even her blue eyes compared to her parents' brown ones could be easily explained by simple recessive-trait genetics. For her, this was just a cool moment and a guaranteed winner at next year's Halloween costume contest.

At that point, mercifully, Amy's chief-of-staff, Dan, walked into the room and signaled that the governor's next appointment had arrived. Amy was happy for the distraction but also sad to have to go so soon, since she knew she would never get the chance to see her daughter again. She made a point to shake everyone in the circle's hand again, pausing just a millisecond when she reached Megan. That connection, that touch, sent chills up Amy's spine simultaneously with a warm relief that the girl was okay.

This chance meeting could have gone so much differently. Just last week Amy had toured the new women's state correctional facility, and she'd be lying if she said the thought hadn't crossed her mind that her daughter might be one of its prisoners. But this, to meet her like this, confirmed to Amy that she had done the right thing. The girl, Megan, was thriving. She was happy, healthy, smart, well-spoken, and well-mannered. Everything that Amy had hoped and prayed for the girl when she gave her up for a chance at a better life.

SIXTY-TWO

As soon as Amy left the soccer team reception, she was shuttled into the budget meeting with state legislators, followed by a senior staff meeting, several phone calls, and then the all-important talk with the CEO of the company thinking of building a factory in Amy's state. It was the kind of day that would normally leave her head spinning and her high-heel clad feet aching, but today Amy was thrilled to have such a busy schedule. It meant that she didn't have time to stop and really think about what had happened that morning. Even though the young Megan Hunter was constantly on her mind.

Amy didn't see her husband Paul until late that night, after the boys had all gone to sleep and Amy finished reviewing some papers for her meetings the next morning. They had had to 'divide and conquer' their parenting duties that night, with Paul attending their oldest son's lacrosse banquet and Amy sitting front row for Graham's end-of-semester school play. Much to LJ's delight, he had been allowed to stay home 'alone' that evening. At eleven years old and with the house full of staff and surrounded by heavily armed state troopers, Governor and Paul Murphy didn't see a problem with it.

It was nearing midnight when Amy finally walked into their bedroom. Paul was still awake, sitting up in bed reading a book about the long-term effects of growing up with an absentee father. Amy greatly admired how her husband had thrown himself into his work as 'First Gentleman,' especially since she knew how much he enjoyed his investigations business and how hard it had been to turn over the reins to his vice president.

Amy walked into the large closet beside their bathroom and began changing out of the suit she had been wearing since 7am that morning. As she kicked off her heels and shimmied out of the pantsuit, replacing it with her favorite cotton pajamas, she called out down the short hallway to Paul.

"Hey honey?"

"Yes?" Paul answered. He too was exhausted after a long day, but he always tried to stay awake until Amy came to bed. He didn't always succeed, and more than a few times Amy had to remove a book from his chest and turn off the light after he fell asleep waiting for her. But he knew that his wife appreciated being able to see and talk to him at the end of the day, even if only for a few minutes. And tonight he had made an extra effort to stay awake, since he knew Amy would want to talk about what happened that morning with the team from Calumet College.

"You know the girl at the soccer reception? The one who looked like me?" Amy asked as she walked back into the room and climbed into bed beside Paul.

"Mmm hmm," Paul answered, nodding his head as he removed his reading glasses and placed them and his book on the nightstand beside the bed. "What about her?"

"I think you know what about her," Amy replied.

"You think she's the baby you gave up for adoption?" Paul asked, conscious that this was the first time he had truly spoken openly about the topic with Amy since their honeymoon.

"I do," Amy said, nodding her head as tears began to fill her eyes. "There was just something about her, Paul. I just knew."

Paul Murphy slid over and put his arms around his wife as she cried, much like his father-in-law Jack Millhouse had done so many years before when Amy's mother cried during the kidnapping. "It might have been her," Paul replied, careful to not shoot down Amy's belief while at the same time recognizing how unlikely it was that the baby his wife had given up for adoption twenty-one years ago had miraculously shown up in their house this morning as a member of a conference champion soccer team.

"I want to know for sure. I mean, I know *in here*," Amy said, pointing to her heart. "But I want to know up here too," she declared, motioning then towards her head.

****

Paul sighed in response to his wife's comment. "I had a feeling you might say that." While most people's response might have been that it was impossible to know for sure, Paul knew that wasn't true. It was possible. He had spent nearly half his life building a business that centered around discovering information that people didn't want discovered. "Sweetheart, you know I shouldn't do that," Paul said as he continued to envelope Amy in a bear hug. "I turned everything in the company over to Jared after we won the election. I don't even have keys to the office anymore. And I can't exactly call up my former vice president, who is coincidentally also one of my best friends, and ask him to look into someone's life without him wondering why."

Amy knew her husband was right. The man running Murphy Investigations now, Jared Smith, was even more naturally curious than Paul. Any request to check up on some cute young college co-ed would undoubtedly only lead to trouble. "Isn't there any other way to run a background check on her?"

"I'm afraid not," Paul responded, and the disappointment in his voice was genuine. He too wanted to know more about the young woman who looked exactly like every college picture he had ever seen of Amy. "You were okay with not knowing where the girl was or what she was doing until this morning. You'll just have to go back to being okay with it."

"Easier said than done," Amy responded as she reached over and turned off the lamp beside the bed. "Easier said than done."

SIXTY-THREE

Paul Murphy had already made up his mind about calling his old company even before he talked to his wife the night before. But he didn't want Amy to get her hopes up in case the project failed. So he told her he wasn't going to contact Jared, even though it was the first thing on his to-do list this morning.

Paul made the call using his cell phone, not wanting anything to trace back to the official, tax-payer funded phone lines in the Governor's Mansion. There technically wasn't anything wrong with what he was doing, but he knew that if the media got hold of the story they would spin it to say that Paul and by implication Amy were using their ties to a private investigations business to check up on their political enemies. A ridiculous charge, Paul knew, but one that could nonetheless ruin his wife's career.

Jared Smith answered the phone for his direct line on the second ring. "Well hey there, Mr. First Gentleman," he said with a grin, having recognized Paul's phone number on the caller ID. "How's it goin', buddy?" Paul had known Jared since college, and even though the other man had technically been his subordinate for over a decade, the two still managed to remain great friends.

"Are you busy?" Paul asked to open the conversation. "I can call back later if you are."

"Nah, man, never too busy for you," Jared responded, his Southern California roots evident in his still noticeable surfer-boy accent. "What's up?" He could tell that his former boss was nervous about something, and naturally wanted to know what he could do to help.

"Well," Paul began, rising from his office chair and pacing the floor as he spoke. "I have a favor to ask. And I feel terrible about asking, because I know I promised that as long as Amy was Governor, I'd only use the resources of the company in an above-board, public way."

The way his friend was talking made Jared nervous, and he knew Paul must really want the information if he was willing to go back on his promise to steer clear of his old company for as long as

Amy was in office. "What's wrong, Paul?" Jared asked, cutting straight to the point.

"Nothing, nothing," Paul answered quickly, almost too quickly for Jared's liking. "Amy and I are just really curious about somebody and were hoping you could look them up for us. That's all."

There was very clearly a missing element to Paul's story, but Jared figured that the odds were he would find out what it was in the course of his investigation. "Sure, no problem. I'd be happy to do it." One of the perks of running a private investigations business was that, any time you were curious about somebody, you could easily run a computer search using the company's advanced technology. Jared and Paul had done so countless times before, and the company's new CEO didn't see anything wrong with it now. In his mind it was nothing more than a really advanced Google search. "Who is it?"

"A girl named Megan Hunter," Paul answered, spelling out the name. "She plays soccer for the Lady Wolverines at Calumet College." Wanting to justify his request, Paul then gave a little more background. "The team won their conference championship and came to the Governor's Mansion yesterday for a photo op and reception. This girl, Megan Hunter, was the spitting image of Amy. It was crazy. So we were just curious about who she is." Then, hoping to throw Jared off the trail, Paul added: "maybe they're distant cousins or something like that."

"Ok, so you're not looking for anything too in-depth. Just a standard software search," responded Jared. "Shouldn't take too long. You want me to email you the results or call?"

"Probably better to just call my cell. Thanks, dude. I owe you one."

"Anytime," Jared said before hanging up the phone.

****

It wasn't until late that afternoon that Jared called his former boss with the results of his search on Megan Hunter. He hadn't really found anything interesting, although he did agree that the girl in the pictures looked exactly like Paul's wife. One thing that had triggered his attention was that the girl was adopted, and just for the heck of it, on a hunch, Jared had even run a search of hospital records around the time the girl was born to see if there was any overlap between Amy and Megan. But just like everyone else, he had no reason to suspect that this Megan Hunter had any biological connection to Amy Millhouse Murphy. So when he found nothing from the hospitals, he figured the adoption was just a coincidence.

Paul had been waiting for Jared's call all day, and when his cell phone finally rang just before four o'clock, Paul quickly excused himself from the meeting he was having with his staff and walked outside onto the small balcony off his office. "Hey Jared."

"Hey man," came the response from the other end of the line. "I ran the search for you. Not much came up, but I can give you a quick overview of what I found." Paul then listened intently as Jared ran through a list of information about the young woman that Amy thought might be her daughter. He didn't want to write anything down, but was careful to keep detailed mental notes of everything that his friend was saying so he could relay the information to Amy. When Jared finished talking, Paul thanked him profusely before promising to get together sometime soon to catch up. The state's first gentleman then hung up the phone, convinced that his wife the governor had been correct: barring a very strange set of coincidences, the girl they had met the day before was indeed Amy's biological daughter.

SIXTY-FOUR

Paul knew that his wife's schedule that day was less hectic than the one before, so he decided to go deliver the news to her right then instead of waiting until later that night. He made the short journey from his office to the other end of the second floor and entered the suite of offices that housed Amy's staff. "Hi Robin," he said brightly, smiling at the middle-aged woman who occupied the first desk in the office and consequently served as a traffic cop of sorts. "Is she in?"

Robin knew that the 'she' referred to the governor, since anyone else would be called by their first name. "She is. Just finished up a conference call actually. You can go on in."

Paul maneuvered his way through the desks and cubicles filled with staffers to reach the large oak door that separated his wife's work space from the rest of the area. Pausing only to issue a brief annunciating knock, Paul opened the door to enter Amy's large and stylish-yet-comfortable office.

Looking up from her desk, Amy was a bit surprised to see her husband there in the middle of the afternoon. It was a welcome surprise, though, and she politely dismissed the policy advisor who was in the room. "Hey honey. What brings you to this end of the house?"

Waiting for the staffer to leave the room, Paul then closed the door behind him and motioned for Amy to join him in sitting on the couch that lined one corner of the office. He couldn't help but smile as their lovable, goofy Saint Bernard, Macy, ambled over from behind Amy's desk and sat down in front of him for an ear rub. Macy was technically the family's dog, but it had been obvious from Day One that his wife was Macy's favorite.

Amy knew that whatever Paul had to say must be important if he wanted her to sit down for the news. "What is it?" she asked again.

Paul gave Macy one last pat on the head and then took a deep breath as he sat down on the opposite end of the couch from Amy, crossing one long leg over the other. "I called Jared this morning."

The announcement took Amy by surprise, since she had fully expected Paul to follow his declaration from the night before that he wouldn't contact anyone at his old company. "What did he f-find out?" she asked nervously, struggling to get the words out.

Paul then stood up and moved to sit next to Amy on the couch, taking her hand into his and resting his other arm behind her head on the back of the piece of furniture. "Well," he began slowly, "based on what Jared told me, it looks like you were right. All signs point to Megan Hunter being the girl you gave up for adoption."

"Oh my God," Amy whispered as tears filled her eyes and she used her free hand to cover her mouth. "I can't believe it. I mean, I can, but I can't," she mumbled incoherently.

"I know," said Paul softly, knowing how emotional this must be for his wife. "You never thought you'd see her. And then there she was."

"Tell me about her," Amy said, her request helping to brighten the look in her eyes from shock to curiosity.

"Jared ran a software search on her. Nothing really in-depth – just what we would normally be able to find out about a person at first glance." Amy nodded her head in understanding, since she was well-acquainted with the way that Paul's company conducted its investigations. "There wasn't much, to be honest," Paul continued. "Most of the information available was actually on her public player profile for the soccer team. She's 5'10". Was a junior this year. Plays center-mid for the Lady Wolverines and got first-team all-conference honors this year and last." Paul paused, looking over at his wife to see her reaction to the information. Amy had long since wiped away her tears and was now listening intently, soaking up the details like a sponge.

"What else? Isn't there usually a 'personal' section?" Amy asked.

"I was getting there," Paul said with a slight smile. Amy always had a way of cutting straight to the chase. She, more than most people, knew how precious every second was and hated beating around the bush or wasting time on anything.

"Her full name is Megan Patricia Hunter. Her parents are Dr. and Mrs. John Hunter. It says she's an only child and played soccer and basketball in high school. She's majoring in Spanish -" Paul stopped mid-sentence as Amy issued a noticeable gasp of surprise.

"Spanish. She's majoring in Spanish. Like me," Amy said. She couldn't quite believe it. But then again, there were a lot of things about the past day and a half that she couldn't believe. "Is that it? Did Jared find out anything else?"

"She's listed in the adoption records database." Paul knew that revelation would undoubtedly frighten Amy, since inquiring minds might try to tie the date of the adoption to the timing of Amy's kidnapping. "Don't worry," he said, squeezing Amy's hand more tightly in his own, "there's nothing in there aside from the fact that she was adopted. No hospital records, no nothing. Jared told me that the adoption is listed as sealed, but from what you've told me, even if someone somehow got it unsealed, the paperwork would probably still read 'biological mother unknown.'" Amy nodded her head in agreement, feeling a little bit better about her chances of keeping the pregnancy and adoption a secret.

"He also did a quick search on her parents," Paul continued. He saw the slight flinch in Amy's face as he said the word *parents*, but he knew better than to say anything about it and instead continued his recitation of what Jared had told him not fifteen minutes earlier. "Dr. John Hunter is an orthopedic surgeon, specializing in injuries to young athletes. His bio says that he met his wife when she was a nurse in the same hospital, but it doesn't look like she works outside the home anymore. He is listed as a deacon at Mt. Zion Methodist in their hometown." Paul then leaned back on the couch, his story complete. "And that's all Jared could find. He even ran a search for political affiliations or contributions, but that came up empty too. Sorry they aren't supporters," Paul quipped with a slight smile.

Amy gave a small grin in return, then got up from the couch and walked over to stand in front of the large French doors behind her desk. Paul could tell that she was processing what she had just heard, but for once he didn't know which direction her thoughts were headed. Was she happy to have the information? Sad that she now knew so much more but couldn't do anything with it? Paul's questions were answered though when Amy turned back around to face him, the tears that were glistening in her eyes contrasting with the broad smile on her face. "Thank you, Paul. I really needed to hear all of that."

Governor Amy Millhouse Murphy then pulled out the large leather chair in front of her and sat back down, reaching for a file folder on the top of her desk and preparing to resume her work. Paul breathed a deep sigh of relief, recognizing from his wife's actions and demeanor that finding out about her long-lost daughter had been a good thing, since it provided a measure of closure that Amy hadn't even known she was missing.

As her husband nodded his head in acknowledgement of her thanks and walked towards the door of her office to leave, it was Amy's turn to issue the sigh of relief. *That's done now*, Amy thought contentedly.

Time to move on.

Please consider writing a review on Amazon.com!

ONE

Joseph was fuming. Absolutely livid as he paced around the hardwood floors of his kitchen in his standard everyday attire of khaki slacks and a button-down shirt. "I should've won that award," the doctor hissed to no one in particular. The kitchen was empty except for him, as was the rest of the house. Joseph lived alone. He preferred it that way. Having someone else always underfoot was messy. Inconvenient. And, more than anything else, it got in the way of his research. "Research that deserved to win!"

The slender, well-dressed man in his mid-forties was yelling now, but he was angry enough to yell. All of his hard work, five years spent in his research lab working on a cure for malaria, and he had nothing to show for it. Sure, Joseph had created an excellent prototype for a vaccine and recently sold it to a large pharmaceutical company for several million dollars. But Joseph didn't care about the money. He wanted the fame. The respect. He wanted to be known not only in the science community but also the general public as the best infectious disease researcher alive. Joseph was the best. He knew he was the best. Now the rest of the world needed to know it too.

When he finished pacing, the bachelor doctor walked over to the island in the middle of his kitchen and pressed a security code into the keypad located just underneath the granite countertop. Seconds later, a hiss-pop sound let Joseph know that the secret door was unlocked. Swinging open what to an untrained eye was just the end of the kitchen's island, Joseph ducked his buzz cut, salt-and-pepper colored head and slowly descended the now visible stairs into his private research lab. Originally built as a safe room for his house, Joseph had long ago decided to use the bunker for the research projects that he didn't want anyone to know about. Financed by the money he made from selling drug prototypes to big pharmaceutical companies, Joseph had another small workspace set up on the second floor of his suburban home that other people were allowed to see, on the off chance he happened to have visitors. But this lab was special. This was Joseph's sanctuary. This was where he was working on the project that would force people to recognize just how brilliant he truly was.

It wasn't a new idea, really – the one that Joseph had to make a virus that could kill people. Doctors and researchers put together new viruses all the time. They called them recombinant viruses. Gene therapy techniques were based on the idea. All that was required was a vector (the viral capsid or shell) and the right arrangement of DNA or RNA. That combination of genes would then create proteins to fight against a patient's disease. When done correctly, miraculous things could happen, like new treatments for skin cancer, Parkinson's disease, and leukemia.

Or, as Joseph predicted, very dangerous things could happen. It was his plan to take the tried and true method of gene therapy to engineer a virus that would express a deadly protein. The virus would then be delivered to the body through blood transfusions, although Joseph was still figuring out the best way to get access to that much human blood and deliver it to hospitals. This entire project was a big challenge for him . . . the man who had spent the past several decades of his life focused only on helping patients and curing diseases now had to plot and plan and scheme for not only how to make a new, deadly virus but also how to avoid police detection in the process. It was thrilling, this new adventure of his.

As Joseph sat in his secret underground lab, working to find the right combination of vectors and genes to express the exact deadly protein that he wanted, he couldn't help but get excited about what was to come. Operation Respect, as he had labeled the enterprise, would take a lot of time and effort. Years, perhaps. *But it will also be fun*, he thought with excitement. *Exhausting, a little terrifying probably, but also really, really fun.*

****

A full year and a half passed without Joseph making any significant progress on his secret virus. A lesser man, a lesser doctor, might have gotten frustrated and given up. But Joseph had learned from a very young age how to be patient. His parents, a trauma surgeon and a socialite, hadn't been at all interested in raising their only child. Joseph was convinced that he was only born to satisfy his grandparents' desire for an heir. So he learned to be patient while waiting for his parents to notice him. Or his nannies to feed him. Or a teacher to walk by and let him out of the locker that he was inevitably shoved into at school. Yes, Joseph was a patient man.

Nevertheless, the scheming doctor hadn't anticipated how hard it would be to make the new proteins do exactly what he wanted them to do . . . every time Joseph thought he was close to having it figured out, something would go wrong. The virus would kill too slowly, or wouldn't kill at all. Several prototypes killed like Joseph wanted but would have been way too easy for hospitals to detect and treat.

Part of the problem was inherent in the complicated virus-making process itself, but a large portion of Joseph's troubles were self-imposed. Because he couldn't just make a killer virus and be done with it. If that was the case, Joseph would have been finished with this research stage of Operation Respect several months ago. No, Joseph's virus needed to be more than just a killer. It needed to be a silent killer. Untraceable. Indeed, the image that always came to his mind while working late at night in his safe room-turned-lab was that of military fighter jets. Those highly complex, high-functioning airplanes were endowed with stealth capabilities to keep them from being detected on enemy radar. Joseph, for his part, was creating a stealth virus.

"And both my virus and those flashy airplanes will work in the service of our country, won't they?"

Joseph posed his question to a cage full of little white mice that he was using to test his new viral concoctions. In Joseph's brilliant yet warped mind, what he was doing – designing a virus that would kill, at minimum, dozens of people – was actually a favor to the United States. The victims of his plan, the ones who would die, were unfortunately just the collateral damage in his creative destruction. "America needs to know how great I am," the doctor continued confidently. "They need to understand the groundbreaking quality of research of which I am capable. They don't understand it right now. But they will. And we'll all be better off once they do."

****

"It's ready," Joseph declared as he inspected the results of his latest test run, nearly two years after he first decided to teach the world a thing or two about respecting him and his medical abilities. "It's finally ready." Trial after trial had come up short of what Joseph wanted to create, but now he had finally managed to find the correct combination of vector, gene, and protein. Joseph knew that if this was a professional lab and the project was a new drug, it would need to undergo human trials first before being declared 'ready.' But he was working in different circumstances, and mice testing would simply have to do. Joseph had told the guy at the store that he had a pet snake – how else can you explain needing to buy mass quantities of little white mice? He always paid in cash, too. He couldn't afford to leave any kind of trail.

"Yes, we're ready," Joseph said again, talking as if the deadly virus sitting in vials on the table in front of him was another person, a partner in crime. It was much more fun that way. Instead of a weapon, he had a partner. An assistant in Joseph's bid to finally gain the respect he deserved. No one ever respected him. Not his surgeon father, who thought that doctors who don't cut aren't real doctors at all. Not his mother, who was so in awe of his father that Joseph was merely an afterthought. She skipped her son's medical school graduation to sit in the gallery and watch yet another of Joseph Sr.'s surgeries. No respect. Not the kids at school growing up who always picked on the skinny kid with glasses. No respect. But that would all change soon.

Now I just need the blood, Joseph thought as he stood up from his swivel stool and walked across his secret lab to the small refrigerator in the corner. Opening the door, Joseph inspected the plastic pouches of his own blood that were stored inside. He had donated two pints of his blood to the cause yesterday. Since Joseph was O-negative, or a universal donor, his blood was perfect. It was almost guaranteed to be used.

"But we need more donors, don't we?" Joseph said as he shut the refrigerator door, walked back over to his work station, and lightly stroked the virus vials reverently. "Not a problem, of course, as long as we do it right. It shouldn't be too difficult to find some vagrants who nobody will miss. And then we'll be doing the public yet another favor, won't we? Yes we will," Joseph purred to the deadly concoction on the table in front of him. "A few fewer eye sores on the streets."

The scheming doctor shook his face and shoulders to clear his mind of the thought of dirty, homeless menaces to society. Joseph had absolutely no sympathy for anyone less fortunate than him. "Just natural selection carrying out its work," he declared as he put the vials containing his virus back in the specialized silver cylinder that kept them fresh and clear of any contamination. Joseph then climbed back up the stairs and entered the code that he needed to exit his secret lair. There was a different code for entering and exiting – just in case someone did manage to find out about the room and get down into it, the homeowner wanted to make sure that they never got to leave.

"Time to find myself some blood," he announced.

Like what you're reading? The rest of *Do No Harm* is available for purchase on Amazon.com!

ABOUT THE AUTHOR

Danielle knew she was born to be a writer at age four when she entertained an entire emergency room with the – false – story of how she was adopted. Inspired by a dream in which she was kidnapped, *Safe & Sound* is her first novel. Danielle lives in Georgia with her husband, daughter, and two dogs.

Printed in Great Britain
by Amazon

56669939R00136